Second Thoughts

Tales of Horror and Suspense

Richard Moule

SECOND THOUGHTS
RICHARD MOULE

Spinetinglers Publishing
22 Vestry Road, Co. Down
BT23 6IIJ, UK

www.spinetinglerspublishing.com

www.richardmoule.wordpress.com

First published by Spinetinglers Publishing August 2012.

Illustrated by Patrick Nolan

www.patrickpnolan.net

ISBN: - 978-1-906755-49-2

Printed in the United Kingdom

'Do you think that they are just as scared as us, as we are of them?'
Said the troll to his brother, both of them sitting perched under the
bridge, while the sound of little children's footsteps echoed above
them.

Contents

The Vending Machine

Justin was sitting down on the long sofa in the canteen next to the sink, when the old-ish looking lady from one of the offices upstairs walked in to fill up a kettle. To Justin, old-ish meant anybody over 30, and he guessed that the lady was either looking good for her age or a young 30's singleton who had let herself go. Either way, one thing was for certain - Justin despised this lady.

She placed the kettle under the sink and turned on the tap, which gave out a hellish scream like it was being tortured. Once filled to the brim, the old-ish looking lady turned the tap off and walked back towards the canteen exit, giving Justin a half-hearted smile. Justin returned the gesture over the top of the metro newspaper somebody had left behind on the coffee table. And then, he heard it.

The dripping. The tiny trickles of never ending water droplets, hammering down into the sink bowl, which echoed throughout the room. Every time the old-ish looking lady came into the canteen at lunchtime she would fill up her kettle (Justin presumed it was her job to do so, tasked by the other members of her office; possibly to get rid of her annoying presence for a few measly minutes each day). And every time she would walk away from the sink, she would leave the tap on, running ever so slightly. Justin always found this completely irritating. The first time it happened he tried to ignore it, or hope that somebody else would eventually go to the sink to stop the constant drips. But Justin soon discovered that nobody else would turn up within his hour lunch break. In fact, he soon found out that nobody else ever went into the canteen at all; at least not to stay in there for long. He was the only one in the whole building who ever ate his lunch in the office canteen.

Justin slammed his newspaper down on the coffee table, got up and, like so many lunch times before, turned off the leaking tap himself. The worst part was that it didn't take a lot of effort to stop the dripping. It wasn't a loose tap; in fact it was very strong and sturdy. If only the old-ish looking lady could be bothered to check then Justin wouldn't have to get up every lunch to turn the dam thing off.

He slumped back down onto the long sofa and picked the metro back up. After looking through the back page sports section he threw it down again. He rhythmically slapped his thighs a bit before looking at his wristwatch. He still had another 18 minutes left of his lunch break; which his boss insisted he spent the entire hour out of the office. Justin always found this quite a challenge, especially when there was nobody else to talk to from the other offices. He had no idea where they went on their lunch breaks either.

He had already eaten his sandwich and was pleasantly full, but out of sheer boredom Justin decided to grab a packet of crisps from one of the vending machines to pass the time.

He shuffled around in his pocket for some loose change and found a 50p coin to arm himself with. He decided to go for the Worcestershire sauce flavoured crisps. Justin usually went for a standard Ready Salted, or even Cheese and Onion if he was feeling a little more adventurous, but he decided he might as well experiment while he had the time.

He put in the coin and punched in the numbers, C13. The vending machine began to make a whirling noise in recognition of this, but failed to drop any bag of crisps. They stayed motionless behind the see-through glass. Justin once again looked at his wristwatch. He still had 15 minutes left, which he thought could now be best spent by either getting his 50p back or his Worcestershire flavoured bag of crisps.

He looked around to see if the coast was clear, but then soon remembered that he was more than safe in the empty canteen. He then pushed his back up against the side of the vending machine and began to tilt it slightly, and then let it go to give it a jolt. A large clumping sound soon followed. A sound that was heavier than a bag of crisps and a 50p coin falling. Justin thought he might have bagged himself one of the chocolate bars instead, which at 60p each he could have got himself a bargain. He knelt down and put his hands in the flaps at the bottom of the machine to retrieve his bonus prize.

The moment he touched the 'thing' that landed at the bottom, Justin felt as though something was wrong. The object felt nothing like a bar of chocolate, a packet of crisps or any sort of snack in a vending machine.

As he pulled the object out to reveal itself, he literally shrieked out in utter horror and dropped the human hand onto the canteen floor. It looked as though it had just been freshly cut off, with the stump still glowing a blotchy, shiny colour of red, with the tips of the white bone sticking out of it.

He was momentarily dazed and petrified at what he saw, all the while not realising that he was still airing out a string of screams. He ran out the canteen, barging the double doors of the entrance aside, and bolted it towards the end of the long hallway. There didn't seem to be another soul in sight, much like every other lunchtime.

He reached his office and threw himself in without knocking first, despite being told to always do so before entering.

'Good Lord Justin! What's the rush? And aren't you meant to be on your break?'

'Mr. Hayes...' stuttered Justin, almost out of breath. 'There's... there's...'

'Now, now Justin, we have been through this.' Said Mr. Hayes, while putting down his sharpened 2B pencil and getting up from his spacious office desk. 'I admire your enthusiasm, I really do; but there is a reason why you have to take your full lunch hour.'

'But Mr. Hayes; I've just seen... there's a-'

'Look young man.' He said, putting a rested hand on Justin's shoulder. 'If it was up to me I would have you working throughout the whole day, I really would! But nowadays it's health and safety gone mad. You work 9 'til half 5, which entitles you to 1 hour's lunch break, which you have to take. If you injure yourself within working hours in the afternoon and you haven't received your break then the company gets sued! And not just by you, but by the bloody unions as well!'

'But there's something in the canteen!'

'And the reason you can't have your lunch in the office,' continued Mr. Hayes, ignoring Justin, 'is that if you were to injure yourself in here, technically you're not in working hours so it would again come back to us! So Justin, please, enjoy the rest of your lunch and I shall see you at 2. Not a minute before!'

'But, Mr. Hayes; I have to show you something!'

'It can wait until 2 Justin, now please...' Mr. Hayes escorted Justin back out the office door, gave him a wink and a smile before closing it behind him.

Justin stood in the hallway, alone. He wasn't sure what to do. Should he run into one of the other offices and tell them that he had found somebody's decapitated hand in the vending machine?

Nobody would believe him; and nobody knew him well enough to even find it laughable. *What a good first impression that would be*, he thought.

But then another thought quickly drove itself into Justin's mind. *What if somebody else sees it? What if they go for help and tell everybody? What if they give it to the police? What if the police find fingerprints all over it? What if the only fingerprints on it were his?*

Justin walked briskly back towards the canteen. He couldn't run, as there was a part of him that didn't want to see the horrid sight of the bloody hand once more. He couldn't hear any other screams, or any sound of unusual commotion. *Why did nobody come running when he screamed? Surely at least one person in the whole building would have heard him?*

He got to the doors of the canteen, and peered through the see-through glass, glancing at the canteen floor. Justin could not see any misplaced severed hands anywhere. With fear erased by confusion, he boldly entered the canteen and searched the floor, puzzled. There was no sign of any stranded body parts whatsoever. It was spotless; all except a bag of Worcestershire sauce flavoured crisps.

It had been over two weeks since the vending machine incident. Justin had still not settled into his new position. Partly because of not knowing exactly what the company actually did (he was pretty sure it was something to do with importing goods from overseas, but not entirely sure what the goods were; all he saw in regards to this each day was numbers), but mainly because he could not get his mind off the dead person's hand (he presumed that the owner had to be dead). Justin was on edge thinking that somebody had found it, handed it in and the police would come investigating any day. But this thought soon evaporated; news like that would sure to have spread around the offices like wildfire. Now he was left with the concern of his mental health. *Did he really see what he did? Was it all just in his head? But he touched it... He had held it... He felt it...*

'What are you day dreaming about young man?' Said Mr. Hayes, while pointing the rubber end of his 2B pencil at Justin.

'Sorry sir,' Apologised Justin after realising that he had been staring into space for a while. 'It won't happen again.'

'No no, don't apologise Justin. You were day dreaming away there nicely. Means that you're thinking about something. And at least you're thinking! Hell, half the assistants I've had before were just mind-numbingly dull zombies who would jump on demand; ask how high, you know the type. At least with you, you're a dreamer. You have something to think about. You're your own person with your own thoughts. Yes Justin, you'll go far in this company.'

A silence glazed the room. Justin was not sure whether a thank you or any other response was necessary. The office only consisted of the two of them, and sometimes the stillness made the room feel claustrophobic to Justin.

'Thank you sir.' He managed to croak out, followed in return with Mr. Hayes' trademark wink and smile that put Justin at ease again. Mr. Hayes glanced over at the large clock on the wall.

'You got 5 minutes until your lunch as well – plenty of time to day dream there.'

Lunchtime soon arrived, and Justin planted himself in the same position in the canteen as he did every working day between 1 and 2. The offices were sat on an industrial estate far out of town, and with no car for transport there was nowhere else to go, unless Justin wanted to spend his hour outside in the freezing cold wind and rain or walk up and down the corridor to pass the time (which he had tried briefly a few times).

The old-ish looking lady came along and filled her kettle up, like she did every lunch. And like every lunch, she would give him a half-hearted smile and still leave the tap annoyingly dripping away. Some days it would be such a faint tapping she would leave, and other times she would leave the dam thing splattering all over the side of the sink. Each time Justin had no choice but to tighten it and turn it off. *One of these days he was going say something… One day soon*, he thought.

He sat there eating his ready salted bag of crisps (he was not thrilled with the more exotic flavours as once tried before) while thinking about how he thought his new job was going. Despite the whole hand incident it was going pretty well, although the job title 'Office Assistant', as specified when he applied, should have been more accurately put as 'PA to Mr. Hayes'.

He didn't mind Mr. Hayes though. He was a nice guy. He had his funny little sayings and habits, like he once stated that he had never used a pen in his whole life; always a pencil. He would say that 'you can always rub pencil out, but pen will always leave a smudge.' Justin didn't quite understand this wisdom, but liked it all the same.

While day dreaming (as instructed to do so), there was a sudden sound of a heavy clunk that echoed throughout the canteen, alerting Justin. It had come from the vending machine.

Justin stared at the vendor inquisitively. He was certain he had heard something drop down, and deep down he knew what it was. He didn't want to look, but curiosity and the desire for self-assurance persuaded him to go over and see what it was, to rid his worries. He knelt down and placed his hand into the machine. He was hoping to feel the cold ice of a can of fizzy-drink, but instead felt something soft but firm.

He knew what it was.

Justin instantly took his hand away and lifted up the vending machine flaps to peer through. Sitting at the bottom of the machine was the same human hand as he had seen before, only this time it looked as though it had been rotting over the past two weeks, with a small amount of colour left in the skin. He could see a faint wave movement, which he soon discovered was the crawling of maggots around their small carcass. Not only could Justin see the wretched hand, he could also smell the terrific stench of decaying corpse wafting through, making Justin heave in disgust.

'Problem there, fella?' Said a voice directly behind Justin. He turned his head around and up to see a man with a sharpened pencil balancing on his left ear, wearing a stained white t-shirt tucked fully into bright blue jeans. 'You finished with the vendor?'

Justin looked wide-eyed at the man who did not appear to be affected by the horrid smell that had got stuck up Justin's nostrils the minute it hit them. Instead, the man looked impatient at him, as if he had lingered long enough around the machine and now it was somebody else's turn. Justin, quite surprised to actually see another person on his lunch break, did not instantly recognise the man. He did not look like he was from one of the offices upstairs. He had to be an electrician, or a builder perhaps, or something to do with the maintenance of the building.

'Well?' Said the man. 'Are you done?'

Justin realised he was still crouched on the floor with his hand in the vending machine (and he could still feel the hand inside of it too). He pulled his hand slowly out, got up, nodded at the man and took a step back from the vending machine. For some reason he could not tell the man about what was in there. He wanted him to find out for himself, so he hadn't had to explain it to him. He wanted the man to see it with his own eyes, maybe even scream at the sight the way Justin did. He wanted someone else to acknowledge it.

'It's like a bloody ghost town here at lunch time ey.' Said the man, while putting his money into the vending machine and tapping in the buttons in no time. He was clearly an expert at the procedure. 'There's not a soul in sight, not even in the canteen. Seems odd to me, sure it's not a big space but at least it's somewhere to sit and chat. Why everybody drives out for lunch seems strange to me.'

The machine began its whirring sound.

'You on the this floor?'

Justin nodded. He couldn't yet get the power back to speak. His eyes were still fixated on the vending machine flaps, and his nose still picked up the awful scent.

'Yea, we'll be working down here after too, once we're done upstairs.'

Justin nodded again, although he wasn't entirely sure what it was *they* were doing upstairs.

A heavy thud landed at the bottom of the vendor. *This is it,* thought Justin. The man knelt down and put his hand through the flaps, began to feel and then frowned in confusion. *This is it!*

'What the…' The man lifted the flaps and peered in. 'Well, bloody hell.'

Justin's eyes widened even further. The man turned and looked at Justin. His confusion however slowly turned into a triumphant smile.

'Looks like it's my lucky day.' The man then pulled out two packets of crisps; a cheese and onion flavour and a Worcestershire sauce flavour. 'Two for one!'

Two months went by. Justin had considerable doubts about his state of mind growing every day that went by, although he had not seen the hand since the last incident. It was like the dam thing went to rest for a while, all the time poised ready to pounce whenever the time felt right. His mind was far from being in a stable place. Justin could brush off the first time he saw the hand as a one off, a freak occurrence, his senses cheating on him for just a split second. *But it happened twice...* Twice meant that there was something fundamentally wrong with himself. *Why could nobody else see it? Or were there others like him who could also see it? And if so, why haven't they said anything either?*

Justin's confusion never got in the way of his work though. In fact, in a weird way it had helped him. He used his work as a temporary escape, to pre-occupy himself from his current problem. And it paid off for him. He passed his probation period. He had gotten a slight raise; well respectful for the short time he had been there. Mr. Hayes had given him extra work and more responsibilities (even though Justin still hadn't quite grasped what it was the company did just yet). He was thankful for the trusted confidence Mr. Hayes had in him.

But in the back of his mind, no matter how hard he tried to shake it off, he could feel it. Justin often had nightmares of the hand crawling up across his back and reaching round to strangle him. He would wake up in blind panic, and could still feel the presence of the hand as though it was underneath his sheets, gently tickling away at his feet to remind him that it hadn't forgotten about him.

Justin knew that he was going to see the hand again. Logic, although nothing he had seen provided any clear sense of the word, told him that it had to come back eventually. Things like that always do, until you finally find out the route of the problem.

He knew that it had to come from the vending machine again. Logic again told him this. And he also knew that whatever this thing was, it wasn't any good. It had to be pure evil. Justin knew he should try to forget about it and steer clear from the vending machine in the canteen. He knew he should, but he couldn't...

It felt as though something was pulling him in towards the canteen each day. Perhaps it was curiosity; naïve curiosity. No matter how hard he tried to resist, he knew that deep down he wanted to see it again; that he had to see it again. Questions had remained unanswered. *What was it doing there? Why could he only see it? Was this the reason nobody went to the canteen at lunch? Or was there another reason? What secrets lay between the walls of the building?*

So each lunch Justin would remain brave in his rightful position in the canteen. He would from time to time inspect the vending machine carefully, almost waiting for something to happen. Every day the annoying old-ish looking lady would leave the tap running for him to turn off, which gradually evolved into another of his daily tasks.

He would wait, poised ready for something to happen. He would go through in his head what he should do when the time comes, but could only think of keeping hold of it long enough to see it disappear again.

He obsessed over it, he yearned for it, and eventually his longing finally paid off…

Justin sat in the canteen; eyes fixated on the vending machine, while the annoying old-ish lady finished using the sink and began to walk away with her filled up kettle. *This leaking tap business was really starting to get to him now…*

When she left, Justin was once again alone in the canteen. And then it happened. He knew what the sound was, and he jumped up from the sofa in an instant; part with anxiety and part with excitement. His heart began to race as he made his way over to the vending machine. Although it had only happened twice before, he knew exactly what had fallen in the machine straight away.

He knelt down and peered through the flaps. There were no crawling maggots this time. There was no rotting flesh. The hand was there all right, but it had decayed even more. It was now purely bone, stretched out like the grim reapers hand offering death to its customers. To Justin, this was the most real and gruesome sight he had seen so far. It conveyed the portrayal of death perfectly, clarifying that this hand once belonged to somebody that was no longer alive.

He grabbed a handful of blue roll next to the sink, plucked up the courage and then gently picked up the skeleton hand as though it was a rare sculpture. He held it close to its chest, like his prized possession he wanted to keep hold of. *If he kept hold of it, then it can't disappear again. But what was he going to do with it now? Who was he going to show it to?*

There was only one person who Justin knew in the whole building – Mr. Hayes. He kept the bundle tight against him as he walked carefully out the canteen back towards his office. As usual, being lunchtime, the halls were empty. *Not a soul in sight,* thought

Justin, as the builder or electrician or whatever he was had said before.

He carefully opened the office door and shut it behind him quickly, still making sure nobody else was about (he didn't want to take any chances. It would be just his luck that on this day everybody would decide to step out of the offices for a change of pace).

'Justin?' Questioned Mr. Hayes, poised over his work with his 2B pencil. 'You're half an hour early. Now you know I like your enthusiasm but…'

'Mr. Hayes,' butted in Justin. 'I've found something. It came out of the vending machine.'

Justin placed the bundle on Mr. Hayes' desk.

'It's a hand sir. A human hand! It's been in the machine for ages now. I've seen it… well… rot. It's been rotting away for a while; it's only bone now. At first I thought I was going crazy, but I have it now! I have it!'

Justin almost chuckled slightly at this thought, spurting out a slight sputter as he did so. Mr. Hayes looked at the parcel that lay in front of him, speechless.

'Somebody must have been keeping it there, hiding it away.' Carried on Justin. 'Maybe it's the vending machine people; you know… the ones who change over the snacks every week. Maybe it's one of them! Whatever it is, I needed to tell someone, and being that you're my immediate boss sir; and the only person I know around here, I had to show you.'

There was an elongated pause between the two of them, just the sound of the small hand on the clock overlooking the door ticking slowly on every second. Justin wanted a reaction. He wanted to rip off the blue roll and reveal the horror, but did not want to startle his boss too much. *He had to see it for himself… He had to unravel it in his own time…*

'So….' Started Mr. Hayes slowly. 'So you say that you have seen this hand before? And you say that it came from the vending machine?'

'Yes!' Said an eager Justin, as though he had guessed an answer right.

'And it has been rotting in there, we presume, for a while now?'

'Yes!' Another question answered loudly. He didn't care how his sanity looked now. *He had the dam thing in front of him.*

'So, is it a male or female hand then?'

'What sir?'

'What gender does it belong to?'

This question stopped Justin's bold eagerness.

'I don't know sir…'

'And is there any ring on any of the fingers Justin? Was there any fake fingernails, any tattoos seen before it start to "rot away"?'

'Well, I'm not sure…'

'You see Justin; I'm just trying to make sure that what you said you have seen is actually right here in front of me. You don't just see a hacked off hand and not notice if it was a man or a woman's, or if there was any ring at all.'

'But sir… I… The thing horrified me. I didn't want to look at it for more than two seconds…'

'Nonetheless you claim you have seen it. I'm just trying to figure out exactly what you have seen. You see… Our imagination can sometimes play tricks on us Justin. Sometimes it can make us think we have seen something that isn't actually there. What it forgets to do is remember all the little details about that certain something. Say you were in a boiling hot desert, and you suddenly see a swimming pool. What you don't see is the water tank, the water ducts, and the concrete foundation, not even the bloody on duty lifeguard. What you see is just the water, because that's what your imagination wants you to see.'

Justin's enthusiasm began to wear off. His heart began to slow down, as though it was getting its breath back from the sudden high of triumph it had recently encountered.

No… He wasn't going to let Mr. Hayes think he was mad. Who cares if he gets a little shocked?

'But sir, just look at the dam thing!' Justin flung up the blue Roll and threw it behind him like it was a bouquet at a wedding. A bag of Worcestershire sauce flavoured crisps came flying up with it, and landed on Mr. Hayes lap.

'But… but…' Justin searched the desk, searched all around the floor but could not find the skeleton hand. 'But I had it!'

Mr. Hayes sighed and got up from his desk, putting one hand on Justin's shoulder to calm him down.

'Come on young sir, let's go and finish your lunch together. I think I've got some explaining to do to you.'

Mr. Hayes came over from the bar with two full pints of beer, a lager for Justin and a bitter for himself. Justin originally said no to the alcoholic drink, but Mr. Hayes insisted he could use one. After little consideration Justin agreed with his boss that he did.

'I should have told you form the word off Justin.' Said Mr. Hayes, while sitting down on a small bar stool next to their table. 'I just didn't want to spook you, that was all.'

Justin took a quick glance around the pub as if somebody might have been trying to listen in, took a good gulp of his beer (which tasted amazing), and faced back to Mr. Hayes to pay attention to what he was about to say.

'You ever wondered why you don't see anybody around at lunch time Justin?' He continued. 'It's because they're all afraid. Health and safety says that our staff can't be hanging around the offices on their lunch breaks, so the only place they can go in the building is the canteen. But nobody wants to go there. That's why they all leave to go to the shops or to the local supermarket, the café, the pub, anywhere but the canteen.'

'Why?' Justin asked, with his eagerness now beginning to become restored.

'It's because of what has happened in that very room. Back in 1984 when the building was first used as office space, Robert Tanford, one of the senior managers working there at that time, drowned one of the receptionists in the sink in the canteen. They had to prize his arms off her when they found him, screaming, "she had it coming".' Mr. Hayes took a sip of his smooth bitter, which left a faint white froth moustache on his top lip, before continuing. 'Then in 1991, quite a few years on, another incident occurred. This time it was Margaret Smith in Human Resources. One day she walked into the canteen, while everybody was sitting on the sofas nattering, and pulled out a pair of scissors and repeatedly stabbed old Mr. Cotton, who was in the finance department, to death with them. The others bravely pulled her off, while she screamed, "He had it coming". And finally, in 2006, over a decade later, one of the young apprentices in marketing was found in the rubbish bin outside, all crumbled up as though he had been bashed up real bad. The police got called in, searched all the offices only to find Mr. Kerr, head of the marketing department, proudly sitting at his desk with a fire extinguisher covered in blood by his side. He

was stated as saying, "He had it coming". A fire extinguisher ey...
Now how's that for health and bloody safety?'

Mr. Hayes nearly chuckled out a little laugh to himself over his
last comment, but soon stopped in respect for the talked about
deceased.

'So, what are you saying? That the canteen has a curse on it or
something?' Questioned Justin, while gulping down more of his
beer for support.

'All I'm saying is that it doesn't take too much for people to
become superstitious. Hell... I'm one of those people!' Mr. Hayes
put up his hands in acknowledgement of his own gullible guilt. 'All
incidents occurred in the canteen. 'You know how fast gossip and
rumours spread after events like that? Well... apparently each of
the murderers admitted in questioning that they heard voices
coming from the walls, from the sink, from the sofas, from the fire
extinguisher. It was as though there was some force that egged
them on to commit such acts.'

'Force?' Said Justin. 'Are you suggesting that the canteen is
haunted or something?'

Mr. Hayes shrugged and raised his eyebrows as if to say that
Justin had answered his own question.

'There are some things, Justin, some places, that cannot be
explained. And the canteen in our building is just one of those
many places.'

'But why haven't they just knocked it down?'

'They tried to!' Laughed Mr. Hayes, nearly spitting in his bitter.
'After the second death in 91', the owners at the time wanted to
knock the canteen down and move it elsewhere. I suppose they
wanted to wipe the whole place clean, so there was no trace or
memory left. But soon after the builders started the work, several
of them suffered injuries that couldn't be explained. Needles to say
that their suspicions arose quickly, and soon quit the contract.
Another building company came in, and the same thing happened
again. Soon enough, they couldn't get anybody in there! So... they
just left it and tried to move on; as well as trying to hush up the
building catastrophe.'

Justin had nearly finished his pint, but savoured what was left, as
Mr. Hayes was still only halfway through his bitter.

'So... what does all this have to do with me then? And why do
I keep seeing this... this hand?'

Mr. Hayes looked down into his bitter, and then gulped the rest of it down before answering.

'In truth, I don't fully know. Take it how you wish, but that canteen has a bad vibe about it. Maybe it's subconsciously trying to tell you something, and if so, then do not listen to it. My advice would be to steer clear of the canteen for a while. Try and forget about it and focus on your work. Nobody I know stays in there for more than five minutes anyway. The weather's meant to clear up soon, so the benches outside will be fine to use again.'

Mr. Hayes took a quick glance at the clock above the bar, and flicked Justin's glass as a signal for him to finish it.

'Come on, lunch is over. Let's get back to work.'

But Justin couldn't stay away from the canteen. He mustn't... No matter how much he tried to steer clear, forget about it, he couldn't. He shouldn't... It was like a magnetic pulse, an unbreakable attachment between Justin and the canteen. It spoke out to him. It lured him in. The walls spoke to him... whispered intriguing propositions. And the more he listened, the more it all made complete sense to Justin. He must always go there at lunchtime. He must stay there the full hour. He must look after it... He must protect it.

After all this time not knowing, Justin had finally worked out what his job role was in the building. He was to look after the canteen. He was the keeper, the watchman, and the guard on duty. It was his job to look after the canteen, to protect it, to nurture its needs. It needed him there... without him the canteen could not survive, could not thrive into the greatness it could become. Just like his predecessors before him, he must sacrifice everything and anything for the canteen; and it was once again hungry.

It had been asleep for too long. It needed wakening up. He could hear it suffering. It was in pain. The people of the building did not understand (they would never understand). They simply discarded the canteen as a place of evil, as a place of malevolence, so they chose to ignore it. And maybe they were right... Maybe it was a place of evil. Perhaps it was destined to feed on the suffering of those around it. And so what if it did? Who the hell were they to say what could or could not happen? Don't they know that in order for good there must be evil in the world? It needs to be at a constant balance. How dare they! How dare they just shun the place out, as though they can just turn away from it and pretend it doesn't exist? Who the hell do they think they are?

The canteen needed reviving, that was obvious. People needed to know it was still there. They needed to fear it once more, instead of this childish superstition which people found entertaining. People love to pretend they're scared of places, especially if everybody else feels the same way. They are just blind sheep, following each other around waiting for one to jump so the rest know how to follow. It needed to be reborn. It needed a sacrifice…

It had been trying to show Justin; through the vending machine it had been showing him the future of what was to come; the inevitable fate of what will happen; that must happen. It must happen…

As the weeks grew, the hand voluntarily showed itself. It wanted Justin to see it. It wanted Justin to look at it, and show him who the hand belonged to. Each time he saw it, it became clearer. His vision became stronger. The hand slowly revealed itself. It showed him who it belonged to. The sacrifice…

He was prepared all right. He was prepared to chop the sacrifice up into small tiny pieces, to hack off the hands, arms, legs, feet, head and feed it to the vending machine. The vendor was the canteen's pet, like Cerberus to Hades. And it was hungry…

He could knock them out with the fire extinguisher (the fools had not even bothered to remove the perfect weapon of choice even after the last time), and then use his father's garden shears from the shed at the back of the garden. Nobody would hear the screams. And even if they did, Mr. Hayes was right… nobody would dare go near the place anyway. But the sacrifice would know what was happening. The screams would nourish the room plenty, enough for it to build up and rise again. The perfect sacrifice… who?

It was someone who had mockingly used the canteen from time to time, disrespecting it. Using it for their own good and discarding its use after, like a cheap-throwaway service station. Not like the proud area that it once was (and will be again!). It was someone who would annoyingly leave the tap running endlessly without caring what would happen if nobody turned it off. And one thing Justin was dead certain about; she had it coming…

Something under the stairs

When I want to watch a movie, and I mean *really* watch a movie, then I always want to do it alone. That doesn't mean that I would ever go to the cinema on my own, or have a screen viewing all to myself (that would be too creepy), plus the busy atmosphere is important for the 'going-out' cinematic experience. No, I am talking about getting a movie to watch at home, in the comfort of your own front room. That's when I want to watch it on my own, if I *really* want to watch a movie. There is nothing more annoying than sitting through a film when somebody is talking all the way through it, asking what happened when and why, what was going on, who is that person again? I don't need that, not when I'm trying to watch something. It ruins the mood, and you can't get into the story. If it's a movie I'm not entirely enthusiastic on watching, then yes, I don't mind having a group of friends watching with me. But on this certain night, I had the night to myself and also had a movie that I *really* wanted to watch. But looking back now, I wish I had called a few of my friends round to be there with me. *At least somebody would have believed me…*

'So where did you say you were going tonight?' I asked Cathy as she was hurrying around the living room, trying to find her misplaced phone. I was stretched out on the sofa, waiting for her to leave so I could get on with watching my movie.

'That new Italian on the high street, are you sure you're ringing it?' Said Kerry.

'It's ringing; you've got it on silent again. What's it called?'

Cathy was digging deep down under the armchair. 'Oh I don't know, La Piazza or something? I'm not sure whether it's meant to be any good or not.'

'Wanna know how to find out if it's good or not?'

'I'd rather find my phone David; I swear I didn't put it on silent, but I should be able to hear it vibrate if I did though shouldn't I?'

'When you get in to the restaurant,' I carried on, 'before you sit down at the table, go straight to the toilets. You can always judge on how good the food will be by the condition they keep their toilets in. If the toilets are dire, then go safe with something simple on the menu, as chances are it's all going to be pretty bad. If, however, the toilets are in perfect condition, you can risk more exotic looking dishes, as chances are the food's going to be pretty good. If you don't want to seem weird by going to the toilet straight away, you can also check out their drinks menu when you sit down. Look under the beers section and if there are a lot of imported world lagers, I'm not talking Carlsberg or Stella, I mean Amstel or Budvar, then you should be in a good restaurant. You're in an Italian right? Well, if there's a lot of Italian sounding beers you've never heard of before, then that's a good sign too.'

'Look, can you stop blabbering on and help me find my phone?' Said Cathy, standing fully upright with her hands on her hips, looking down at me in one of her huffy looks. 'The sooner I find it the sooner I'll be gone so you can watch your movie.'

I gave in and got up from the sofa. 'Fine; where was the last place you... actually I'm not even going to finish saying that.'

'It was right here on the coffee table,' She answered anyway. 'I put it down while I was hoovering the carpet and then – that's it!' Cathy trotted over in her high heels to the cupboard under the stairs, slid across the single bolt, swung open the wooden door and turned on the small light bulb using the dangling switch inside on the right. She took out the vacuum cleaner stored away and searched the cupboard floor. 'Gotcha!' She held her shiny phone up to me in triumph.

'Woopee,' I said sarcastically, and slumped back on to the sofa.

Cathy turned off the cupboard light and bolted the door shut. 'Good God, we really need to sort that cupboard out; we've got so many boxes in there, I don't even know what's in half of them?'

'We'll get round to it Cath.'

'Like we got round to sorting out the attic?'

'Weren't you in a hurry to get to the restaurant?'

'Oh Christ, I gotta go...kisses!' She blew me a kiss, grabbed her furry coat and car keys from the side of the armchair and made her way out of the front door. 'I'll be back around eleven.'

'Just make sure you're back before twelve; we don't want another pumpkin situation again now do we.'

'Very funny, I'll see you later.' She blew another kiss and hurried out the front door.

I picked up the television remote, switched it over to the DVD input and undid the DVD tray. Sitting next to me, still in its original wrapping (there's something utterly satisfying about keeping your DVDs neatly preserved until the Big Day), was *Creepshow*, my choice of entertainment for the evening. I saw it in the Horror section at the local music and film store called *Culture* on the high street. A rush of guilty pleasure soon spread all over me as I picked it up, looking with excitement at the casing. It was years since I last saw it (it was never shown on any television channels as I could recall), and soon remembered seeing an old VHS copy of it in my Dad's collection back when I was a child. He tried to hide it on the top shelf, but that only made it more mysterious to me. I had stayed up all night, waiting for my parents to go to bed, and then gently crept downstairs, retrieved the video and began to watch it on the lowest volume, so not to wake my parents up. I remember thinking that it was a masterpiece. It was petrifying but satisfying at the same time. I remember being scared, but intrigued. It was something that I had never seen before. So, in the *Culture* music and film store, having that same force of delightful emotions in the grasp of my hand, £8.95 didn't seem too extortionate (I usually refuse to buy a movie nowadays for anything over £5).

I unwrapped the DVD, slowly, careful not to scuff up the casing (I was already planning on watching it again sometime in the future. That's why you buy movies instead of renting them, right?). After quickly checking the disc for any scratches and finding none, I popped it in the DVD tray and closed it. I got up and turned off the main light overhanging nearest the television, so not to get a glare, and dimmed the backing lights so to give the best atmosphere without being in pitch black on my own; after all, it was still a horror movie I was watching, and I am only human. I pressed play on the DVD menu and sat back on the sofa, positioned the perfect distance away from the screen. The movie began to load up. I grabbed one of the beers from the cooler sitting to the right of the sofa at an arms reach away, and a handful of nachos from the pre-prepared bowl on the coffee table, ready and waiting, but not once touched until the film had started (I didn't want to get up and re-fill halfway through the movie).

I felt cosy, warm, ready and excited. I've been called a movie geek before, and at times I will quite gladly own up to that title, as I was always the most relaxed and comforted when watching a movie; to forget about the constant worries and boredom of the real world, and get lost into a far more exciting story; something unbelievable, unimaginable, unworldly. This was my idea of a perfect Friday night…

But, after this night, I can tell you; I no longer have that same comfort.

And so began the first scene of *Creepshow*, with the mood set perfectly eerie and wonderfully dark. I scoffed down another handful of nachos excitedly, and whisked down a heavy gulp of alcohol to give my backbone courage. And then, the home phone rang. Too predictable to be scared by, I quickly jumped up, paused the DVD and picked the receiver to get rid of the interruption quickly.

'Hello?' I said, probably sounding a tad impatient. After all, there was nothing worse than having to pause through a movie, no matter what stage of the story it was up to.

'Hey, it's me,' said Cathy down the other end of the line, sounding in a rush. 'Listen, I forgot to pick up Trish's purse she leant me the other night. She needs it for tomorrow but is busy all of the day, so she's going to stop by and pick it up tonight, okay?'

'She's what? Oh god, fine… what time?'

'The purse should be sitting on top of my dresser table.' Said Cathy, ignoring my timing concern. 'I have to run. We're just about to go into the restaurant, love you!'

'Is she coming round soon then?' I tried to get in, but got a dead line for a reply. I put the receiver back down hard. 'Damn…'

That was all I needed, one of Cathy's friends stopping by to pick up her bloody handbag or purse or whatever. I knew Cathy's friends pretty well. Well enough to know that 'stopping by' meant a good natter for about twenty minutes about God-awful crap that I have no interest in whatsoever. She would probably want to go through what her plans were for Saturday night, as if I gave a flying crap what her plans were. At this rate there was no chance of me even thinking about watching my second film I had managed to stumble on in the shop, called *From Beyond the Grave* starring the legendary *Peter Cushing,* an idea I had been flirting with all day but decided to play it by ear before committing and getting my hopes up too soon. Back to back movie watching is all well and good as long as you have the energy to give each film the complete focus it deserved. But there was no chance in hell of that happening this night now, not after news of Trish the chatterbox paying me a little visit.

After sulking to myself about the situation for a while, I unpaused the DVD and continued to enjoy my night, quickly forgetting I had a visitor knocking at any time.

But soon enough I was interrupted again. Not by the phone this time, but by a slow rumble. It was like a vibration of some sort. I paused the movie and listened out for it. Something was fidgeting around, like the sound of rats scurrying. No, it sounded more like it was on its own. Perhaps it was a giant rat? Either way I soon noticed that the weird scattering was coming from the cupboard under the stairs.

It was the vacuum cleaner, that was my first thought. There was a plug just inside of the cupboard that it was plugged in to when Cathy did the cleaning in the living room. I figured that she must have accidently turned it on as she was looking in the cupboard before she went out. I got up from the sofa and started to walk towards the cupboard to switch it off, but I suddenly stopped walking when I spotted the vacuum cleaner sitting just outside of the cupboard, with its extension lead wrapped round its handle unplugged.

I stared at the cupboard, which was still projecting a strange, eerie noise. *What the hell was in there?* There was a lot of boxes stacked up inside, so I presumed that it must have been some electronic gizmo that still had its batteries in it; probably some weird Christmas present that was still in its packaging and trying to break free. I cautiously slid the bolt across and opened the cupboard door (why cautiously I don't know at this moment, but now very glad I did so). I switched on the one light bulb by the dangling switch on the right, which gave out a mist of yellow light, displaying the floating dust perfectly. It only shone through by the doorway, as the other light bulb hanging nearer the back of the cupboard had gone out a couple of years back. I could see row upon row of stacked boxes, looking like they were never-ending as they faded into the pitch dark. *Just my luck*, I thought. The sound could have been coming from any one of those boxes. A simple knock to one of them nearest the door could easily trigger a tidal wave of vibration, causing every one of them to shake some electronic gadget on and off.

The rumble was still apparent. I gave a quick shake at the nearest box, hoping that it would cause the end of the noise, but to no avail. I gave another nudge, this time heavier than before.

And then that's when I saw it…

Technically I didn't see the whole of it, but what I saw was good enough proof for me. From the dark shadows at the back of the cupboard glistened two white spots. At first I thought it was one of the bulbs coming back on, but as I looked closer my vision became clearer.

I saw its eyes...

They were like a cross between a pair of snakes and a gorilla. They seemed to have that wide glow of green in between the white of them, but the stern shape of something wise and ancient. It was nothing I had ever seen before. The eyes grew bigger as they appeared to be coming closer towards me.

I jumped back, collapsing over one of the boxes out of the cupboard, and scampered to my feet. I got to my knees, which I thought was close enough, crawled out and slammed the cupboard door shut, bolting it locked. I didn't move back straight away, as I was struck stupefied in curiosity.

What the hell was it? It looked like some kind of animal; a big animal; an animal that shouldn't be living in somebody's downstairs cupboard! I sat back in silence, staring at the wooden doorframe, trying to listen for more movement. The air seemed too thin to me, and I was finding it hard to keep my breathing quiet.

There was no sound for a while. Whatever was in there had stopped moving momentarily. I stayed by the door, contemplating my next move. *What the hell was I supposed to do? Was I meant to call the police?* And tell them what exactly?

"Hello Mr. Policeman, I believe that there's some sort of monster in the cupboard under the stairs, can you please come along and remove it for me pretty please?"

Perhaps I was just imagining it? Was I? Did I actually see anything in there at all? I looked back at the television screen, which was paused on a floating skeleton hanging outside a little boy's window. Had my imagination just got the better of myself? It would make sense really, a more logical and realistic explanation than something living under our stairs.

I plucked up the courage, slid the bolt across and slowly undid the wooden cupboard door again. I suddenly felt stupid for thinking that I had seen something in the first place, but at that point even more stupid for looking to reassure myself of this. I felt like one of those idiotic curious teenage kids in *Halloween* or *Nightmare on Elm Street*. Why couldn't I just laugh it off and go back to watching my movie? Why did I have to prove to myself that nothing was there?

In any case, I undid the door fully and turned on the small light. Nothing. Just the same stacked up boxes as before. I peered closer towards the dark shadows and empty blackness at the back of the cupboard, but saw no signs of any movement whatsoever. For some reason I whistled. Looking back I'm still not sure why I decided to whistle, for truthfully I didn't want anything returning the call and running straight at me. Perhaps it was just a necessary caution to confirm that nothing was there. In any case, my own actions did make me laugh and satisfyingly made me feel at ease again. I shut the cupboard door and jumped on the sofa, picking up the remote and getting back into my film.

Looking back I have to admit I had brushed off the whole incident pretty quickly, as though imaging a pair of beast's eyes in a cupboard was a natural occurrence, a situation that most people must have found themselves in at one point or another in their lives. Perhaps it was because I was still eager to watch my movie and didn't want to waste any unnecessary worrying about the state of my mental health. Either way, I really should have anticipated that the night's ordeal was far from over...

I was about half an hour in and I had already gotten through the entire bowl of nachos and about two and a half beers (I tended to eat and drink more when I got excited). Jon Lormer had arisen from the grave to wreak havoc on his family in the first story, *Father's day*, when the noises re-appeared in my ears. It sounded as though something was scraping across the wooden floor, like some sort of sharp object. I immediately turned towards the cupboard to find in horror that the sound was once again coming from inside it. It was creeping closer towards the door, sounding like a giant sloth stretching its paws out slowly, one step at a time. Whatever it was, I imagined straight away the sharp scratching on the floor surface had to be a claw of some sort. There was a sound of boxes toppling over, one at a time. My heart completely stopped (cliché I know, but that is the only was of describing it. It felt as though somebody had come up to me and literally held my heart tightly and wasn't letting it go).

The sound was so clear. Something was alive under the stairs. It was a fact. Not my imagination, not through excessive drinking, or any type of out of date nacho, but a stone cold fact. Something was inside that cupboard, and it had woken up.

I thought about jumping behind the sofa, but wondered how effective that tactic would be were the thing to escape the cupboard. I just froze, not moving any inch of my body, staying perfectly (and more importantly, quietly) still. My mind traced back to the Tyrannosaurus Rex in Jurassic Park.

Don't move… it can't see us if we don't move…

I looked at the cupboard door, concentrating on the single bolt trying to figure out how sturdy it was. I hadn't even paused the DVD, so not to arouse any suspicion of the room's ambience. The second story of the anthology was beginning, but I couldn't keep my eyes off that dam bolt.

I remembered Cathy moaning about why we needed a bolt across the cupboard door in the first place. She insisted that it would stay shut on its own, but I noticed it slightly ajar at times so decided to put one on anyway. There's something not right about a door that's neither fully open nor tightly shut. She complained that it made the door look old, rusty and heavy (probably the reason why the cupboard had been neglected all these years). I was so glad I didn't listen to her on that occasion now, and half of me at the time resented her for even arguing about the bolt, the one thing that may stop this thing attacking me. But as I looked intently at the bolt, I was beginning to consider just how good of a job I did on it…

The slow, agonising creeping came to a halt. Whatever it was, it had to be at the door of the cupboard; surveying it's surroundings, considering its options. I let a gasp as I inhaled in, in which I was answered by a weighty grunt. I let out a small shriek at the sound of this. This was England, not bloody Australia! There were never any dangerous animals here. Sure, now and then you would get an angry badger or fox growl at you (some countryside hikers would even consider this a rare treat), but not a crocodile or a bear or a tiger or a snake or a gorilla or whatever other dangerous animals there were in this world. So I don't really take any shame in saying that yes, I did indeed let out a small shriek.

The door moved slowly. It was nudging it, trying to open it, trying to get out, but being held back by the single bolt, my single bolt I put on myself. The bolt rattled looking as though it could come swinging off at any second; at least I thought I saw it rattle… I thought I saw the door move as well. I could have sworn that something was trying to get out, break free, but as soon as I saw these movements the sooner the room fell silent again. All the noises had vanished, leaving the faint humming of the television still playing *Creepshow*. I managed to free my right arm from its state of stunned stature, grabbed the remote with my newly working hand and paused the movie.

Had the creature decide all of a sudden to give up? I listened further for any more grunts or scrapes of any kind, but nothing. There was not a sound coming from the cupboard. Gone. The thing had gone.

Another thought crossed my mind; perhaps an even scarier thought. What if there was nothing there? What if I was imagining it? Some would consider this to be a blessing, the idea that a potentially life-threatening experience could be so quickly overridden by the relief of nonsense imagination. Not me. I had an uncle Peter who said he heard voices when he was on his own, telling him naughty things that nobody should speak of. He spent his last remaining years locked up in a nuthouse, along with all kinds of other whackos I spotted when visiting him every other week. So no, this was not a good sign at all.

I jumped up off the sofa and headed towards the kitchen. I searched the drawers for some heavy objects, something I could use as protective weaponry. I got as far as a rolling pin and gave up searching. I wasn't living in the house of flying daggers, so this was probably my best option without accidently stabbing myself.

Carefully, I crept towards the cupboard once more, this time armed. Half of me wanted to find something. I wanted to come across a fox or a dog or some sort of animal that could justify making all that noise (even though I knew that those eyes were not ones of either of those animals, or any other animal I had ever seen). But as I opened the cupboard and switched on the light all I saw was the same dusty sight as before. No boxes were overturned, no claw marks on the wooden floor, no sign of anything hitting the door.

Nothing.

I immediately poured the remainder of the beers away in the sink, threw the last bits of crumbs from the nachos into the bin and put on the kettle for a good strong cup of hot coffee. Maybe there was something in the beers or food that had a bad effect on me, disagreed with my digestive system. What was it that Ebenezer Scrooge said: nothing but an indigested bit of beef, a blot of mustard, a crumb of cheese and all that? *Old Scroogie was wrong about that though wasn't he?*

I balanced the steaming hot cup of coffee in my hand as I sat back down to watch the rest of my film. Monster or no monster, I was adamant I was going to finish the end of *Creepshow*.

Half an hour and two cups of coffee went by with no interruptions. Then out of nowhere a loud banging noise made me jump out of my skin (another cliché, this time I didn't actually do this). My eyes darted towards the cupboard door, which stood still, not moving at all.

It was all in my head, I kept saying to myself, which didn't feel me with any more comfort. *It was all in my head, it was all in my head...*

'David? Are you home?' I soon heard murmuring through the front door. 'David? It's Trish? You in?'

I sighed in relief; probably the only time I ever did that after hearing Trish's annoyingly painful high-pitched voice. I got up to open the door and when I did was greeted with a flash of cherry red lipstick smiling directly at me.

'Hello David!' She gave me a kiss on each cheek and trotted in with her high heels, her furry coat brushing my face as she walked past. 'I thought for a moment you weren't home? Did Cathy warn you I was popping round?'

'Yes, she did; sorry, I was watching a movie.'

'Oh, I'm not interrupting am I?'

'No, not at all.' I lied. 'What was it again you were after? You're purse isn't it?'

'Yeah,' she said. 'I left it round here last time I was round here; you know, that time me and Cath came back from Swankys?'

Swankys was a bar that played loud annoying music in town. A place I got dragged to on several occasions, and despised.

'It's upstairs on Cathy's dressing table I think; I'll just go up and get it for you.'

'Thanks David.' I walked up the stairs without offering Trish a seat or a drink. I didn't really want her hanging around for too long. Trish was okay in small doses, but for any lengthy amount of time she proved irritating. I found the purse on the floor in our bedroom. I knew it had to be Trish's, as it was coated with glitter and looked absolutely hideous. If it belonged to Cathy I would have definitely noticed it by now and complained about it.

'Is this it?' I asked while holding it up to Trish as I walked down the stairs.

'That's the one! What am I like ey? I can't believe I left it here in the first place.' She said, a bit too excitedly. 'I'd lose my own head if it wasn't screwed on! God, it's the only purse that will match my outfit for tomorrow.'

'Right,' I said while handing over her revolting purse, careful not to ask her what the occasion was. I also wondered what in the hell would match the disgusting thing.

'It's Lloyd's work do tomorrow,' said Trish anyway, 'they're celebrating a big deal they've just signed. I'm not sure of the ins and outs of it, but it means we get to celebrate; so it must be good! We're going to this fancy restaurant up town, famous for its seafood. Can't remember the name of it, but I think it's just off of Upper Street. I'm not a big seafood lover myself but it's a night out isn't it?'

I nodded, looking at the front door that was still open, trying to hint in a polite manner. I didn't really want to hear about Lloyd's successful business achievements. I had met Lloyd before, and thought he was a complete arsehole. He was arrogant, smug and very good-looking. He liked to show off his fortune every chance he got. One of the ways was by dressing up with trophy wife Trish like a Barbie doll. *He probably thought he was a dead ringer for Ken as well.*

'Yeah, the business is going really well for him, but he works very hard for it. He's always working late in the office, I hardly ever see him until the weekend and even then something usually comes up. Still, gets me my shopping money doesn't it ey?' She gave a cheeky wink with her over the top fake eyelashes and let out a cackle of a laugh. 'Oh, what am I like?' I restrained from answering that, instead just doing my best fake laugh I could.

And then, the noises from inside the cupboard began again.

It started with the slow scraping on the wooden floor, following by heavy footsteps. I looked at Trish to see whether she acknowledged it at all, but she carried on yapping about god knows what.

'...I said to Cathy she needs to come on one of my shopping sprees at Blue Water, but Cathy said she couldn't bear to watch me in action! She said she'd have to join in the spree with me! You'd love that wouldn't you David! Oh, God I'm a terrible influence aren't I...'

Trish was standing directly in front of the cupboard. *How could she not hear that?* It was nearly deafening. The slow thuds of the steps were getting louder and louder. Faster the sounds came, growing towards us. *The thing inside was coming at the door again, trying once more to get out...*

'...I mean I know most of it I'll never use, but what's money good for if you can't spend it ey David?' I nodded politely in agreement. *What if it was all in my head? She couldn't hear it could she? She would have said something by now surely?*

A heavy knock on the cupboard door echoed throughout the living room. I looked at Trish for some sort of response, any reaction at all.

It was all in my head wasn't it. It was all in my head; it was all in my head...

'What am I like ey David!' Cackled Trish. 'God you must think I'm awful don't you David, I'm such a... What's that noise?'

Trish looked behind her at the cupboard, nearly filling my mouth with her fur coat as she turned around. As much as I was relieved that she could hear the sound and that I was not going insane (at least not on my own anyway), I was stunned speechless, as if embarrassed by it; like it was my secret noise that I kept under the stairs myself.

'I think there's some strange noise coming from in 'ere David?' Said Trish, putting her ear close to the cupboard door (she had to hold aside her dangly earring to listen). The cupboard door thumped loudly, almost knocking into Trish. She jumped back slightly. 'Something's in there David, do you have a naughty little doggy you've locked up? Let's have a look...'

Before I could even react, Trish's glossy fake fingernails were unlocking the rusty bolt, holding back whatever was behind it.

'Trish, no!' I tried to grab her, to stop her... *to save her...* But I was too late.

As the door swung open a flash of bright light that filled the whole room immediately blinded me. It was though I was caught in some sort of a trance; although I was fully aware of myself I could not seem to move. I felt like I was floating, but my feet were still firmly on the ground. I tried to move towards the cupboard, searching with my arms to find Trish. The light cleared, like fog finally settling, and then I saw it again…

I saw its eyes again…

They came from within the darkness of the cupboard and were wider than before, as though it was now fully awake, fully aware. It seemed to back off deeper into the cupboard, its eyes still staring directly into mine. *It was looking at me, challenging me, eyeing me out…*

And then it was gone, faded completely out. The shining light glared strongly one more time and then lifted completely. As my eyes refocused, I saw that the cupboard door was once again closed, *and bolted shut…*

'Trish?' I shouted out calling for her, once I had fully recovered and could move again. 'Trish?'

What the hell had just happened? Had I just blacked out? Did I dream it all? Was it all in my head? The living room looked exactly the same, the cupboard door was bolted shut; did Trish even come round?

Perhaps I was going crazy after all. I looked at the television screen. *Creepshow* was still running. It was on the third story now, the one with Leslie Neilson in it. My cup of coffee was sitting on the table next to the sofa (although I didn't remember pouring myself a third cup…). I sat down, mostly because I was exhausted, as well as wanting to return to my original position before any of this madness had happened. I looked around the room, darting backwards and forwards. I was in the living room, but it didn't *feel* like my living room. The only best way I can describe it is that it was like when I was younger being back at school when it was dark; on nights like parents evening or school plays. I knew where I was, but at the same time, as I walked through the same corridors I would walk through every day, I would feel disorientated by the exclusion of light. That was how I felt at that moment. The only sanctuary I had was from the television screen.

And then my eyes spotted it.

On the floor next to the cupboard door was Trish's God awful purse and one of her dangly chandelier earrings.

It happened! Oh God, it happened! She was here. Trish was here. But where the hell was she now? I thought, as I looked towards the cupboard doors…

I drank the third cup of coffee, pacing up and down the living room, keeping my distance from the cupboard. I stopped pacing for a second, grabbed a chair from the dining room and stacked it against the cupboard, wedging it tightly shut.

All this time, I had loved horror movies, novels, comic books, games, anything to do with the genre. I always imagined what I would do if was ever in such a predicament, secretly longing to find out. And now that I was in my very own horror story, I soon discovered that I did not like it one bit.

So what the hell was I supposed to do? Should I call the police now? Was this now the correct occasion to do so?

I picked up the phone and called Cathy; after all, it was her friend.

'Hang on Hannah... Hello?' She said after finally picking up. 'Who is this?' I wasn't sure why she asked who it was, as I was pretty certain our house number would show up on her mobile.

'Cathy, don't panic; but something's happened to Trish!' I said, doing my best trying not to sound panicked, but still with a sense of urgency.

'What's that about Trish?' She said, half yelling over the sound of a noisy restaurant where everybody was socialising, eating, drinking and having fun. Pretty much the exact opposite of what I was doing. 'Has she picked up her purse yet?'

'Yes, I mean no; well, she came round anyway... she might even still be here...'

'What?' She yelled, and then laughed; probably due to something funny one of the girls on her table had said to her. 'Sorry, I can't hear you that well David.'

Then just bloody move to somewhere you can hear me!

'Cathy...' I hesitated, but then thought I'd best just come out with it. 'Cathy... there's something under the stairs.'

Cathy giggled. 'What did you say?'

'There's something under the stairs Cathy! It's in the house!'

'It's probably the vacuum cleaner David; you know, that thing you rarely get a good look at?'

'Cathy, listen to me. Trish came round. There was something in the cupboard that came out and now she is gone. She could be in the cupboard with this thing. What should I do?'

'He's saying he locked Trish up in our downstairs cupboard,' Said Cathy to her friends around the table, which they responded by giggling.

'Keep her in the cupboard David!' One of them shouted down the phone.

'Throw away the key!'

'Cathy, no, listen! I don't know what to do. Should I call the police? Should I tell Lloyd about Trish?'

'He's been watching scary movies all evening, trying to freak me out before I get home.' She informed the table. 'Look, all you need to do is chuck a bottle of vodka in the cupboard and she'll be fine for the morning. I got to go now David; our mains have just arrived. Kisses!'

'Cathy? Cathy!' She had hung up. I ran towards the front window, looking outside to see whether one of our neighbours was out walking past that could help. We didn't speak to them much at all, but now was a good a time as any.

But there was no one out there. No sign of movement, apart from a few cars cruising by on the road. I then saw Trish's convertible parked directly outside our house. I knew it was hers from the last time I saw it. You can't really forget a car in a hurry that's bright pink all over.

People were going to know that she was here. Whatever happened now, it was plain and clear that Trish visited.

I picked up the phone again and dialled 999.

I told the police everything. To hell if they thought I was mad, I knew I wasn't, and this was an emergency. I told them every little detail I could think of, and then started to ease off every detail once I could hear the concern for my own sanity on the other end of the phone. I told them enough though, and that they needed to come round right away. They said they would be there as soon as they could... I slammed the phone down by accident, and then curled up protectively on the sofa, staring towards the stairs.

There was no way I was going to look in that cupboard again; at least not on my own. That ugly beast was waiting for me to do so; I just knew it.

And just as I thought about it, the cupboard began to shake furiously. It was as though whatever it was inside there could hear what I was thinking, and wanted to come out and tell me what *it* was thinking. The chair seemed to be securing it nicely, although the single bolt still didn't fill me with confidence, as it rattled away helplessly. I looked around the room for another object I could use to block the door, something, *anything...*

I could see our old wooden chest of drawers that we kept all our CDs, DVDs in the first drawer, and obsolete formats such as VHS and cassette in the bottom one. God knows what we kept in between the middle two, but there was no way I was moving that on my own. I thought about using the globe drinks cabinet sitting in the corner next to the kitchen, but remembered how I had found that in spitalsfield market and bought it on an impulse purchase. Cathy loved it and was completely shocked by my spontaneity. Such nostalgia could not be dragged across the floor without fear of damaging it. And then I saw the coffee table… a practical item, but it wasn't my most favourite piece of furniture in the house, so I began to drag it across the floor towards the cupboard. It was probably going to be the best supporting obstacle anyway, and could easily hold that thing at bay until the police arrived.

I have to admit, looking back, I am very surprised as to how calm and collective I was at this stage. Cathy's friend Trish, as far as I knew, had just been sucked into our cupboard under the stairs by some wild monster that was now trying to break free and take me in there too. I was being very responsive, very matter of fact about the situation. I was working logically, trying to keep this affair from occurring. As long as I held this *thing* back before the police arrived, they would know what to do with it, I would be safe from harm, they would find Trish and there would be a rational explanation for the whole of this. After all, this was Britain…

But then something happened that threw my entire plan out of the window and crashing down onto the pavement floor with a horrendous smash.

The bolt broke free…

The dam flimsy thing couldn't hold on any longer, the screws holding it together pinged out (one nearly hitting me in the face I was that close with the coffee table) and it just snapped off. I shrieked (yet again) and threw myself at the mercy of the cupboard door, with my back helping the chair keeping it shut.

The door was banging against the back of my head at a frenzied pace. *It knew what it had done. It could taste the freedom. Or even worse, it could taste me…*

I could hear all sorts of crazy noises now. There was snorting, scratching, hissing, growling. I thought of Jurassic Park again, of the sounds that the Velociraptors had made in the film. *Perhaps*

Stephen Spielberg himself had a similar problem in his own downstairs cupboard before...

I was strong, but not that strong. I was getting the better of it by holding the door back, but this was mainly due to the added support of the chair. If that chair got knocked over, there was no chance that I could keep the door shut.

The banging stopped. I stopped. I paused and listened. The sound of its movement was getting thinner. It was retreating.

I had won! I had beaten it!

But as I listened further I could hear the sound of movement travelling louder at an alarming rate.

It's taking a bloody run up!

A thunderous bang sent me flying head first onto the floor. I knocked my head pretty hard, and thought for sure that I was bleeding, but could not see any blood. I pushed my back against the cupboard door, but something was blocking it shut. Something was half in and half out. My eyesight was still blurry from the hit I took, but could feel whatever it was trying to swing for me.

It was an arm, or a tail, or tentacle, or something hideous trying to grab me. I shielded myself as best I could, being partially blind for the moment.

My doorbell went. I had never been so happy to hear that God-awful chime before in my life. I wanted to run over and throw myself in the visitor's arms for protection, but I knew I couldn't move now. Not with this thing so close to breaking free. I needed to stay put for now.

'Help! I can't move!' I shouted over the deafening noise.

'Hello sir, this is the police! Are you okay?' Said a stern voice from outside.

Am I okay? Am I okay? Oh, no worries officer, everything is just peachy around here, sorry for disturbing you now.

'I can't move! You're going to have to break the door down!'

'I'm going to have to break the door down sir,' said the stern voice again. *I was so glad they sent the best of the best round...* 'Move away from the door!'

If I was near the bloody door I could open it you idiot!

The sound of the front door cracking was simultaneous with the sound of the cupboard door giving way. Each hit on the front door lost me time in the cupboard door. I was slipping away; my socks were beginning to slide across our living room floor. The thing was louder than ever. I knew I didn't have much time left. My arms were growing weak, as was my legs. The pain in my back was getting worse. *I couldn't hold on any longer…*

The chair slipped away, and the cupboard door swung open at the exact same time the front door swung open. I dived onto the floor shielding my entire body, waiting for the monster to attack.

'Sir? Is everything alright?'

I looked up and saw a concerned looking policeman staring down at me. He looked too young to be a policeman to me, but then again I didn't know what the starting age was.

'Get away from the cupboard!' I shouted at him, trying to pull him down to the ground with me (not sure how that was going to help him actually, but it seemed like the thing to do at the time).

'Sir!' He said, taking my hand off him. 'Sir, calm down. Now we've had a report that there's a missing woman here; is this correct?'

I nodded while sitting up. I looked over at the cupboard, which was open; but there was nothing there, only the vision of the first stacked boxes. Another policeman had walked in; a little bit older, and picked up my DVD remote and turned *Creepshow* off.

Hey, *I was watching that bozo…*

'And, we have also been told that there's a man who thinks that there's something in his cupboard under the stairs, which may have took her?'

I nodded again. The policeman then looked at his colleague and nodded to him. The older policeman then grabbed my arms gently and pulled me up.

'There, there now, why don't you come with me while officer Williams has a look around?'

'Where are we going?' I said.

'Just to the car sir, I need to ask you a few questions.'

They thought I was mad, that was the bottom line. Nobody believed me. Not the police, not Cathy, not Trish's husband Lloyd, not the Jury, not the Judge, not even the nutters they threw me in with. They didn't believe my story at all.

After taking me outside, officer Williams had searched the downstairs cupboard and found Trish. Now, I didn't like Trish very much, but I do have a bit of respect for the dead, so I'm not going to go into detail as to how they had found her, or at least what was left of her. And as I was the only one there at the time, guess who they blamed for the whole thing on? Oh, and my side of the story didn't exactly help me win over any fans either. They thought I had gone crazy.

. The judge at the trial told me that I was 'a danger to myself and to others around me' *(bloody cliché...)*. I can never forget Cathy's face at that place. She couldn't even look at me. It was a though someone had drained her completely. She looked so pale, timid, *and ashamed.*

So they locked me up, but not in prison, oh no. They put me in some nut house for the criminally insane. It was like being in Arkham Asylum. I keep expecting the Joker or the Riddler to jump out at me at any moment. The other prisoners (or patients as they like to call us), even the guards, all keep their distance from me. It's as though I'm some sort of monster walking amongst them, like I was Mike Myers, or Jason, or Freddy Krueger *(I have to admit, I do like the idea of that; like I am the invincible killer in a horror movie...).*

But my immortal thoughts have soon vanished as of late, as there's something here with us that I have seen. Something that keeps tormenting me every time I walk past. I know it's there, *it* knows I know as well. I can feel it, hear it. It is in the janitor's cupboard under the stairs. The janitor's been missing for a few days now. Only I know what's happened...

It's trying to get out now. I need to warn someone, but I fear that they will think that I'm insane, like my good old uncle Peter. *Perhaps he would be able to hear it too if he was here?*

Either way, everyone here is in big trouble, as I know for a fact that there is something under the stairs... (Not a cliché yet, but I fear it will become one very soon)

And I still haven't had a chance to watch *From beyond the grave...*

Barry

'I say, Charles darling? Could you be a sport and snap some leaves off of Barry would you? There's a good chap.' Projected Henry towards the living room, whilst pouring the red wine vinegar across the diced up pieces of tomato in the kitchen.

'Of course Henry.' Said Charles, who put his broadsheet paper down by the side of the armchair and got up; his pipe still smoking proudly in the corner of his mouth. He strolled his way over to the living room windowsill at the front of the flat, where their beloved basil plant was growing boldly towards the light. He picked off a few of its leaves and then walked through the open doors into the kitchen.

'There you go dear.' He said, while planting an affectionate peck on Henry's cheek and handing over the basil to him. 'Dinner nearly ready then I presume?'

'Oh yes Charles; bread's just come out the oven, strips of beef have been marinated and cooked, half rare for you and half medium to well done for me, the mint yoghurt dip's on the table and I'm just about ready with the tomato salad.'

'You're a clever one aren't you Henry.'

'I know, I know, just as long as you do some of the washing up afterwards. And don't try and sweet talk your way out of it this time.'

'Alright…' Sighed Charles, and then went over the sink and poured a glass of water. 'I think I'm going to give Barry a bit more to drink.'

'Good lord Charles; you look after the basil better than you look after yourself. It doesn't look as though it's ever dropped a single leaf on it's own yet.'

'And you know why? It's because of the special attention and care I give to it. All a plant needs to thrive is good, honest nurturing.'

The pair laughed in unison. Charles left the kitchen with the full glass of water and made his way over to his prized foliage. He gleamed admiringly at his achievement, while pouring the water in the shallow bowl at the base of the plant pot. Barry was a healthy plant that was for sure, growing well over double in size since they bought him. He was a magnificent basil plant to behold. His stems were fully erect; strong, sturdy roots; his leaves were fully green and vibrant. There were no signs of fusarium wilt, bacterial leaf spot, basil shoot blight, downy mildew, or any of the other basic basil plant diseases (Charles had looked all these up just to make sure what to look out for). Most basil plants only lasted for a year, and Barry had been with them for a good 10 months with not one leaf being dropped in all that time.

'There you go Barry... a little more water for you; soak it up old boy.'

But as he carefully touched Barry's leaves, spreading them aside, something caught Charles' eye in midst of the base of the stem.

'I say...' Said Charles, while looking slightly puzzled at his herb. 'Henry? Henry, come over here for a moment would you?'

'I'm just finishing the tomato salad Charles, don't be so impatient.'

'No, no Henry; come in here for a second. Come and have a look at this...'

'Good lord Charles, what the devil is it?' Said Henry, carrying out the tomato salad to put on the dining table in the living room. He met Charles, who was bent down next to Barry in a still glaze. 'Well?'

'Well you see; I don't really know. But have a look at this.' He lifted up a few of Barry's leaves to reveal something else growing out of his stem. 'Now what does that look like to you?'

Henry knelt down to observe, and couldn't believe what he thought he saw.

'I say...'

'That's what I said.' Chuckled Charles.

'Is that what I think it is?' Questioned Henry.

'I think it might be.'

'But this doesn't make any sense. Basil plants don't grow a set of teeth do they? No plant does! I mean, I don't even think Venus flytraps grow real teeth. Barry looks like he's got a full set of choppers hidden away there.'

'Well how about that, our little Barry; one of a kind!'

'What's that play called Charles?' Questioned Henry again, this time clicking his fingers to spur some remembrance. 'You know, the one in the flower shop...'

'Oh you mean Little Horrors?'

'Yes, yes... No, it's not called that... Little Horror Shop...'

'Little Shop of Horrors?'

'Yes! That's the one. We've got ourselves our own little shop of horror haven't we?'

'Well, he's hardly big enough to eat anybody now is he.' Charles sniggered.

'You never know… The plant in the play started off small, but sure grew after that. You said it yourself before that Barry was growing faster than most plants usually did.'

Charles nodded in acceptance, and then a silence of pondering momentarily filled the room.

'Just as long as the blasted thing doesn't start singing to us!' Laughed Henry. Charles blushed slightly, not entirely sure he should tell Henry about occasionally singing to Barry while doing the ironing. 'So what do you think we should do about it? I mean, we should tell someone right?'

'No, no…' Said Charles protectively. 'Barry's our little plant. If we tell someone they'll take him away.'

'They could give us some money for him? Maybe he's a rare find. Could be worth something Charles…'

'Oh? And what would they do with our poor Barry then? They would put him under every lamp and test him until all his leaves fall off. No, no Henry; Barry stays here.'

Henry sighed in acceptance. There was no use arguing the point. He knew that he wasn't going to persuade his Charles into parting with his beloved plant; not after all the effort he went through looking after Barry. For Charles, to give him up to somebody else, even for a good sum of money, would be unthinkable.

'So what do you think we should do with our little friend then?'

Charles bent down further to inspect the strange growth, while taking a good pull of his pipe to concentrate. Henry loved it when Charles smoked his pipe. He always looked so sophisticated; like a handsome Sherlock Holmes.

'Well, I say we keep guard of old Barry and see how he develops; see how big he gets, and see how big *that* gets.' Said Charles, pointing towards Barry's set of teeth.

'Why? Do you think it could turn dangerous?'

'It? He… Henry. Barry has a name you know.'

'All right, do you think Barry could potentially be dangerous then?'

Charles took another drag on his pipe.

'Not yet... But there's definitely potential. How about we give him some of our beef strips?'

Henry gave him a stare, but then went to the kitchen and came back with a piece of rare beef (Charles' half). He handed it to Charles, who then carefully dangled it over Barry's teeth. The pair stared in amazement as the set of chompers began to move in curiosity, edging closer towards the strip of meat.

All of a sudden, Barry's teeth started frantically gnawing away at the beef as if it had been starving in the desert for months on end. It swallowed it down in a matter of seconds, causing a startled and unbalanced Henry to stumble backwards over their antique coffee table, which was followed by a loud thud.

'Good lord!'

'Henry, are you alright?' Said Charles, hurrying towards Henry's aid.

'Yes, yes. It's only me being clumsy as usual. But my word! What a hungry little fellow we have. I was not expecting that!'

Charles held out his arm and helped lift Henry to his feet.

'Looks like we'll need another placemat around the table!' Laughed Charles, soon followed in harmony by Henry.

There was a heavy trot of footsteps that was coming from their ceiling, which escalated downwards until ending up at the front door of their flat. A thunderous repetition of banging on the door quickly averted the pair's attention momentarily away from Barry and towards their visitor. Charles, still with his pipe hanging out his mouth, opened the door to their landlady Mrs Badger.

'Ah, Mrs Badger, what a pleasant surprise this is. How are you?'

'What the bleedin' 'el's been 'appening down 'ere then? I 'eard a commotion? Woke me up from my kip!' Said Mrs Badger, letting herself in and nosily inspecting the place.

'Oh, that was I Mrs Badger.' Said Henry, putting up his arm in apology. 'Just me being clumsy.'

'Well I've 'ad it with you two down 'ere. I can't keep up with all this noise all the time. Your tenancy agreement's over next month, and I want you two out of 'ere! You understand me?'

'Now, now old girl... be fair. This is the first time you have ever complained about any noise.'

'Don't you "old girl" me!' She snapped, shaking her bony finger at Charles. 'It ain't natural. Don't think I'm stupid, I know what you two are! Two men sharing a flat together?' She pointed at the open door to one of the bedrooms. 'I notice there's no bed in that one? I know what you two are up to. You're a pair of fags aren't you?'

Charles and Henry exchanged shocked looks. It wasn't as though they had kept it a secret.

'We didn't know you felt like that?' Said Henry for the both of them.

'Well of course I do! It ain't natural!' She repeated. 'If I'da known what you two were I would have never of let you stay 'ere. I mean, look at this place?' She pointed at the antique furniture and then at the paintings. 'It's like your living in your own little weird *queer* world? You're a pair of freaks! Next month, you're out; you 'ere me? Out!'

She glanced at both of them strongly, before letting herself out. 'Start packing, you pair of queers!' She turned and said before slamming the front door shut.

Henry gave out a heavy sigh and slumped down onto the armchair. 'Good God; you think you know someone…'

'That's probably what she's thinking about us.' Laughed Charles, holding on to Henry's hand for comfort. 'Oh dear… what are we going to do?'

'I suppose we need to start looking for somewhere else to live.'

'We'd be lucky to find anywhere else in this town. We can't buy, not with the money we've got, and where else in this town rents out? Let's face it, we won't find another place like this.' Said Charles. They both worked in the town centre, just a short walk away, and without neither of them being able to drive would make it difficult for both of them to live any further away.

'So what are we going to do about that old bag upstairs then? She's pretty much made up her mind. We've got a month left, and we're out.'

Charles now gave a heavy sigh and sat on the sofa opposite. He picked up his pipe that was sitting neatly in the ashtray and re-lit it. It took a few puffs to get it going and then he shook off the lit match. He sat back and pondered.

'We need to get rid of her Henry.' Charles whispered, aware that Ms Badger was probably trying to listen in on them.

'What are you saying Charles?' Whispered back Henry.

'I am saying that our lives would be at lot better if that old girl wasn't around. Think about it; she has no family does she?'

'That we're aware of Charles.'

'Well that's something we can look into in a bit more depth now isn't it, but as far as we're aware of, I haven't seen a single guest enter this block of flats for her, not even once; not to mention her ever leaving here for a few days.'

'We would be so lucky!'

'So,' continued Charles, 'that means she either doesn't have any close relatives or she has fallen out with the ones she has.'

'Meaning?'

'Meaning, that if she were,' he whispered even more so than before, 'God forbid to ever have a serious accident, or go missing; how many people would really miss her?'

'Charles…' Said Henry in a disappointing tone. 'You can't say such things darling. We've come across bigger bigots than that old trollop upstairs.'

'But none of which he have had to move because of.' He pointed his pipe at Henry, backing up his argument. 'There is no way I am moving because of who we are. People like her upstairs do not deserve anything; and you agree with me Henry, I know you do.'

Henry let out a sigh in acceptance. *There was no use in arguing the point.* '…So, how do we do it?'

'You mean…'

'Yes, you know what I mean.' Said Henry, signalling to keep his voice down.

'Killing her? That's the easy part.' He said it anyway. He knew Henry didn't want to hear it, but thought he had better get used to it as a matter of fact. 'You saw how she waltzed in here; she's not afraid of two queers now is she?' He said sarcastically.

'Invite her round and then gag her? Strangle her? Stab her with the kitchen knife?'

Charles chuckled. 'Well, I'll let you use your colourful imagination there sir; you seem to have a few ideas already. No, the tricky part is getting rid of her. We can't have her in the cupboard under the kitchen sink waiting for the police to find. We need to get rid of her so she vanishes.'

'Like she wasn't even here…'

'Exactly…' Charles pointed his pipe at Henry in agreement. Henry leaned his head back, trying to think; or perhaps to take it all in, what he was actually agreeing to do.

'How do we get rid of her then Charles?' But before Charles could answer, there was a soft rumble, like a small vibration, that came from the windowsill. The two men looked over and saw that the sound was coming from Barry.

'Oh dear, I forgot about our hungry little friend over there Charles.' Laughed Henry while holding his forehead. Charles jumped up from his seat, as if shouting eureka, nearly spilling his tobacco over Henry.

'That's it!' He heavily whispered through his teeth. 'That's it! Barry!'

'What?' Questioned Henry.

'Barry. You saw how the old boy went through the meat earlier; he didn't leave a trace of it after, did he?'

'Well, I would like to think that my marinated beef is a bit more tasty to get through than Mrs Badger.' Said Henry, folding his arms in protest.

'But what better way is there to get rid of her Henry? Think about it; there wont be a trace left of her. What do you say?'

'What about bone Charles? Do you really think Barry can gnaw through human bone?' And at this, Barry rumbled again, shaking his leaves as though seeming to accept the challenge. Henry and Charles exchanged glances.

'I'll go defrost the chicken legs from the freezer…' Whispered Henry. 'Just to check…'

Two months later, the two of them were sat round their old wooden dining table eating Henry's chilli prawn noodles; both using chopsticks elegantly. They had *Leon Russell* softly playing over the speakers in the background.

'How's the noodles darling?'

'Superb as usual Henry; superb!' Complimented Charles; after dabbing the side of his mouth with the napkin. 'You fancy throwing a prawn over for Barry? I think he may be hungry again.'

'Of course.' Said Henry, and then picked up a prawn from his plate and threw it like a dart across the room into the corner where Barry sat patiently in his large floor standing pot. The tips of his roots were now almost touching the flat ceiling, his leaves were bright green, looking healthy in colour, and his teeth had grown stronger and pointier. The prawn was gone in a matter of seconds.

'We overfed him slightly didn't we Charles.'

'Slightly,' agreed Charlie with a smirk across his face.

'You don't suppose they're going to be a tad suspicious when they come to search here for Mrs Badger and see Barry now do you?' Said a concerned Henry.

'If they want to take a closer inspection of Barry then they can be my guests.' Said Charles, holding his hands up innocently.

Henry let out a deep sigh in acceptance. 'Fine,' he said. 'But I mean it; the damn thing best not start singing to us…'

Ashes to Ashes

'Jesus Christ!' Blurted out Charlie Simms, while swerving his Mitsubishi Jeep around a poised pigeon in the middle of the motorway. Luckily there were no other cars on either side of the road, so he straightened up the wheel, gave out a breezy sigh and relaxed again. If truth were told he was soon thankful for the feathered hazard, as it helped to wake him up a bit and stopped him falling asleep behind the wheel.

He grabbed his coffee container and took a large swig to make sure he stayed alert from then on. Charlie never liked long distance travelling, and especially did not like travelling on his own. He could go stir crazy talking to himself, and with no decent radio frequency, CD player or MP3 port, he was stuck on his own.

Technically though he was not *completely* alone. Sitting comfortably in the front passengers seat next to Charlie was a briefcase. Strapped inside the briefcase tightly was an oval shaped urn, and inside the urn was a sealed bag. Inside the sealed bag were the ash remains of Arthur Horton, Charlie's father-in-law.

Together they were on their way travelling from Buckinghamshire down to Cornwall, to a quaint little village called Tintagel. This was Arthur's childhood home, and it was on his deathbed that he requested to be scattered at sea there, commemorating the days he spent fishing off the rocks with his father and old school friends.

Charlie had been given the task of having to transport Arthur down to Tintagel, where Charlie's wife, Carol, and the rest of her family had already gathered. Due to a misunderstanding at the funeral traders, Arthur's urn was not entirely ready when the grieving and very angry widower Mary, Charlie's mother-in-law, went to collect her husband. As they had a schedule to stick to for the ceremonial weekend (distant relatives flying in and all) and Charlie, not being able to get time off work on the Friday morning, immediately got nominated in collecting and taking down Arthur for the Saturday morning scattering.

So here he was. Or rather, here they were: the pair voyaging down to the West Country together.

'I tell you what Arthur; these dam pigeons are getting braver.' Commented Charlie, whilst looking across his shoulder to the passenger seat, pretending to talk to his father-in-law. He much preferred talking to him like this than before. 'Why I remember when pigeons used to just fly away at the roar of an engine. But now, well now they just sit there. Heck, half the time I don't even know if they're ever going to take off at all. It's as though they want to test you, to see if you *would* run them over, like they're playing chicken. Ha! Imagine that Arthur, a pigeon playing chicken!'

'Giss on! You don't arf tork some rubbish when you're on ya todd Charlie boy.' Said a thick Cornish accent, coming from inside the briefcase.

Charlie had to do a double take. He could not believe it. He knew that voice anywhere.

Surely he hadn't heard it? But it was so clear? Now he knew that the drive was making him go stir crazy.

Baffled and quite disturbed, Charlie decided to ignore what he thought he heard and focused on his driving. The sooner he got there, the sooner he could have a drink. He had a heavy week of work and it was obvious now that it was catching up on him in a big way.

'So what, now that arm 'ere ya don't wanna say 'ello ta me?' Said Arthur's voice again, questioning Charlie's hostile behaviour Charlie nearly jumped out of the seat and his eyes flung in the direction of the suitcase. He banged his head a few times with his left hand, trying to force the voice out of his mind, and then breathed in and out heavily. He did not want to believe it.

It was all in his head. He needed a drink...

Charlie washed down the remainder of his coffee supply without even touching the sides.

'Cam' on Charlie boy; talk ta me! Arv Been bored stiff all journey.'

'Go away!' Snapped back Charlie for the first time. 'You're not real! You're in my head. I haven't had much sleep lately... that's it. I've had late nights at work and the stress is getting to me. I'm just talking to myself here...'

'Oh, sure you Ahh. Arm just a figment of your imagination! Arm not real at arl am a?' Said Arthur, very sarcastically. *'Ya never was good at getting' things right first time were ya?'*

'I'm not hearing this...' Assured Charlie to himself.

A signpost for services flashed by the side road, which Charlie anxiously examined. There were two miles remaining until the next stop. He decided to turn off at the next one and get some much-needed fresh air. He was feeling claustrophobic. He also found that he was perspiring heavily.

'So ya just guna ignore me right? If you ignore me I'll jus go away? That ya plan?' Questioned Arthur.

Charlie stayed silent, concentrating on getting to the service station, trying to keep it together.

He only had one more mile to go.

He could see the turnoff in the distance up ahead. He was almost there. He could not help but to keep glimpsing over at the passengers seat, staring at the briefcase. Half of him was expecting to see it start moving or shaking around, but it stayed completely motionless, bar the occasional jerks caused by bumps in the road.

The Jeep finally pulled into the services car park. Charlie's seatbelt was already off before the ignition stopped. He leapt out, slammed the door, and then breathed in the fresh windy air. He wiped the sweat from his brow and tried to air out his shirt. Charlie knew that he had been suffering from stress as of late, but never knew how badly it would affect him.

After grabbing a snack from the sandwich bar and re-stocking on coffee, Charlie started to feel more at ease. He had not heard from Arthur for a good twenty minutes.

Perhaps it was just all in his head?

Charlie worked as a labourer in one of the large industrial factories just outside of High Wycombe. His work entailed mainly unloading lorries and sweeping anything that needed sweeping. It meant long shifts, low wages and little holiday time. He was not the worst employee, but by no means the best. It was not Charlie's plan to be there. After many years of trying to get into his true passion, to become a sport's journalist, but failing miserably, he eventually caved in and got the only job he could in order to help support the rent.

His wife Carol on the other hand had been given more luck in her bank position, being recently promoted, and was therefore the main provider of the house. Fortunately with no children there was no immediate rush or worry about Charlie's income.

Carol's father Arthur however, had an entirely different point of view on this. He had always looked down on Charlie and saw him as a waster, with no real manual drive in him. Arthur often commented on his failing writing career and constantly reminded

Charlie that '*if it wasn't up ta Carol bein' so socksessful, you'd both be lucky for a roof ova your 'eds.*'

Although not the easiest father-in-law to have around, Charlie was of course upset when he passed, more for the sake of Carol than his own grievance. But the last thing he needed right now was to be talking to dead people's ashes, *the least of all that criticising old fool's.*

Charlie cautiously got back into his Jeep. He slowly turned the key, as if not to wake Arthur up again. He pulled out of the car park, down the slip road and back onto the motorway. Once he reached seventy he eased off the accelerator and leaned back into his driver's seat. There was no sign of any voices. Charlie smiled to himself, and even managed a slight chuckle.

'*Ya miss me then Charlie boy?*'

'Jesus!' The sound of Arthur nearly made Charlie go head first through the sunroof. 'No, no, I'm not listening to you Arthur, you're not here!'

Charlie desperately searched for another sign by the side of the road, hoping for another service stop, or even a junction to pull off at: anything that would let him get out the car again.

'*Stap being a baby and talk ta me Charlie. There ain't another turnin' for a while now, so ya can't jes get rid of me.*'

'How are you back in my head? I thought I got rid of you?'

'*What? At the services!*' Arthur gave out a roaring laugh. '*Ya think I was guna waltz in there with ya? I'm a gonner here son, there's no foxtrots where I am now ya no.*'

He wanted to believe more than anything that he was going mad. He wanted to believe that it was all in his head. It was the most logical explanation. It was the one that made sense. The only other alternative was that Arthur was indeed talking to Charlie from beyond the grave, and communicating to him through his ashes.

'What do you want from me then?' Said Charlie defensively. His hands were going white from squeezing the steering wheel so hard. He could feel the sweat starting to build up again underneath his hair.

'*Can you jest relax for one moment Charlie boy; I ain't gonna hurt you am I? How can I ey? I'm in a bloomin urn.*'

This surprisingly did make Charlie a little less scared. It was true, Arthur was dead and inside the urn, which was inside the briefcase, that was seatbelt fastened tightly to the passenger seat.

Even if he managed a special Houdini escape trick, he was still just a pile of ashes.

'So… What do you want?' Asked Charlie; still uncertain as to whether he was questioning Arthur, or himself.

'Well, I know that me and yourself have never quite seen eye to eye, but seein' as it's you who's takin' me down to my berrin, it's you I'm guna 'af to ask a favour off of.'

Charlie huffed sarcastically. This was the same person who openly opposed his and Carol's engagement, so strongly in fact that he did not even turn up to the wedding. *And now the same person wanted a favour off of him?*

'You see Charlie boy,' Continued Arthur. *'As it stands, I am currently du' to be scattered at sea tomorrow by my dyin' wish. However, I have since had a change of 'art. I bin' talkin' to some of the others 'ere and they…'*

'Others? What others?' Interrupted Charlie. 'They're not here with you now are they?'

'Other dead people Charlie boy! We all talk to each other still. We all still ave a good natter. Well, they ave warned me 'bout burials 'n' scatterings at sea. They say that my ashes needs to stay all togetha' in one place, keeping myself in mind, body and spirit. If I'm spread at sea I'm goin' to be all ova' the place ain't I.'

'So what do you want from me then Arthur?'

'Well Charlie boy, I sorta' need you to call off the sea chuckin' for me. Let 'em place me in a nice graveyard somewhere instead.'

'So you want me to tell everybody that you, Arthur's ashes, have told me to call off the sea scattering?' Laughed Charlie hysterically, now more intrigued with his own sanity than disturbed. 'And it's because you want to be kept together, so you can keeping having a good old natter with the other dead people? They would think that I've gone mad. Maybe I have gone mad! I'm talking to a dead guy for Gods sake!'

The sign at the side of the road indicated another exit within three miles. Charlie contemplated whether or not to stop again. He wondered if it was worth it, or whether it would be better if he carried on so he got there quicker. Either way, he knew that one thing was for certain; Arthur was not going anywhere for a while.

'How about you jus' say you forgot to take me? You could jus' bury me by the side of the road and fill the urn up with soil? Nobody will notice will they ey?'

'I'm sure they'll notice the difference between soil and ashes Arthur. And anyway, why should I help you out with this? If I remember rightly you never helped me out once. You hated the fact that Carol married me and you used to constantly remind me that I was a failing journalist. Why should I help you out at all?'

The car fell silent for the first time since Arthur had spoken. Charlie looked to the slip road he was passing by, and then turned his eyes back to the road in front of him.

The initial fear of insanity had now passed. Although still very much in the back of his mind, it was now replaced with resentment, sparked by the remembrance of his father-in-law's spite. And now, after all those years of abuse, the shoe was indeed on the other foot. It was Arthur pleading for Charlie's aid. This was Charlie's chance to get even.

'I'll tell 'er what you did.' Said a very controlled Arthur.

This made Charlie uncomfortable. Him and Carol had no secrets between them. They shared everything together, their ups their downs, it did not matter. All of the boyfriends and girlfriends were a thing of the past, to which they could still discuss to each other about. Any past history of health problems or drug taking as a youngster was dealt with the first time they got into their first deep conversation. In Charlie and Carol's relationship there were no secrets. Apart from one...

'Oh really, what did I do then Arthur?' Said a protective Charlie, although he knew full well what he had done.

'Don' play dum' with me Charlie boy, I know what you did. And the others 'ere know what you did too. We all talk 'ere Charlie boy; we all talk. We all know 'bout you 'n' your mates.'

Now it was Charlie who fell silent. The car turned claustrophobic. He felt trapped, confronted. He knew what he had done, and he also knew that so did Arthur.

It was the early spring of eighty-eight. Charlie Simms had set off on the road in his ford Escort with his two best mates, Barry Goodman and Paul Jacobs. They were driving down for their Easter break holiday to Brighton. It was threatening to shower that day, although the sun was still beaming strongly. The ground was still damp from the weeks before heavy rainfalls, but the weather report was looking good for the following days ahead. The car itself was full of optimism and excitement from the three friends, crammed in with their entire luggage, along with Paul's spacious surfboard, even though he could not even stand up on one.

It was their first trip away from home as teenagers: old enough to drink, but still young enough not to worry. Barry sat in the passengers' seat alongside Charlie behind the wheel, while Paul sat in the back, constantly having to keep his head ducked to make room for the luggage: occasionally swapping seats at the service stations.

The whole journey they spoke about how many girls they could each pick up, where they could watch the football matches, how big they thought the apartment would be, what food and drink they should purchase at the off-licence to see them through the week, the amount of money they were going to spend. All basic questions with reasonable answers, but to them these topics were the foundation of their holiday. They needed to make sure they got each one right in order for a successful and memorable trip. The trip did indeed turned out to be memorable. Neither one of them forgot what was about to happen to them.

The side windows were halfway down, with Paul's leg spread alongside Barry's seat with his foot half sticking out the car. Barry had the map scrolled out on his lap navigating to Charlie, who was concentrating on the small and windy roads that seemed to get smaller at each turn.

Charlie did not know where they were; Paul did not know where they were; and the navigator Barry did not know what page on the map he was meant to be looking at. After admitting this to the other two, Paul started to hit Barry with his large foot in a playful banter. Barry, who was laughing along with Paul and Charlie, started to wrestle back and restrain Paul's boot. Charlie grabbed the map off of Barry's lap and began to try to figure out where they were while the two continued to scuffle.

Charlie managed to pinpoint their location by a nearby road sign. As he turned to the others to address his success, he was accidently greeted with an elbow to the face from Barry, which saw Charlie being hurled across the driving seat, with his head hitting the opposite closed window.

The Escort, with Charlie's hands still dangling on the wheel, skidded across the side of the road and collided with a thunderous thump on the windshield, to which all three boys jumped up in shock.

Charlie slammed on the breaks as hard as he could. The car slid across the road surface, causing a loud screeching sound, and then finally came to a stop.

As they finally got out of the car, they looked behind them and saw an elderly gentleman, who looked to be a frail old farmer, laid out on the side of the road across the tall grass. He did not move one inch. Each friend thought the worst. Each friend knew the worst. It took a very brave Paul to feel the old man's neck, and then reel back in terror.

They considered getting to the nearest town and calling for help. They considered staying with him until some other car drove past. They considered if anybody witnessed the accident. They considered whether they would be accused of manslaughter, of murder. They considered how long they would go to jail for. They considered driving on, and hope that somebody would eventually find him.

They considered making a pact…

The three friends carried on their holiday, but it did not consist of the fun filled frantic they once dreamed of. Instead it involved heavy deep drinking, arguments, fights, sleepless nights and lack of appetite.

After the holiday the three friends became increasingly distant from one another, until eventually came the point where they went out their way to avoid each other. Each was riddled with guilt for what they had done, but could never tell another soul to repent.

This was the one secret Charlie had that he never told his wife Carol, and never planned to either. Partly because of the pact, partly because of the fear of the reaction, but mostly because he wanted to believe that it never happened: that if he did not speak of it, it was not true.

Charlie hated driving at the best of times. It never failed to remind him of the spring of eighty-eight. And he especially hated driving whilst talking to a bribing, criticising and condescending pile of ashes.

The rest of the journey consisted of constant conflict between the two of them. Charlie, now fully acceptance of communicating with Arthur's ashes, spurted out all the times when Arthur had gone out of his way to cause trouble; how he always put him down in public; how he never showed him an ounce of respect.

Arthur, who all the time was threatening to tell Carol about Charlie's secret, blamed Charlie for holding Carol back: that she could have done so much better; that his career was a joke; and that he and his friends were murderers.

They kept bickering at each other all the way towards Exeter, with Charlie stopping halfway through to put Arthur in the boot of the car. But still he could hear him moan and complain.

This continued through to Launceston, past Bodmin and did not stop until they got to their destination.

A relieved Charlie parked the car along the road next to the cottage they had rented out for the weekend. He made sure that Arthur stayed in the car. He was still not entirely sure whether anyone else would be able to hear him, but did not want to risk it.

He carried his bags inside the cottage and greeted his wife Carol with a large bear hug. Most members of the party were round as well having after-dinner drinks.

Tom and Susan, Carol's sister and brother-in-law, who were sharing the cottage with himself and Carol, were there along with their two kids Daniel and Sarah; Auntie Barbara, Arthur's older sister; Barbara's daughter Christine with boyfriend Nick; The grieving Widower Mary huddled next to her brother Mark; Mark's son Harry and wife Julie, with their young boy Harry Junior; Arthur's cousin Mick and second wife Lucy who had flown in from Spain; Tony and Kevin plus wife Margaret, who were Arthur's old fishing friends that still lived in Tintagel.

Charlie got a well-deserved can of beer from the fridge and hid in a corner seat away from the bulk of people.

Finally, he had a drink...

He tried to forget about the journey down, but could not help in staring outside the window at the jeep every minute or so. Half of him expected to see the boot fly open and the suitcase dragging itself towards the front door. He could faintly hear Arthur still in the back of his head, reminding him that *'e was watchin'*.

Instead of reacting to this, Charlie just kept topping himself up with more beer to drown him out, all the while getting evil stares from his mother-in-law Mary every time another can was opened.

A concerned Carol also watched over her husband continuing to drink and every so often whispering: *I can't hear you in here, you're not real,* and *it's all in my head...*

The night went slowly for Charlie, but soon enough the guests retired back to their own cabins, leaving Charlie and Carol with Tom, Susan and the kids.

That night Charlie got no sleep whatsoever. He tossed and turned restlessly, blaming it on the beer to Carol. Their bedroom was upstairs, with a big window facing outwards towards the road, where Charlie constantly glared. He could hear Arthur rustling away in the back of the Mitsubushi, and kept asking Carol whether she could hear anything, but his wife could not hear anything but the wind.

The morning finally came and Charlie's head was pounding. His headache was a mixture of alcohol and worry; worry divided by the dilemma with Arthur's ashes and the fear over his own sanity.

He started to re-question how stressful his work had been on him lately. Maybe the stress and guilt of his failing career had finally got to him? Perhaps the burden of a failed writer had drove him mad?

Mad enough to start hearing voices? People had been known to do madder acts than that before.

After a few concerned words from Carol about his peculiar behaviour from last night, Charlie was ordered to get ready and then to go get the suitcase from the car. The ceremony was to be held early morning, the same time as Arthur most enjoyed his fishing, so they had to hurry. Normally Carol was hardly ever on Charlie's case, but she could be let off on the day of her Father's scattering.

Following a tight struggle in the petite shower and rummaging through his packed bag to find his creased suit, shirt and tie, Charlie got ready and headed outside towards the car.

It was a beautiful spring morning. The sun was beaming pleasantly; the clouds glowed as white as the sheep in the fields; the flowers were blossomed with bees and butterflies surrounding them; the grass sparkled with the faintest dust of dew covering; the wind was keeping at a mellow, relaxing breeze.

All the bright spring colours seemed to radiate a ray of light directly into Charlie's nurturing head. He walked sheepishly towards the boot of the jeep, with Carol, Tom, Susan and the kids trailing in a conga line. He pushed the open button on his electric key chain and got into position behind the motor. He lifted the boot slowly, expecting a full blast of Arthur's moaning to leak out at any minute.

But strangely there were no voices; no condescending, patronising voices at all. Charlie, who was even more concerned now, hesitated as he stared into the back of the jeep. There was the briefcase, lying exactly where he had left it, but minus the annoyance of Arthur's blabbering.

Charlie got out the briefcase and began to walk with it alongside Carol, who was smiling at Charlie whilst holding his free hand for comfort, up the hill towards the King Arthur's Arms Pub meeting point.

The journey up there was silent. Nobody said a word to each other, not even Arthur. They met the rest of the party huddled in dribs and drabs around the bar. A few more members had been added since the following night.

Auntie Barbara's son Eric and his girlfriend Georgina; Arthur's second cousin Mavis along with her husband Brian; Peter, another one of Arthur's old fishing friends; And Arthur's younger brother Terry, who had a remarkable but creepy resemblance to his older brother.

It strangely had a feel of Christmas to it, although nobody was in a too jolly mood to ruin the occasion. Everybody was drinking heartily while talking amongst one another. The whole gathering was in an optimistic mood, all bar Charlie.

After handing over, with much relief, the suitcase to Mary on request, he bought his cottage a drink each, a Beer for Tom; wine for Carol and Susan; and lemonade and orange juice for himself and the kids: his stomach was having enough trouble just by smelling the alcohol.

A clashing of drinks, raising of glasses, fond words spoken, a few tears swept away, and then the convoy began to leave the pub and make it's way up the hill towards the chosen destination.

Everyone was marching with purpose and enthusiasm, working their lungs to keep up. It was a fair old steep climb, especially for some of the elder members. Charlie trailed as far back and away as he could from Mary and her brother Mark, who was now carrying Arthur in the briefcase. Carol managed to free her hand from

Charlie and make her way through the party, up to her mother for support. Charlie still trailed further, helping out some of the elderly as a good alibi. Although technically he was helping, he still felt guilty in what he was doing.

The big moment had arrived. Everybody had made it to the top of the hill, all gathered round a big stone rock that faced out to sea. The spot where Arthur used to love fishing had eroded over time, leaving only a trace of unsafe surface below.

The wind was a bit choppy and the tall grass was swaying side to side as if drunk. The light breeze of water followed every time the waves splashed like thunder against the rocks below.

Mary's brother Mark opened the suitcase and presented the urn to the crowd.

'Let us all pray in silence in the memory of Arthur Horton; a loving husband, father and dear friend to us all.' Said Mark bravely, in a slightly nervous tone.

Everybody bowed their heads and prayed in silence; even the kids who were on their best behaviour did so too. Charlie bowed his head in unison with the others.

'Come on Charlie boy… help me out just this once.'

There it was; that dam voice again.

He kept his head down. He knew what he had heard but chose to ignore it. In a few minutes it would all be over and he would never hear his father-in-law's voice ever again.

'I need you Charlie. You're the only one who can 'ere me!'

This actually made Charlie relieved. At least he could not tell Carol anything. He guessed that the old bastard definitely must have tried to a good few times.

It had been a good minute's silent, at least for everybody else. Mary signalled to Mark. Mark signalled back, and then slowly undid the lid of the urn. The rest raised their heads up to watch.

'I won' forget this Charlie… I'll tell 'em what you did before I completely loose it! I'll get them, the others 'ere, to haunt you for etern'aty! Ya 'ear me Charlie boy!'

This did not relieve Charlie. What if he really could get 'the others' to haunt him? What if they would never leave? What if he would keep hearing the voices forever?

Mark began to unravel the thread that tied up the bag holding Arthur's ashes.

Charlie began to panic inside. What should he do? What could he say? Stop the burial at sea because the pile of ashes told him to? They would all think he was mad.

If he left it, then he would not hear from Arthur again. Then again, if what Arthur was saying were true, then he would never be free. He had never heard 'the others' talk before, but did not like the sound of them one bit.

'And now, we bid farewell to our good friend Arthur...'

Mark turned towards the sea with his arm fully stretched out. The urn began to tip.

'*Come on Charlie boy...*'

Charlie had to make a choice. They would think he was mad if he told them anyway, so he knew what he had to do.

What followed next was absolute bedlam.

As the urn began to tilt, just before the first of the ashes could get poured, Charlie sprung from the back of the gathering, pushing past cousin Mick and knocked down his second wife Lucy, leaped in front of Mark grabbing the urn off his hands, careful not to spill anything out, and then began to run further up the hill away from the party.

'*That's it Charlie boy! Good on ya! Run! Run as fas' as ya can!*' Spurred on Arthur, as he got carried away under Charlie's arms.

The widower Mary fainted, being caught by her two daughters Carol and Susan; Auntie Barbara and second cousin Mavis plus husband Brian shouted and screamed at the top of their voices; Barbara's daughter Christine and boyfriend Nick were helping Arthur's cousin Mick and second wife Lucy off of the ground; all the kids started running around in circles chasing each other; while Mark, Tom, Terry, Harry, Tony, Kevin and Peter attempted to run up the hill after Charlie, trying to retrieve the urn.

Charlie heard them shouting for him to stop, calling him a crazy fool and to give back the urn. This annoyed Charlie and made him run faster. What would they have done in his situation? How dare they criticise him.

'*Come on Charlie, we can outrun them. Ol' Tony's got a replacement hip, he'll be down soon!*'

Out of all the men, Tom seemed to be gaining most of the ground. Charlie was not a very fast runner, he knew he could outrun the old men but wasn't planning on a high-speed chase against Tom.

He turned round and saw them in the not far distance. He could faintly make out the expressions of hatred on their faces. Charlie was wondering how he would explain this to Carol. He just ruined her Father's burial. Would she understand? What if she didn't?

Charlie started to rethink what he had just done. But then quickly remembered about 'the others'. Would he really of been able to carry on through life with 'them' always watching, always whispering, always stalking?

Probably not...

He also thought of poor old Arthur. Granted he did not like the old git, but banishing him to an afterlife with no spirit was not what he had in mind for him.

'Watch out for Tom! 'Es a quick one ain't 'e! 'E can easily catch you up 'ere Charlie boy!'

Typical, thought Charlie. Arthur always favoured Tom as a son-in-law, even when the other one was trying to save his soul. But he was not lying. Tom was gaining fast. There was no footpath to stick to on the hills, and the slopes were getting thinner. Charlie started to loose balance slightly, just missing the edge of the cliff.

He started to climb higher, holding on to the long grass to pull him up. He looked behind and saw the rest of the party were now all on their feet and joined in the hunt, even the children.

Tony had stopped running completely, with his friend Kevin also stopping for his support. Mark and his son Harry were slowing down, so were Terry and Peter, but Tom seemed to be speeding up.

Why did he want to be the big hero of the day? He used to moan about Arthur all the time to Charlie. Was he trying to show off in front of Susan and the kids? Whatever he was planning, it seemed to be working.

Again, Charlie almost slipped.

'Careful, Charlie! Don't be a clumsy fool now!'

He picked himself up and carried on running. His breathing was getting heavier and his arms were tiring of carrying. Sweat started to drip down across his forehead. He could not keep this up for much longer.

Suddenly he realised that he was at a narrow end. He could either try to climb vertically upwards, or shimmy past a side path towards the next big cliff.

'Come on Charlie! Give it up; we'll pretend like this never happened...' He heard Tom shout out.

The wind in between the rocks was a lot heavier due to the strong waves below them. Charlie knew he could not stop now, not now he had got this far. News would spread of what he had done. He would forever be cast in the shadows. Carol may not even take him back. *What had he done?*

He would have to get a new job, a new home, a new life. Maybe this is what he needed. Maybe he needed this push to jumpstart his sports journalist career again?

But right now Charlie had only one thing on his mind, and that was to get Arthur spread safely on solid ground. He did not want to do it too close to the sea. He needed to go inwards. But the cliff was holding him back. He needed to get past the narrow edge in order to get to the greener, more in-land side. Maybe he could hide somewhere until they all passed, then bury him?

Tom was slowing down, purely because he too was approaching the narrow edge. Charlie, without hesitating, charged towards the other cliff, using all the energy he had left in him.

He slipped for a third time.

Charlie tumbled over the edge, with Arthur still grasped firmly in both hands.

'You bloomin' idiot Charlie b...'

The ambulance came too late after the lifeguard had fished Charlie out of the sea. They drove him to the nearest town that had a hospital, but was pronounced dead on arrival.

Charlie's funeral was relatively small. He did not have much family of his own: only a stepsister and auntie who he had still kept in touch with. Carol also attended, much to the disapproval of her mother. Although he had ruined her father's big day, he was still her one and only true love, and would miss him dearly throughout the coming years.

Charlie, fortunately with no sea burial, was at peace. He was with 'the others' now, who actually weren't bad people at all. They did indeed talk to one another. They knew what he had done, but most of them, as he soon found out, had done much worse. Plus, where they were, you couldn't stay mad at someone forever.

He could have looked back on his life and felt sorrow for the lack of success, achievement or years he had lost out on, but once you are gone, as Charlie found out, you realise how insignificant most things were.

The afterlife was good for Charlie. But every now and then he could hear a string of sentences trying to be put together in an all too familiar voice: a patronising tone that would never try to give up…

'Giss on… ya 'ear me… I'll tell 'er…my dyin' wish… I'll haunt you…get the others…ya 'ear me…CHARLIE BOY!'

Stranger at The Doorstep

Do you know what I have finally come to realise; it is the little things that piss me off. It is the small things in life that get to me. Now I know what you're thinking. So what? Everyone has to deal with the little things in life. It's the little things in life that make the world go round. It's what people call sods law. It's the things that people grow to accept as a fact of life and that everybody should just get on with it. Hey, at least it's not the big things in life that are affecting you.

But that's the difference right there. The big things in life do not piss me off. The big things in life are there because they are so big that nobody can really deal with them; or at least deal with it straight away effectively. It takes a lot of people and a lot of time to get rid of the big things in life. But the little things… They are clearly there just to piss everyone off.

Here is a great example of something that pisses me off. Computer games. Now everybody knows that in order for a computer game to start it has to load up. This takes time. This is worthy of the wait, as there is a reason for the wait. The graphics and screenplay are more technical than before so it needs more power to load up from the disc. What I do not appreciate is when you have to wait a good two or three minutes going through all the gaming manufacturers, producers and publishers logos and adverts before even getting to the loading screen. How arrogant are these people? You would never dream of putting in a music CD and sit through minutes of franchise marketing before getting to the songs would you? I'm sure it takes more disc space and power to get these opening credits loaded than the actual game itself.

I'm not stupid, I understand the reason why manufacturers do this; it just pisses me off.

This was one of my usual pathetic trails of thoughts while I was planning my daily tasks, which insisted of preparing my breakfast and lunch at the same time while my latest computer game was slowly loading in the living room.

In the kitchen I had two rashes of bacon on the grill, two slices of bread buttered, and brown sauce already smothered on. I made sure that I had seven beers in the fridge ready for the afternoon, and a packet of chicken wings out of the freezer ready to be defrosted for my dinner.

I poured myself a large cup of black coffee, just ready in time to take off my rashes of bacon and put them into the sandwich.

I then wiped down all surface areas where I prepared and headed back into the lounge, balancing my coffee in one hand and my sandwich in the other.

By this time my computer game had finished loading, bypassing all the manufacturing logos that always pissed me off, and all I had to do is press the start button to begin. *Perfect.*

(Knock, Knock)

Ah Jesus Christ…

There were two weighty knocks on my front door, loud enough not to ignore or pretend not to hear. It had to be something with a certain amount of importance or interest to me, so I put down my game controller and sandwich, picked up my coffee as a shield and made my way over to the door.

I took the latch off and as I slowly opened the door, the light from the outside blinded my eyes temporarily. As my vision became fully restored I observed a small, stocky man on my doorstep, wearing a black suit and tie, grinning from cheek to cheek and looking directly at me through thick glass lenses.

I had never opened the door to anyone who looked as happy as this guy did before, not even distant relatives that have popped by every once in a blue moon. He stared at me as if I was an old school friend that he had not seen for years. Needless to say I was a little bit curious as to what this stranger wanted.

'Good afternoon sir, how are you this fine day?' Said the stranger, still grinning enormously. I had a quick glance at my watch, realising it was indeed now the afternoon.

I think it may be a British thing but generally instinct tells you to be cautious of those who are too friendly, or smile too much. There had to be a catch. They have to either want something or sell you something. Therefore I was all the more cautious with this visitor, as I had never seen a friendlier looking chap before.

'I'm okay thank you.' I finally replied cautiously. 'Can I help you with anything?'

'I was wondering if I could have a moment of your time to ask you a few questions?' He then picked up his briefcase by the side of his foot, opened it and took out a large yellow folder. Charity worker. I thought he had to be a charity worker.

I did not believe in charity…

'I'm sorry, I don't want to buy anything today thank you.' I started to close the door slowly.

'Oh no, I'm not selling anything.' He said very honestly. 'I just want to ask you a few things, that's all.'

I was slightly puzzled.

'Is it a survey then?'

He chuckled, and I really do mean chuckled; like a playful laugh, for a good twenty seconds.

'No, no... Sorry, let me introduce myself. My name is Michael; I work for the Jehovah Witness Watch-height society. May I ask what your name is sir?'

At this point I started to feel awkward. The minute he mentioned religion I seized up a bit. I was never religious, but at the same time never anti-religious either. I believed that everyone had the freedom of speech, but not to come to my own front door to do so. Although I found this very rude of him, I did not want to seem rude back or appear to disrespect his religious beliefs.

'My name's Matt.' I kind of spurted out on demand for my name.

'Ah, Matthew, a terrific name.' said Michael, grinning even more so than before.

'Listen, I'm really sorry but this is not a good time. I'm quite busy today I'm afraid.' I said, interrupting him before he could go on any further. I did not want to get his hopes up.

He looked me up and down. I completely forgot that I was still in my dressing gown and slippers. He looked quite concerned as to what I was quite busy doing, but he seemed to understand.

'Okay then, another time perhaps?' he said, still sporting a grin but not so obvious as before.

'Okay, have a nice day.' I slowly closed the door; catching a glimpse of him putting away his yellow folder back into his briefcase.

I put the latch back on for some reason, and then went back to my console. It was an action and adventure style game, set on story mode for one player. Just the way I like it.

The next day I was up a little bit earlier, not too early but at least it was not the afternoon. After I showered and got dressed I went downstairs and turned on my game console, then headed towards the kitchen. Same routine as before, but my head was a little bit pounding from the night before, so I limited myself to just four readily chilled beers to put in the fridge for later.

I then sat down with my mug of black coffee and checked all the job sections in the local newspapers. There were a few vacancies I circled that I thought could be for me, or more rather the jobs that I could actually do.

After eating my breakfast and completing another level on my game I phoned up a few of the circled job options only to either be told that the vacancy had already been filled, or that they were looking for someone a bit younger. I think the last job I enquired about even asked me if I had updated my GCSEs? I wasn't even sure that you could do that?

I put down the phone and let out a heavy sigh. I knew that I should stop searching the local papers and head down to the job centre, but I could not stand it down there. It's not that I felt embarrassed or too proud, but more patronised by the staff.

I backtracked towards the kitchen and added to the beers for later. I had a feeling I would need them. I then sloped back onto my sofa and pressed start on the controller. I thought I might as well get another few levels done by the end of the day.

(Knock, knock)

I decided to ignore the door, as I was not in the mood to talk to anyone after my job hunting. I turned the volume up on the television as to drown out any further knocking.

(Knock, knock!)

The knocking was louder and more forceful this time.

Perhaps it's an emergency? Maybe one of the neighbours is in trouble?

I paused my game and thought about it for a second, let out a sigh, and then got up and opened the front door.

Standing there was the same Jehovah Witness as the day before; teeth still beaming like a Cheshire cat. He was wearing the same clothes, even the same tie.

'Good morning Matthew, good to see that you're more awake than yesterday.' His voice sounded generally pleased to see me. Unfortunately I could not say that I was entirely pleased to see him.

'Hi there, Michael is it?' he confirmed by quickly nodding his head up and down, 'Didn't you come round yesterday?' I questioned.

'I sure did. You said to come round another day when you were not as busy. I came round earlier today on the off chance that you had the day off. I presume you are okay to talk now?' said Michael, already getting his yellow folder out of his briefcase.

It was obvious that he was not going to take no for an answer, and even if he would I felt obliged to listen this time, being that I shut the door on him the day before. I assumed that it would not take too long.

'Sure why not, I can spare you a few minutes today.' By the time I had agreed Michael was poised ready with the folder overlapped in his hands.

'That's fantastic. Tell me Matthew, are you a religious man yourself?'

'I'm afraid I'm not, but neither do I criticise other peoples.'

'Ah, an open mind, that's what I like to see.' Said Michael, with his eyes gleaming larger than his teeth. 'Tell me then Matthew, why do you think there is so much suffering in the world, what with all the crime, war, terrorism and illnesses?'

I was more expecting a lecture than an open discussion. I paused for a second to consider my response.

'Well I believe that without any bad in the world then nobody would understand what good is. The evils and the suffering are there to remind us that what we do have is so precious and not to be taken advantage of.' I said, feeling quite pleased with my sophisticated response afterwards.

This proclamation made him ponder a bit himself, while nodding in acceptance.

'Well I truly admire your optimistic perceptive of life. It's... very refreshing.' He then took off his thick glasses and folded them into his front top pocket of his blazer. 'Have you ever had the chance to study the bible and what it can teach us all?'

'I studied it briefly at school when I was younger, learning its basics, but haven't really had the chance to get into it thoroughly.' I honestly said.

'That is a shame. You should really try to spare some time to learn from it. For the bible teaches us that God will bring about changes on the earth, as said in the book of Revelation, chapter twenty one, verse four; "He will wipe out every fear from their eyes, and death will be no more, neither will mourning nor outcry nor pain be anymore".' Said Michael, keeping eye contact with me all through the quote recital.

An awkward silence took place, as though Michael wanted this statement to sink in.

'So… when do you think God will act on this then?' I said to break the silence. He looked at me confused, but ready to educate.

'Matthew… God is acting upon this every day. He is acting through messengers like myself to spread the word of our lord's work.' I started to feel ill at ease whenever he said my name. 'By teaching people the way of the bible only then can we rid the world of evil and get back to the delights of paradise.'

'Delights of paradise?'

'Yes,' he smiled, 'where the first couple on earth were placed; the garden of Eden, from the book of Genesis.'

'Oh yes, I remember being taught about that' I said, while still leaning against my front door trying to find a position that was comfortable. 'I liked that story.'

The moment I uttered those last words, Michael's facial expression suddenly changed, and for the first time I saw his face not smiling. He looked straight at me with a serious look, as though he meant business.

'Story?' he questioned, and then muttered out a sarcastic laugh, which lasted the same amount of time as his recent chuckle. 'It's not a story Matthew. The Garden of Eden is as much of history as Jesus himself.'

I felt a shiver of discomfort flicker over me. I was now in dangerous territory here, upsetting someone's religious views; something that I had never intended to do.

'Yeah, I suppose you're right' I laughed off, without making eye contact with him.

I wanted out of the conversation by this point and to get back to my depressing day of being rejected by any job worth going for.

'Anyway, the day is getting on now so I'm afraid I'm going to have to go back inside. It was nice talking to you Michael.' I said as politely as I could.

His eyes did not budge. Once again the air of awkward stone cold silence filled my front patio. I could not tell whether he was angry, upset or just in deep thought. He did not move either, but just stood as straight and tall as humanly possible. I wanted to shut the door on him, but he seemed too close to the door, even though he was only on the first step. Eventually, Michael's face slowly raised a smile: a very wide, creepy smile.

'The eyes of the blind ones will be opened, Matthew.' He said, very slowly and very surely.

I closed the door a lot quicker this time, hoping that he would now get the message that I did not want to be disturbed from my chamber of solitude. I slumped back down onto the sofa and swiftly brushed off the incident, getting smoothly back into loading my computer game. Having known what was to follow, I would have run away from the house as far and as fast as possible.

'Yes mum… I know… yes don't worry, I'll find a job soon, these things take ti-… I know it's taking longer than usual… I know… well I'm looking in the papers, looking online, I go down the job centre every day, there is literally nothing out there at the moment… so what if I play a lot of computer games? It's not as if I've got anywhere to be now is it? So why should I wo-… so how should other thirty year olds be spending their time then? Down the pub wasting all their money on beer and slot machines? If anything I think I'm being more sensi-… the last thing I need right now is a girlfriend, she would probably nag me more than you do about getting a job… oh, okay, and where am I supposed to go find myself a girlfriend then? … Where? … The Pub?! … Even if I got a girlfriend I couldn't wine or dine her anywhere, no job; remember? … No, I'm not raising my voice… no I'm not angry at you, look I'll give you a ring later on okay, I've got to get down the job centre sooner rather than later… okay… love you too. Goodbye.'

I hung up the phone and launched it the other side of the room onto a pile of clothes that needed washing.

Shit…

I didn't like lying to my mother about going down to the job centre, but I could not take another second listening to her babbling on. I knew that she meant well, but her tone was so condescending. I was her only child and after Dad died I was pretty much all she had to talk about to her rummy friends on card night every Thursday.

I could see her side of it; everyone else around the table discussing their children's high flying jobs, their boyfriends and girlfriends, their grandchildren, even their hobbies or sports that they do. I always dreaded to think what would be said about me. I guessed that my mum probably lied about my career, rather than telling them I got fired. It would not of surprised me if she told them all that I had a girlfriend, or hell, even happily married.

Still, I know she cared, or else she would not have checked up on me all the time.

I spent most of the day contemplating these thoughts and the night crept up on me pretty quickly. I had knocked back quite a few more beers than usual, even having to reload the fridge halfway through. I had a stack of about two and a half packs of beer left in the garage to go through as well, so I was well equipped. Whenever I went shopping I always loaded up on key essentials such as beer, as well as coffee, bacon, bread and frozen meals, so I didn't have to go back for a good few weeks. I hated shopping.

I was in my usual position parked on the couch with the television on, not actually sure what I was watching, whilst peeling the label off my bottle of beer. I was reading the back, trying to translate from German.

Why is German beer over here so much cheaper than English beer? English beer tastes like flattened down yeast soda, yet more expensive than imported lager. Also, why does it always come in big old cans or larger bottles? You drink halfway down and it's gone flat and warm. When are they going to take a leaf out of the European's book? Fucking Idiots...

I sipped my German beer with much appreciation and efficiency. I was reminded of the time when I worked in a local bar back when I was a student at the university in Leeds. The amount of times I poured someone a pint and I got asked to top it up more by some stupid red-faced old git was unbelievable. Comments like 'got a flake to go with that?' or 'give me a full measure, I want a proper pint' always got under my skin.

The head is there for a reason dummy! To keep your shit English pint from loosing its flavour!

I started flicking through the TV channels with no luck in finding anything new. I settled for an old horror movie on repeat that I had seen a few times over, but content with another viewing. It was 'The Brides of Dracula', with Peter Cushing playing a fantastic Van Helsing: it was always worth another watch.

When watching the last few minutes of the movie, I began glazing past the screen and looking towards the windowsill directly behind. On it was my Graduation photo; myself kitted with a cap and gown with a fake grin cast around my face. I never liked that photo. It felt somehow fake or phony, as if I was a fraud. I remembered how everyone congratulated and said how they were so proud of me, and that I should be overjoyed with my achievement.

Achievement? If they call sitting on my arse three times a week in a lecture theatre, not knowing what the hell was going on, drinking myself stupid every night and not working in a single job for three years, then coming out with a below average grade an achievement, then an achievement I have accomplished.

It was not my idea to have my photo frame staring at me as the centrepiece of the living room; it was my once very proud mother's. On occasion I put it out of sight, tried to hide it, even binned it. But each time my mother visited she would immediately ask where it was, so I had to go get it and place it back to where she originally put it. Eventually I gave up on trying to get rid of the photo and accepted its place in the house.

So there it sits, so smugly, grinning right at me. Fucking ugly bastard.

I glanced back at the television only to find the end of movie credits rolling down in front of the burning windmill on the screen. I gulped down the remainder of my (still cold and lively) beer, and then examined the empty bottle for a while, debating whether I needed another. I decided not to, and to save the remainder of the beers for another night, hence prolonging my need to go out and shop that little bit more.

I switched off the television, only to be surprised that it was actually raining, which the noise from the television must have been blocking out. I got up to go to the final bathroom break of the night, leaving my empty bottles on the side table to be cleared up in the morning.

(Knock, Knock)

At first I thought I had imaged it and carried on towards the toilet. I balanced myself while aiming, not splashing the seat once.

Hmm, not as drunk as I thought I was… could have done with that other beer after all.

I shook myself off, flushed and went to go upstairs to bed.

(Knock, Knock!)

That time I definitely heard it. I stopped midway on the third step. I waited, poised for a third knock.

(Knock, Knock!)

Who the hell could that be? It's two in the morning?

I rushed down the steps and made my way over to the window next to the front door and peered curiously through. It was still dark and the rain disjointed my vision. I could make out a faint silhouette of a figure at my front door. It looked as if the window drew attention to my movement.

(Knock, Knock, Knock!)

The three harsh sounding knocks startled me. I got curious and scared at the same time. I never got many visitors, and had never had any at night before. The only visitor I had had for the past two days was the Jehovah Witness.

Shit. That Michael! I forgot about him.

The alcohol had helped in erasing the incident the day before from my mind.

What if it's him again? What does he want?

I felt uneasy, but then a rush of anger soon took over, probably due to the Dutch courage.

Who the hell does he think he is knocking on my door at this time of night? What if I was asleep? What If he has been watching me and knows that I'm awake? The guy's insane.

I crept closer to the front door to see through the peephole. As I looked through I tried to control my eye from flickering. I leaned both hands on the door and pressed my right eye tightly on the hole.

I could not see anyone there.

Christ, am I imagining this?

I started to chuckle softly to myself. Perhaps it was the horror movie that got my imagination flying, along with the quantities of alcohol consumed.

I was still leaning on the door, partially because I had trouble balancing, but also subconsciously waiting for a further knock. I was probably there for a good few minutes before retreating back upstairs. Once I was tucked up in my bed I realised I had forgotten to pour myself a glass of water. After drinking beer I tended to need it during the night in case I got a dry mouth.

As I walked back into the kitchen I grabbed a large pint glass and poured it to the brim with water from the tap. I went to take a few sips to avoid spillage on the way back up when I heard my letterbox flap. It was too heavy for it to be just the wind, so I made my way cautiously back to the door. I noticed a scuffed up piece of paper on the matt that was not there before. I snatched it up and unfolded it, fining out the creases. The piece of paper had on it written in bold black marker pen: "THE EYES OF THE BLIND ONES WILL BE OPENED (ISAIAH, 35:5)"

I got up pretty early the next day, even though I did not get much sleep in the night. I couldn't help but be concerned about the note I received, and there was no doubt in my mind that the Jehovah Witness, Michael, was the one who posted it. This made me feel very vulnerable.

What did he want? Did I upset him that much before? How sensitive is this guy? Is he dangerous?

I skipped breakfast. I couldn't eat. I was too busy thinking the best way to handle the situation. I lied on the sofa, still with the note dangled in my hand. It was obvious that I was going to see Michael again soon; that he still had some unfinished business with me.

And sure enough, he soon came knocking.

(Knock, Knock)

This time the knocking was more faint and not as abrupt, as if he did not need to work as much to get my attention. He was right.

I jumped off of the sofa and headed for the door, with the piece of paper still gripped firmly in my hand. I still had nerves inside me, but there was more anxiety.

I swung the door wide open, and there he was; same suit, same tie, same briefcase, same thick glasses; same annoying grin.

'Hello Matthew.' He said, in a near patronising tone.

'I got your note.' I accused him, while holding it up in his face. 'What's the big idea? Coming to my house at night, knocking on my door in the early hours of the morning? Putting threatening notes through my door? What kind of Jehovah witness are you?'

He stood there still smiling, not denying any allegation.

'Look…' I continued. 'I am deeply sorry if I have offended you or made you mad. I did not mean to insult your beliefs.'

'Mad?' he said, with a puzzled look on his face. 'How can I be mad? I am happy. God has brought me to you so that I can cleanse your soul Matthew. He is testing me. You are a non-believer Matthew, and I have to save your soul. This is God's test for me.'

This guy is actually insane!

'Is that it? You want me to believe?' he nodded his head very slowly, and I nodded simultaneously with him. 'You want me to believe, and then you will move on is that it?'

Again he nodded.

'Well then Michael... I believe!' I said, probably not that convincingly. 'I believe in God. You have made me see the light.'

'Oh Matthew, It's not that simple. You have to help me spread God's word in order for you to truly believe. I am your new teacher, your mentor, and you are my pupil. Together we will rid the world of non believers and soon enough there will be new heavens and a new earth, the one that we are awaiting according to promise, and in there righteousness is to dwell.'

I was speechless for a while, although I was trying to spit something out, anything that could stop him talking.

'Look... I'm really sorry; I'm a busy person. I have commitments I need to fulfill, I can't just abandon everythi-'

'Don't lie to me Matthew.' Interrupted Michael. His voice dropped to an angry level. 'Lying is a sin. I know you lost your job a few months back now, and I know that you haven't had a days work since. I've been watching you. You need my help Matthew. Whether you want it or not, either way I am going to help.'

'Is that a threat?' I questioned.

'No sir... that's a promise.' I examined Michael up and down, and for some reason he looked a lot broader than I had remembered. I was no squirt but was mainly tall rather than strong. Between us I would say he had the strength advantage.

I scrunched up his note that he posted me and threw it in his direction. His eyes followed the paper to the floor, and then turned back at me. I slammed the door with force.

What the fuck?

I felt naked after he had said that he had been watching me all this time.

How has he been watching me?

I ran over to the window to look and see if he was still outside. The wind was picking up, swaying the trees outside, tearing the leaves off, but no sign of Michael. I looked right down the end of my street and could faintly see his briefcase being carried away. He was gone... for now.

I needed a plan. I picked up the phone and thought of calling the police, but I soon backtracked. I had nothing. He had not entered the house, he had not physically harmed me, and hell, the only bit of evidence I had I just threw back in his face. What could I say: *I'm being stalked and threatened by a bible basher?* They would all have a good laugh down at the police station over my expense.

I had heard enough stories about the police not getting involved until it was too late. Old Mrs. Garrison who lived three doors down once told me that some kids from the neighbourhood used to play donkey derby over everybody's back gardens a few years back before I moved in. She said that when the police were phoned they didn't act on it until one child got injured on the barbed wire Mrs. Garrison put up next to her geraniums. She got a police record complete with a hefty fine and had to pay for the child's hospital bills. That's police justice for you.

No, I had to think of a way out of it myself. I got dressed, grabbed the nearest bag I could find and started packing my essentials. To be fair, there was not a lot to pack, just a few spare clothes, toiletries, my wallet, keys and my portable game console, complete with charger and spare games. I decided to make a visit to my mother's house, and hopefully this whole thing would blow over by the time I returned. I needed to get out of the area for a while. Hell, it wasn't as if I desperately needed to be in my own home while unemployed.

My Mother lived about thirty miles north from me, about half an hours drive on the motorway, not too far away but far enough. I guessed that even if Michael had seen me drive off, he could not follow me very quickly on foot, although I was not totally sure that he didn't have a car.

Surprisingly my Mother was pleased to see me. I suppose it had been a while since I last visited. She made me a good healthy dinner of pork chops, runner beans and roast potatoes, followed up with apple pie and custard. I could not remember the last time I ate so well.

We both had a glass of wine each with our dinner and talked about old memories, mostly fond ones from when my Father was still around. She did not mention my unemployment situation once, probably so not to scare me away. I did not mention anything about Michael so not to worry her, but more because I did not want to talk about it. If I forgot about it, I hoped that it would just go away.

I helped wash and clean up the dishes, even though my Mother insisted on doing it herself. It ended up a system of her washing and me drying. It was nothing special, but I enjoyed spending time with my Mum again. Once finished, we both sat down in the living room and started to watch one of her TV crime dramas she liked to view. She asked how long I was planning on staying; I said I had no date restrictions, to which we both laughed. I felt at home again.

(Knock, Knock)

I nearly jumped up from my seat. My mother got up as well, making her way to the door.

'No! Don't answer the door.' I said, signalling to my Mum to stay seated.

'Don't be silly Matthew.' She carried on towards the door. I stayed low in my seat, ready to pounce up if needed.

What if Michael had followed me here? Son of a bitch…

'Mum, wait!' she paused. 'Let me answer it.'

She looked confused, but trusting. I got up and put myself in front of her. I grabbed the door handle. My heart started racing. I was not totally prepared for this, not so suddenly after the last meeting. I turned round to check on my Mum's position and got a very concerned look from her. I turned back towards the handle, pumped up my chest, swung the door wide open and leaped outwards, ready for a confrontation.

I almost gave Betty, one of my mother's rummy night girls, a heart attack. I apologised, invited her in and made her a cup of tea, along with a couple of biscuits on the side as a peace offering.

I stayed at my Mother's for a good week, all the while not letting her know the main reason I visited. I think she knew that something was wrong, and that I did not want to discuss it; call it Mother's intuition. She gave me a bag full of food, consisting of mainly fruit. She offered me some money but I really could not accept it. I still had enough of my own saved up to last me a good while. I wasn't sure for exactly how long, but I didn't need any handouts.

The roads were surprisingly clear on the ride home. *Typical*, I thought. *The only time I'm not in a hurry to get home…*

As I cautiously drove into my street I scouted the pavements, looking for Michael. I could not see him, or anyone else for that matter. I parked on my drive, got out of the car and made my way to my porch, while still circling around, keeping guard. I turned the key in the front door and tried to go in, but something was blocking the entrance. I pushed hard on the door, forcing my way in, only to find a stack load of papers all scrunched up, with a few letters thrown in the mix as well, piled up on my matt. There had to be over five hundred sheets. I immediately grabbed one of the pieces of paper and unfolded it. It read: KEEP ON KNOCKING, AND IT WILL BE OPENED TO YOU (MATTHEW 7:7).

I picked up another sheet and opened it up: KEEP ON KNOCKING, AND IT WILL BE OPENED TO YOU (MATTHEW 7:7). I pick up another: KEEP ON KNOCKING… all of them had the same message, all was written on in the same marker pen, in thick, bold, black letters.

'And this man has visited you now on a few occasions you say?'

'Yes,' I answered to Police Constable Haroldson, who sat upright on my adjacent sofa. He was a large man, but well groomed. His eyes seemed to carry age, but I guessed he was only in his early thirties.

'And you say he has not actually set foot or forced his way into your home?' Said Constable Millins, who was sitting cosily next to her partner. She seemed less confidant, but more understanding.

'No, but the harassments are getting worse. It started off with just one preaching letter, now I have a stack load of them.'

'All you know is that his name is Michael?'

'Yes, and he works for the Watch-Height Jehovah's society, or something like that?'

'Okay, I will see if we can get in touch with the society and ask after him. Unfortunately though Mr. Richards, we will not be able to push any charges on him without any concrete evidence, or any eyewitnesses of these harassments. So far nobody, but you, has claimed to see him. We will keep you in touch if we find anything.'

I thanked the two constables for their time and saw them out. Mrs. Garrison was right… the police were a waste of time. I was pretty sure the two were standard 'on the beat' cops who got radioed to practice a call in to a distressed member of the public. I was pretty sure that I would not hear from them again. Something in their mannerisms told me this; maybe it was the shifty body language or the full up and down stares that they both gave me, but either way they thought I was nuts.

Another week passed and there was still no sign of Michael visiting again, or any word from the police. I had to hand it to Michael; he bided his time well.

I got on with my daily chores around the house; now and then I drifted off and forgot about him, but not for too long. There was still no luck on the job front, with adverts getting fewer and fewer as the days went by. Luckily this gave me plenty of time to prepare for another appointment with my Jehovah.

I managed to buy a cheap video camera from the local pawnshop, which I set up by the window facing my porch, carefully hidden behind the curtains. Each day I would switch it on record and let it run through, having to change tapes at least twice. I would then rewind and watch these on fast-forward using my old VCR machine, spotting for any sort of movement.

Soon enough I became obsessed with it. As I replayed the tapes, half of me was glad not to see Michael near my house, but the other half was drawing more anxious to see him again. If I could get him on camera then I had at least something to show the police.

I was going insane. I needed to get my life back to normal again, with a normal job, a normal social life and no religious freaks trying to convert me.

It was the afternoon. I had just finished away the remainder of my second bottle of beer after completing the last level on my latest computer game. I threw my controller on the floor in triumph and headed towards the kitchen, with my empty drink still in my hand. My chicken wings were just about defrosted, ready to be put in the oven.

(Knock, knock)

I dropped the bottle onto the floor, shattering it all over my kitchen tiles. I ran through the living room, scuffled over to the front door and peered through the eyehole.

It was Michael all right. I could see the last rays of daylight bouncing off his big, baldhead. I felt jittery. I had him on camera, as last! I could prove his existence.

I was so excited he had returned that I completely forgot why he had done so. This was the same guy who had been hassling me all this time. Although he had not physically assaulted me yet, I had felt threatened. He had not yet crossed the line, but part of me believed he was about to, and soon.

I braced myself and opened the door.

'Hello Matthew,' he smirked, 'I presume you have been expecting me?'

'You know God damn well I have. You've hardly given me a choice not to.' I folded my arms to show I wasn't impressed.

'I'm guessing from your blasphemy you still haven't changed your ways. But no fear, your guardian angel has returned to show you the light. Our teaching begins tonight.'

'Tonight? Then what the hell have you been doing all this time before?' I purposely blasphemed just to piss him off: this did not impress him.

'I have been preparing you for what is to come; giving time to let your destiny sink in, but it seems we're going to have to take more drastic measures with you aren't we now Matthew.' His smile began to slowly grow again.

I could not help but notice his physique. He seemed again bigger than before, as if he had been working out or getting into shape. His arms appeared to be just two great big biceps, and his shirt seemed to be having difficulty holding in his powerful chest. I had no idea what he did during the day, probably worked out down the gym every moment he wasn't knocking on unfortunate people's doors.

'Now listen, I have had the police round here and they know about you. Take this as your final warning; do not come round here again or else it will be in the hands of the police to deal with you.'

'Only God can judge me for my sins, and right now Matthew I am working for the lord. The way I see it, I have nothing to be sinful about. Soon enough you will see the light, and the lord shall give you hope and strength, just like the lord bestowed upon to me.' Said Michael, with his hands being used expressively, as he was preaching to me. 'Your time has come Matthew, to join us in the fight to banish the world of serpents and rebels. In this age we live in, people commit sins on a daily basis. God did not purpose that the earth should be as we see it today. God wants us to rid the world of evil, and those that are left shall be his children. The righteous themselves will possess the earth, and they will reside forever upon it.'

'So you want me to help you brainwash everyone is that it? Look, you've left me with little choice here Michael. I am going to go inside, shut this door and phone the police. If you think that you have done nothing wrong, please try to explain that to them when they arrive. If your God knows you have done nothing wrong I'm sure he will tell them and you will be let off.' I slammed the door as fault of habit and made my way over to the phone. I picked it up and dialled 999, but there was no ring tone. I tried it again, but still nothing. I checked that the phone line was connected properly to the wall socket and then tried dialling another number. The phone was dead.

Shit, he's cut the phone line! When did he do that?

I went upstairs to get my mobile phone, which was in my bedroom somewhere. I found it lying on the floor to the side of my bed, where it must have slipped down. I tried switching it on but it had no battery. I had not used it for months. I rummaged through the top of my chest of drawers where I kept all electrical bits and pieces. I found the phone charger, unravelled it, and plugged it in the nearest socket and into my phone. No response. There were no bars shown or any sign of lights flashing or charging at all. I tried another socket, but the same occurred. I then tested the main light in the bedroom. No lights.

The fuse board has gone.

I ran downstairs, with my mobile and charger in both hands, towards the back of the kitchen where the fuse board was. I opened up the lid only to find all the switches up. I switched down and back up the main switch, but nothing appeared to come on. I plugged in the phone charger to the nearest socket in the kitchen but again nothing came on.

Power cut.

He must have just cut the power as well, the son of a bitch.

I then had a sinking feeling in my stomach.

The Camera!

I had kept the camera plugged in just in case the batteries had run out during the day. They were re-chargeable ones that I didn't really trust.

I ran over to the front window where the camera was placed. I snatched it off the stand and inspected it. The recording red light button was still on. I breathed a sigh of relief. I stopped recording and started to rewind it for roughly five to ten minutes. I pressed play and fast-forwarded slowly.

Sure enough, there was Michael walking up to my doorstep with his briefcase in hand. I witnessed him knocking on the door and myself answering. I paused the camera, and zoomed in on Michael's face.

'I've gotcha now Mickey!' I said to myself, in a triumphant tone.

'No Matthew, I've got you.' Said an all too familiar voice directly behind me. All of a sudden I felt a sharp blow to the back of my head...

As I restored consciousness, I tried to support the back of my throbbing head with my hands, only to find that I was restrained.

'Hello Matthew, how are we feeling?'

My eyesight was still out of focus; all I could see was a bright light. As my vision slowly restored, I could see Michael's face, grinning directly at me.

'Are we feeling better now Matthew?'

I was still dazed and could not respond. I looked around and noticed that I was fully tied to a chair in my kitchen. I could faintly see Michael rummaging around in his briefcase. His sleeves were rolled up as if he meant business.

'I'm sorry it had to come to this Matthew, but you left me no other alternative. I hope you can eventually forgive me for busting the lock on your back door, I will see to repairing it after we are done here.'

I felt weak, as if I had been drugged. I tried to wriggle free, but the rope was tightly wrapped around my arms and legs.

'There's no use in trying to struggle Matthew; you have been given a highly strong dosage. Save your strength for the Lord's work.'

I was so frail I could not even move the chair. Michael stopped looking through his briefcase, sat down on a chair opposite me and folded his arms.

'Do you know what the name Michael stands for Matthew? It stands for the Archangel Saint Michael, the field commander of the army of God: the very Michael who led Gods army against Satan's forces during his uprising. I am that same spirit, in mortal form Matthew. I have come down from heaven to once again battle with

Lucifer.' He got up and started walking around the chair I was tied to.

'Do you know what the name Matthew stands for?' he waited for a response from me, but I was still too weak to do so. 'It stands for Saint Matthew, one of the twelve Apostles of Jesus, and one of the four Evangelists. And also just like yourself, he used to be a tax collector before joining Jesus and his followers.'

He had done his research well.

That was my profession for a good twelve years, before the recession hit in and cut backs had to be made. I couldn't complain too much at the time, as they had given me a very generous redundancy package, most of which helped me with the upkeep of the house while I lounged around it all day, as well as paid for all my beers.

'You Matthew, are the perfect candidate. You are the man I need to help me rid the evil out of God's earth, to help restore paradise once more.' He paused for a second, and his grin dropped. 'However, I know your mind is not willing. You have been wasting your life away drinking, playing computer games and lounging around in your own filth. You are a sloth Matthew, a great big dirty sloth. But that's all about to change Matthew.'

He reached into his briefcase again and got out his yellow folder.

'Now you accused me of trying to brainwash people before didn't you? Well, I'm afraid to say you were not that far away from the truth there Matthew.' He held up the folder, letting it unfold downwards, revealing a black and white spiral wheel.

'Because your mind is weak, we will have to take strong measurements to make sure you give yourself over to our Lord fully. In short, we are going to have to convince your mind to believe.' He gently spun the wheel with his left hand, whilst holding the folder directly into my face. 'The Lord is your shepherd, and whose name is Jehovah are the most high over all the earth! You shall worship our Lord God, our Saviour Jesus Christ!'

'You... bastard.' I stuttered out, and looked away from the folder, closing my eyes. 'You can't hypnotise me... I won't look!'

He put down the folder and gave out a frustrated sigh. He then reached into his briefcase and pulled out a roll of duct tape.

'Why can't you make this easier on yourself Matthew!' he shouted at me, then opened up my eyelids and stuck two strips of duct tape on both eyes, forcing them to stay open. I could feel my eyebrows stretching as they were being pulled back. I shrieked as much as I could, but I had no energy. I could feel my body going into shock. Michael picked up the folder again, spun the black and white wheel directly into my face.

'Trust in the Lord with all your heart; do not depend on your own understanding. Seek his will in all you do, and he will show you which path to take...!'

I felt my eyes watering up rapidly, wanting to give way, but I could not even move my head now. My eyes were transfixed on the spiral.

'It is because of him that you are in Christ Jesus, who has become for us wisdom from God, that is, our righteousness, holiness and redemption!' Michael was shouting the verses at me, and they were sinking in.

I could feel myself drifting off. Everything became blurry. I had given up. The crazy bastard had won. All I could hear was his voice...

'And your God shall supply all your need according top His riches in glory by Christ Jesus! No power in the sky above or in the earth below, indeed nothing in all creation will ever be able to separate us from the love of God that is revealed in Christ Jesus our Lord! No temptation has seized you except what is common to man. And God is faithful; he will not let you be tempted beyond what you can bear! So now there is no condemnation for those who belong to Christ Jesus! If we confess our sins, he is faithful and just and will forgive us our sins and purify us from all unrighteousn-...'

(Knock, knock!)

'Mr. Richards, it's the Police! Open up please sir! It's Constable Haroldson!'

I could faintly hear the calls from the front door. I started to come to again, this time to a worried face of Michael's.

(Knock, knock!)

'Mr. Richards, if you are in there, don't panic. We are going to force our way in.'

There were three heavy poundings on the door. Michael was startled and furious at the same time.

'Our work is not complete!' He ran past me over towards the kitchen drawers, and as he ran back I could see a knife in his right hand, along with the yellow folder still clenched tightly in his left. He knelt down to his knees in prayer.

'Give me strength my Lord.' He whispered to the knife, then rose up again

There was a final heavy blow and a crashing sound at the front door.

I was still dazed and tied to the chair, with the strips of duct tape still over my eyelids, which I could feel were loosening from my struggles. Michael ran out of the kitchen into the living room, towards the front door, with the knife in an upright position.

'Police! Freeze!'

'Our work is not complete!' I heard Michael shout out. I then heard the sound of four or five gunshots and a heavy thud on the floor.

The strips of tape on both eyes had simultaneously come loose from my struggles, and with one final mighty effort I could finally shut my eyes. I then fell unconscious once more.

I turned over the two rashes of bacon on the grill, smothered the buttered bread with brown sauce readily prepared for them, and then poured out a large mug of black coffee.

I fished out a frozen lasagne ready meal from the freezer for my dinner later on, and then returned to my bacon.

I made my sandwich, wiped down all surface areas, and then sat down at my kitchen table with my breakfast, where my morning paper was already folded out on the second and third page. There was a small column on the seventh page as I flicked through, which headlined: JEHOVAH WITNESS SHOT DEAD OVER HOSTAGE SITUATION.

It had been nearly over three weeks since the incident had happened, and I still found it hard to believe the whole ordeal only managed a tiny column within the day's stories. My whole life-threatening experience summed up within a few sentences. It made me realise just how insignificant one person can be. *They must have run out of news and needed a little extra to fill up the blank pages,* I thought.

When they had found me tied up and barely breathing, due to shock, they had quickly called for the ambulance to revive me. As I finally came round, the first face I saw was Michael's. Only it wasn't him. It was Constable Haroldson.

As soon as I was well enough to talk, he visited me a few days later to explain how he had managed to come and rescue me. He said that they looked up the Jehovah Witness Watch-Height Society, or the WHS, but could not find any existing members by the name of Michael. They did however, got told of a member named Mitchell Huson, who had been banished from the Society for 'too radical views' on religion. Coming from Jehovah Witnesses, this was a pretty big statement.

They looked up Mr. Huson and soon discovered a back history of reports and statements of his threatening behaviour. He even had a brief spell in prison for trying to cattle prod a burning cross onto a Jewish Butcher from East London, who began getting frequent visits from him.

He got let out for good behaviour by helping out with the prison ministry. After he was out, Mitchell Huson was no longer heard of again, presumed to have changed his identity in order to protect himself from any Jewish community backlash.

The moment Constable Haroldson found out this information, he said he had a patrol car waiting by my house to keep a clear observation. The last visit Michael gave me confirmed it was the same man as before, only now with a baldhead and glasses on: but still a complete resemblance of the police photo the patrol car had been given.

They saw him walk round the side of my house after I had slammed the front door shut. After they realised that there was no walkway, just my garden fence, by the side of my house, they instantly called for backup.

I thanked Constable Haroldson greatly, and apologised if I had seemed a bit off with them on the first visit. It looked like Mrs. Garrison had just been unlucky with her police experience, but I could not argue one bit with mine.

It was all over as fast as it had all begun. Something in me felt as if it was not finished: but as if it was just the beginning...

After I had breakfast, I washed up my plate and mug, and then got dressed ready for the day. I had no time to play any computer games anymore either. I was making my way over to the Jehovah

Witness Watch-Height Society. I still had not found a job, but it did not bother me. I had a new meaning in life now.

I was one of the Lords children, and he had chosen me to complete his work here on Earth. I needed my disciples to help me rid the evil out of this land, and there was no better place to shepherd my flock than the WHS.

And on this day I no longer went by the name of Matthew. From this day, I would be known as Michael.

The House Special

Agnes collapsed through the front doors of the tavern, falling to her knees onto the hard wooden floor. The locals that sat in the armchairs and stools turned and stared at the arrival of this new stranger, still clenching their ales and bitters tightly in their hands. Agnes looked up in aid of support, to which three men that where sat perched along the bar stood up, put their drinks down and walked over to help. As they picked her up off of the tavern floor, all three men noticed that she was trembling considerably. There was a cold breeze blowing through the night, but this shiver was not of the temperature. This, the men soon noticed, was of fear.

After ramblings of mad unworldly behaviour and much convincing that the doors and windows were tightly shut and secure, together the three men managed to sit her down onto the nearest available chair. One of the men, whose name was known in this tavern as Gray, fetched a cushion to support her head.

'Would you like a drink madam, to calm your nerves? I'm afraid they're out of the House special, but I could offer you some brandy if you like? It will warm you up madam.' Said Hoffman, one of the other men, who looked the youngest out of the three, although still an older gentleman compared to Agnes. Her panting had slowed down, and she managed to nod her head in response. Hoffman walked to the bar and picked up the drink, which had already been poured by the barman, who was listening in on the event with the rest of the tavern. 'There you are. Get this down you madam.' Hoffman passed her the drink, which she gulped down within seconds.

'Thank you,' Agnes managed to sputter out, looking grateful at all three men. She felt safer being with others than on her own outside. 'Thank you all so much; I'm sorry for my unpronounced burst. I was so glad to see the light from afar I just ran as fast as I could from the woods.'

'What was it that startled you so, young madam, if I may be so bold to ask?' Asked Manning, the third man of the three.

Agnes would tell them what she had, or had not, seen in the dark woods. But she would not tell them everything. She would not tell them that her father, a proud English Lord, had married her off against her will to a gentleman who was seemed to be of wealth and good fortune. 'What has love do to with marriage?' Her father would tell her on many occasions. 'He will provide for you. You are a lady now, and I cannot provide for you any longer.'

And so it had been settled. She had got married to the gentleman, named Henry Bathering. He was a good man, kind and generous; but she did not love him. And for that, she despised him. He must have known that there was no love, but, like her father, this was not of a concern for him. 'What has love got to do with marriage?' He said, the same as her father had done so, when confronted by his wife about her feelings. This, to her, was the last straw. That very night she would get up from her slumber, sleeping next to her façade of a husband, go downstairs to the kitchen, pick out the sharpest knife hanging, go back upstairs and stab her so-called husband through his heart. His eyes met hers as he drew his last breath. She would never forget the expression of shock, guilt and despair all in one look.

Disposing of the body was more hassle than expected, as Henry was heavier than she thought, as she slumped the body over her horse, and rode towards the nearest lake. He sank well enough though.

When Henry was reported missing, years went by with Agnes living off his wealth 'waiting' for her husband to return. But the money did not last long. It was soon apparent that Henry was not in as good fortune as once presumed. With no husband to look after her, it appeared Agnes was to be penniless and poor, having to become a maid to get by. It was about this time when she also got the news of her father passing away in his sleep. Their mother had been dead many years before, so his fortune would go to his children, which was she and Percy, her younger brother. But it turned out that her father, not knowing of Henry's disappearance before he passed away, had left his entire estate to his only son, Percy.

Agnes would not tell the men at the tavern why she had travelled to their village in the first place. She would not tell them that she had knocked on the door of her beloved little brother's cottage and stabbed him in the heart using the same knife she had kept hidden safely on her self, the very knife she had used on her loving husband. She would not tell them that she had no regrets in doing so, that she had always envied the respect and freedom her little brother had been given from their father, and that she was glad that she had ended his worthless life before their father's estate had been finalised, leaving her the last heir to his wealth.

She would, however, tell them this.

'I was riding through the village trying to find my way back home from visiting a dear friend of mine. I must have somehow got lost and ended up going through the woods.' She drank more of her brandy before continuing. 'That was when I saw it.'

The three men gazed at each other. 'What did you see ma'am?' Asked Hoffman for the three of them.

'It was a beast.' She answered. 'A hideous, foul, monstrous creature, that swooped down from the trees. It looked oddly human formed, but both eyes were of an animal, not of a human. And the teeth, oh those ghastly teeth! They looked as sharp as knifes, with two pointy canines sticking out profoundly above the rest. It attacked my horse, causing me to topple over on the ground. I managed to get myself up and run as fast I could, leaving my bags behind.' The bag that contained her trusty knife to be precise, but that wasn't as important right at this moment. 'I could hear the monster growling, snarling and tearing at its kill. I could then hear it start to move, as though it was beginning to pursue me. I ran as fast as I have ever done so in my life, jumping over the branches and fallen trees, searching for an exit in that never-ending forest of yours. That was when I saw the tavern's lights burning brightly, and… well, you all know the rest from there.'

The three men exchanged glances at each other once more.

'You've had quite a shock, haven't you now.' Said Gray. 'Can't say I've ever heard of such a beast roaming our woods before though.'

'Not to worry, you're safe in here now madam.' Added Manning. 'Why don't you go and clean the mud off of your face in the lavatory.' He pointed towards a door the far side of the tavern, which had a silhouette of a woman hanging above it.

'Thank you… Thank you all so kindly. Yes, I think I shall go and wash up. It was dark outside, so very dark. I may have been mistaken out there; perhaps my mind was playing tricks on me from the long ride. Why, I bet my horse just stumbled, and is safe and sound galloping around amongst the trees, wondering where it's owner has run off to.' She tried to laugh, but was still too soon for the incident to be taken lightly. Agnes made her way over towards the lavatory, with the three men (along with the rest of the tavern) watching her. She was now wondering how she could retrieve her bag that contained her trusty knife. How foolish she must have been to just drop it like that, and scatter off scared without even thinking about reaching for it before she ran. It could have been used for protection against whatever animal, if there was such a thing out there, which had chased her.

As she opened the door, Agnes immediately noticed a strange thing. Directly in front of her was the sink with a mirror hanging above it, but there was no reflection of the rest of the locals. She turned round and saw them all smiling pleasantly at her. Agnes returned a polite smile and then turned to face the mirror once more, which only displayed the bar, the tables and chairs, the stools, the drink glasses topped up with ales and bitters, but nothing of the three men or of the rest of the locals.

Agnes walked in, closing the door behind her.

Vampires! They were vampires! She had heard tales of such creatures before, thought of them only to be mythological. A vampire had no reflection, and she could not spy a single person's reflection from the entire tavern in that mirror. It made perfect sense now, that thing that attacked her in the woods must had been one of them. But they were so friendly? Did they know that she *wasn't* a vampire? After what she had told them it had to be pretty obvious.

She observed the rest room. There were four thick walls and no windows on any, and only one door that led back out towards the tavern. She had to make a run for it if she stood a chance of getting to the front doors without one of them attacking her. Friendly or not, there was one moral to the stories she had been told about vampires; do not trust a single one.

She washed her face, so to not arouse suspicion, and bravely opened the door, facing the smiles of plenty, who seemed to take no further interest in their own full drink glasses.

On the count of three in her head, she ran towards the door. The three men, Gray, Hoffman and Manning, all stood up on their feet, but did not chase her. They were still smiling those goofy, crooked smiles at her.

Agnes made it to the front doors and swung them open. She froze before running into the blackness of the night, for there standing in front of her was Percy, her beloved little brother that she had watched die after being stabbed through the heart, or as close to the heart as Agnes had believed.

'Hello my dear sister.' Said Percy, grinning a wide set of razor sharp teeth, with two long distinctive canines at the front of his mouth. Before Agnes could ponder her last thought, Percy drove a knife into her heart, the same knife that had killed her husband Henry, and, supposedly, her brother Percy. He then sunk his teeth into the side of her neck, and blood began filtering out of the wound.

'Looks like the house special is back on for a while,' noted Hoffman to Gray and Manning, as they each, along with the rest of the tavern, grabbed an empty glass to fill.

The Great Allando

The curtain came falling down at the Blackpool Grand Theatre, followed by a cheering roar from the crowd, eager for another encore.

Always leave them wanting more, thought The Great Allando. He took a moment's pause, relishing the crowd's echoing claps and whistles. He could have stayed there all night listening to that sound.

And this was only the new shows first night!

The lights went up, and the crowd's applause soon vaporised and got replaced with the noise of people shuffling along the aisles, trying to find an exit. The Great Allando took a deep sigh of joy, and then made his way back to his dressing room, receiving handshakes and high fives off some of the stage and lighting crew as he walked by, all praising his fantastic performance.

He had requested that after each performance that he would be left alone for an hour in order to regain his strength back; to which everybody at the theatre company honoured this agreement.

He opened the dressing room door shortly after admiring its hanging star sign, which boldly spelt out his stage name in bright gold, and then locked the door behind him. He took off his shiny blue cape and tossed it playfully over the stand-alone coat hanger. The Great Allando then retired to his dresser chair, facing his own reflection in the mirror and smiled a goofy grin. Overhanging the dresser table mirror was his very own promotional poster of himself performing in all his stage outfit, which read in bright colours 'THE GREAT ALLANDO: GIFTED MEDIUM EXTRAORDINAIRE', and underneath he could still just make out the venue and dates information, for diagonally across the large poster in thick red was the best letters he always loved to read: 'SOLD OUT'.

He had made it all right. He had finally made it. After working all the small clubs and bars, all the grotty pubs and restaurants, he had finally made it to the big league. All those years of playing to the crowd, learning better techniques, understanding a variety of human reactions, and taking abuse off local idiots and doubters had finally paid off. He was now a 'somebody'. Everybody wanted to come and see him, witness his magnificent powers and hope to get reacquainted with their loved ones.

'Stupid fools,' The Great Allando muttered under his breath while undoing his tie.

There was one solid knock on the door. The Great Allando waited patiently, midway through untangling his top shirt button. Another three fainter knocks soon followed. He scrambled to the door and opened it quickly.

'Quick, get in.' He said, before fully seeing who was waiting there. Paul walked in casually without rushing himself, with The Great Allando trying to push him in faster. 'Did you make sure nobody saw you walk out backstage?'

'Of course I did Alan, don't worry yourself.'

'Don't worry myself?' Questioned The Great Allando, checking outside the door before shutting it. 'If one person, just one person clocked that you are in on the act then I wont have another booking in this town. They will call me a fraud. And news will soon spread around other areas! Soon enough I wont have an act at all!'

'I know, I know. But like I said, I made sure that nobody saw.' Reassured Paul. 'Great show tonight Alan! You blew everybody away! You were spot on with everybody you spoke to. I still don't know why you insist on me continuing to come to these gigs? You don't need me there at all. You have the gift!'

Allando laughed, and then tossed his undone tie on the hanger on top of his cape.

'Well you know me Paul; I always like to have a safety net. Having you there gives me that extra-added boost. If I throw a name or a letter out to a crowd and nobody answers it looks pretty bad. If it happens more than once it looks dreadful. I know I pick easy ones, but I had to use you tonight still didn't I? Even to a crowd as big as that one.'

Paul nodded in agreement, staring wondrously at his idol.

'I mean, it's simple really isn't it.' Continued Allando. 'I just throw a name of somebody's mother into the crowd and pick anyone in the audience at random. If the next question doesn't fit, then I simply go on to the next raised hand. And with audiences this big Paul, it's safe to say the odds are in my favour, especially if I keep playing to gullible saps like this lot today.'

Allando proudly sat back down in his dresser chair and began to rub off his eye makeup with a wet wipe. But Paul's admiration however, soon deteriorated.

'So... you do not believe in it at all then? I know you use me as a scapegoat for when you sometimes get it wrong, but...'

The Great Allando interrupted Paul with a howl of patronising laughter. He wasn't surprised by his questioning, as he knew that Paul was simple minded, but found it hilarious that after all the shows they had worked on, he still believed.

'Don't be so naïve man! Good God, you're as stupid as the rest of them! Let me tell you something Paul; all us mediums, all us psychics are all fakes. We are all just simply magicians. Nobody can really speak to spirits or read people's thoughts. It's all to do with reading people's reactions and body language.'

Paul looked at The Great Allando half disappointment and half offended, to which Allando replied with a gentle apologetic sigh.

'Look, let me tell you something Paul. Have you ever heard of The Great Harry Houdini?' Paul nodded. 'Well, after his mother died, Houdini missed her so much that he visited many psychics and mediums, searching for someone who he could contact his mother through. But each person he visited and met, he could quickly expose as a fraud, due to Houdini's training in magic. He spent most of his last years debunking these self-proclaimed people. Well, people like me really!'

Allando poured himself some water from the jug into one of the glasses that was placed on the dresser table.

'Well, before Houdini died,' Continued Allando after taking a large gulp. 'He and his wife, Bess, agreed that if Houdini's spirit could communicate to her, he would utter the phrase "Rosebelle believe" as a sort of codeword to prove to her that it was actually him. I think it was a snippet from a play Bess was in or something like that. Anyway, when The Great Harry Houdini finally did die, Bess held séances for ten years after his death trying to communicate with him, to which she never got one response. Now, what does that tell you? Still think it's all real?'

Paul paused for a moment, staring at the self-claimed medium with a newfound feeling.

'I think you should go back to being a magician.' He suggested bitterly.

'What! Ha!' Allando stood up from his chair in dramatic disbelief, nearly knocking over the jug of water in doing so. 'You really are nuts! Why the hell would I want to go back to being a magician? You need so many props, lighting and stage assistants.

If you're a magician, the audience always wants to be dazzled by the latest and greatest trick out there, something that they have never seen before. The medium act I do, I pretty much do at every show; yet nobody gets tired of seeing it. It's pure gold dust.'

'But you're giving people false hope.' Argued Paul.

'If anything, I am giving them what they want to here; some sort of comfort that their relatives and loved ones are doing alright.'

'What about that lady in the front row you told that her Grandmother had unfinished business? And the gentleman sitting on the side rows near me? You said that his brother was still upset about their fight? He didn't know what you were talking about until you actually convinced him that they actually did end on bad terms.'

Allando huffed out loud.

'Well… Well that was just part of the act wasn't it. You have to throw in some bad messages as well. If every message was the same like "don't worry I'm fine" or "there happy where they are now" then people would not buy it would they?'

Paul did not answer. Momentarily the pair stood facing awkwardly at each other. It wasn't tension that was separating them, but more a sense of distrust.

'And anyway, who are you to judge? You're part of the act! Ever since we met in that dainty little tavern you've been my plant on every show I have done, and you have always gone along with it. I know you're a superstitious man, but why have you decided to change your mind so suddenly?'

Again Paul did not answer. Instead he slowly made his way to the door and opened it slightly to check that nobody was walking by. When he saw that the coast was clear, he began to exit, but before he made his way fully out, he turned back to The Great Allando.

'I think you should stop while you're ahead now Alan; before you upset too many people.'

The door shut, leaving Allando staring at another one of his 'THE GREAT ALLANDO : GIFTED MEDIUM" posters stuck to the back of the door. He sat back down and stared at himself in the dresser mirror.

Was what he was doing so wrong? How much different was it to his magician days?

He sighed and cupped his head forward in his hands. As he tilted his head he saw a large bunch of flowers sitting on the side with a note attached to them. He ripped off the note and opened it up. Inside it said: "Congratulations! You are finally home." He looked at his reflection once more, this time once again with pride.

This is what he did. This is why he had practiced and performed so hard. This is what he was born to do. He was home.

The second night of the sell-out show at The Blackpool Grand Theatre saw the turnout of Blackpool's finest weird and wonderful tourists. As The Great Allando peered through the curtain by the side of the stage he saw old ladies with their shopping bags spread amongst the aisles, groups of young students congregated together wearing similar clothes, as if they all shopped at the same cheap and trendy store, both young and old couples trying to find their seats without letting go of each other's hands. He scanned the packed out crowd. Allando never got nervous about numbers, or ever had stage fright. On the contrary, he thrived on a larger audience, as there were more choices to pick from. But tonight, for the first time, he was nervous; for his safety net, his scapegoat, and his plant, was not there. He could not see Paul in the seat he allocated to him, or any of the seats for that matter.

Was he ill? Did he actually mean what he said the other night? Was that it? Was he not going to show up anymore?

Although he was worried, The Great Allando soon assured himself.

So what if he didn't show up. He was The Great Allando! All these people came here to see him; and by God he was going to give them a show.

He put on his shiny blue cape, adjusted his tie and got into position. The dry ice smoke began to fill the stage floor. The lights dimmed in complete darkness, slowly hushing the crowd into silence. The overhead announcer's booming voice began to introduce the show:

'LADIES AND GENTLEMEN, PLEASE WELCOME TO THE STAGE, THE WORLD'S GREATEST GIFTED MEDIUM EXTRAORDINAIRE; THE GREAT ALLANDO!'

The curtain rose up slowly with a roar of applause and whistles from the eagerly awaiting crowd, and erupted on the sight of Allando appearing from the heavy fog. He stepped forward towards them, absorbing the claps and cheers as much he could.

Silence soon fell again, everybody eagerly waiting to be bedazzled and amazed. Allando walked up and down the front of the stage without saying a single word, all eyes following every step he took. He scanned the crowd, staring at the enthusiastic faces, the impatient stares, the looks of doubt, and his favourite look of all, the gaze of hope. All of which, he could read like an open book.

He owned the show before he had even spoke. He had complete and utter control of every outcome of the performance. It was all his for the taking…

The whole audience gasped as he raised his right hand towards his head in thought, and then closed his eyes tightly. This was his sign. It was in this pose to show the audience when he could "communicate" with the spirits.

The Great Allando held his eyes firmly shut while remembering what he rehearsed earlier, when something strange happened. It was something that had never happened before, something that shocked even The Great Allando into horror.

He actually heard a voice.

(Ask if David Holt is there; it is his father Graham, wanting to communicate with him.)

Alan could not believe it. His eyes opened sharply in fright and he let out a gasp of amazement, triggering the audience to jump at the look of terror bestowed in them. He trembled with fear and anxiety. The thought that he had imagined the message was simply preposterous. It was spoken to him in a way that he had never heard before, as if it came from his own mind rather than through his ears. It was the clearest message he had ever been spoken to before in his life. And there was no denying it.

There were whispers of concern coming from the seats in the theatre, looking on at Alan, who seemed to be suffering from a mixture of a fit and stage fright. He could hear faint voices of doubt from backstage as well.

(Ask if David Holt is there; tell him that his father Graham wants to speak with him.)

The message got projected in his mind again. But this time it did not fear Alan. Instead, he embraced it. This was indeed a miracle. He did not know why or how it was happening, but he was communicating with something of the unknown. He could actually hear what they were saying. He was a real medium!

If only Paul could see him now…

His thoughts spun round his head so fast, considering how great this was. He could prove to the world that his powers were real. No more faking, no more trickery; he did indeed have the gift. His shows would sell out at every venue he went to. Goodbye Blackpool, hello America; hello world!

'I have a message!' He shouted out in excitement, causing the audience to jump once more. 'Is there a David in the room?'

The hands of plenty of men flew up. Alan smiled in delight. On any other night he would be pleased with the numerous options, giving him room to conjure up the next line by eyeing the willing show of raised arms, reading their body language, learning their story by sight. However, tonight he did not need as many. He only needed one. As far as he was concerned, his standard routine was out, and his new gift was in.

'Now keep your arm raised if your name is David Holt?' He said with a smirk grin as he tried to guess which one was indeed Mr Holt.

But the overconfident smile soon faded; as he witnessed all the raised hands in the theatre fall, leaving no volunteers remaining. He never normally did full names in his act. It was too specific. His routine always worked around probability and flexibility; giving him room to manoeuvre around with open-ended questions and letting the audience give most of the answers.

He was so sure of the name though. It was not as if he heard it incorrectly. But there was no David Holt in the audience? And without Paul on stand by, Alan was out of luck.

'No? Anybody with a father named Graham?' Asked Alan in desperation. One man's hand flew up quickly. 'Yes sir! You sir, David.'

'Oh, my name's not David, sorry.' apologised the man, and then quickly reeled back his arm.

Alan was embarrassed. The voice he heard in his head was wrong.

But what the hell was that all about? He had heard a voice!

As time was precious on his lonely stage, he decided to return swiftly back to his normal routine. But before he could, Alan heard another voice.

(Ask for my cousin Rita!)

'Rita! Is there a Rita?' Said Alan, hoping that this one would be correct. He wanted it to work so badly. Either that or he was going crazy.

An old lady nervously put her hand up in the front row.

'Yes! You madam! Have you recently lost a cousin?'

'I have Allando. She was a great loss to the family, and the first of my cousins to go.' The old husband sitting next to her comforted his wife as she spoke.

(Tell her it's me; Helen)

'Your cousin Helen says…'

'No, no,' Interrupted the old lady. 'Her name was Cassandra.'

'Cassandra?' Questioned Alan, but soon nodded in acceptance, thinking to go ahead with it.

(I died very young. It shocked the family)

'Cassandra's saying *(MY NAME'S HELEN!)*… Is saying that she was taken from the family at a very young age?' Said Alan, ignoring the message he heard in between. This comment threw a look of confusion over the old lady.

'She died at the age of 92?'

'Well… was she always young at heart though, am I right?' At least this comment got a nod from the old lady, most probably due to her wanting to believe.

(Tell her I forgive her)

'Cassandra says *(I TOLD YOU MY NAME'S HELEN!)* that she forgives you.'

This again puzzled the old lady, looking to her husband for guidance, which he gave a simple shrug of uncertainty.

'We never argued once, not once.' Replied the old lady. What does she need to forgive me for?'

Alan nervously held his hand towards his head, begging for a response that was actually true for a change.

(Tell her I forgive her for wearing that ridiculous jumper she's got on.)

'I'm sorry Rita; she says that she forgives you because… she was always jealous of yourself and what you have with your husband *(LIAR!)*. She wished that she had someone of her own that was as close and comforting.'

The old lady smiled with joy and tears towards her husband sitting next to her, which gave Alan a sigh of relief, and then moved away to the other side of the stage to avoid any further mishaps.

What the hell was going on? Were these voices mocking him? They weren't getting anything right at all!

Whatever was happening, Alan soon realised that there were plenty of doubtful faces in the audience, all of which not convinced by the show so far. He began back to his normal routine to get things going again, picking out the vulnerable and obvious members of the theatre crowd, and feeding them their own answers. He began to gain back the trust of the show, with a few faces backstage lighting up again as well.

Whatever those voices were, he thought best to not worry about it until after the show, and then he will truly try to figure out what the hell was going on, for his own health's sake. He thought he could maybe learn how to control it and how to use the gift properly. For now though, he had an act to do.

But it was not soon after he had won the crowd over, when the voices returned again. He was halfway through talking to this young widower when the first message popped up in his head:

(Tell this bitch that her husband's having way more fun here than he ever did spending time with her.)

It was a blunt, mean spirited message. It stopped Alan's trail of thought once more.

(Ask where my son Harry is!) Shouted out another voice.

(Where's my wife Susan?)

(Tell Bill I haven't forgotten!)

(Is my mum there? Ask for Maggie!)

(Roger! Where's Roger? Is he in the audience?)

'Stop it! One at a time!' Alan spontaneously shouted out loud. The audience started to whisper concern, which made Alan begin to sweat nervously. He was losing them again. But before he could even think of rendering anything, the voices began piling on top of one another in his mind. They were getting louder and heavier after each one. It was as if they had all formed an angry queue and nobody wanted to stay in line.

(I want to speak with my husband!)

(Can you tell my niece not to worry…)

(Tell Betty I miss her very much)

(If my sister Kate is there, tell her I always hated her.)

(Speak to George for me; I want him to move on with his life)

(This is Tony's grandfather speaking; I want to talk to him about his future)

Alan held his head tightly, trying to squeeze out the voices. They echoed around his head swelling up inside like a balloon ready to burst at any moment through his skull.

'Stop it! Stop talking to me!' Alan screamed, trying to shout louder than the voices.

The audience started growing irritated by this display, with some people leaving out of disgust, muttering to themselves about a demand for refunds. Others just sat and watched The Great Allando struggle. Some of the backstage crewmembers were half on the stage, ready to help on stand by.

Alan was throwing himself across the stage, banging his head against the flooring, trying to shake out the voices in his head.

(What are you doing?)

(Don't you want to hear us?)

(We want to talk to you!)

(You want the gift don't you?)

'No! No I don't want this! Close the curtain!' Alan shouted out, and the curtain dropped, with The Great Allando rushing to make it under. The crowd was a mix of complaints and boos spread across the theatre, all of them wondering why their show was cut so early.

Alan ran past all the concerned stage crew and stumbled his way directly to his dressing room. He locked himself in the room, with everybody worried outside who could only hear the sound of smashing and frantic screaming from Alan, howling over and over again for the voices to cease.

Paul walked casually along the Blackpool front, his sling bag slumped across his shoulder and hands comfortably placed in either pocket. He soon came across the Blackpool Grand Theatre and noticed a man on top of a ladder pasting up a new poster of the next big headline act that was newly touring. He could just about make out that the underneath poster was that of The Great Allando's sold out show, which he heard had to be cut short after just the second show; the only show he never made it to. Paul gave a sigh of disappointment.

'I tried to warn him.' He said to himself.

(We know you did Paul; we all know you did…)

Carriage Fever

We all stampeded out of the over ground train like a herd of cattle, 'we' being my good self and the rest of Joe Public. Everybody was in a rush, much like most Monday mornings. It was the start of the working week, the beginning of the slow and painful stretch back to the weekend and comfortable lie-ins. Yes indeed, Mr. and Mrs. Joe Public hated Mondays with a strong passion.

Walking past me were the usual crowds of people; the same faces I saw every day on my journey to and from work. There was the uptight suit who carried his oversized briefcase that never failed to hit at least one other person who was walking past. There was the dolled-up looking tart that thought she was something out of the apprentice, who always held up the queue at the ticket barriers while she burrowed through her purse looking for her travel card. I also spotted Desperate Dan, the fat-looking gentleman who had a chin on him that always reminded me of the comic book legend from the Dandy. This version of Desperate Dan looked a bit more run down though.

Each working day I would see these same people, and many others I constantly recognised. Now and then I exchanged eye contact with some. I would smile out of common courtesy. Some found this refreshing, and others found it creepy (mostly it was the young women who found it creepy).

Nonetheless, we would always head the same way to work. We all got on the Cambridge to London Liverpool Street train that passed through the same stops. I got on at Broxbourne; Desperate Dan would already be sitting down on one of the few seats. I assumed that he got on at Cambridge so he could take first pick of the vacant seats. By the time it got to my stop at 8.26am I would be lucky if I had a seat to lean against, let alone sit on.

We would all sit and stand and huddle on the train together; go through Cheshunt, Waltham Cross, Enfield Lock, Brimsdown, Ponders End, Northumberland Park, Angel Road, and then Tottenham Hale. The good old Hale....

This was the stop where we all piled out, every man woman and child for themselves, all hurrying to get downstairs to the underground. Rush hour on a Monday morning was the seventh layer of hell. I have always had this thought that if the devil decided to live on earth, he would definitely opt to work in the

London underground. I have no doubt that he would fill pleasantly at home there.

So here I was, the same as I was every Monday for the past eight years. I hurried up the steps to beat the queues of people trying to get through the ticket barriers and guess who steps out in front of me blocking my path through? Who else but the dolled-up tart that always held me up in the morning. She was flapping around trying to find her ticket in her purse while finishing a conversation on her mobile before she lost signal underground.

I looked at her impatiently, to which she completely ignored my disgusted glare. She was going to finish her conversation in her own time. I couldn't butt in on the other ticket barrier queues as now they had built up forming their own lines, with no gaps in between whatsoever.

Don't lose it Rick…

She always sickened me this woman. She looked so plastic. Her hair was always done up proper, she had slapped on piles of make-up, fake eyelashes, boobs revealed under a low-cut top, blazer jacket and trousers to match with high heels that made her taller than me (I always thought that she would definitely be smaller than me if she ever took them off). She fancied herself as a right businesswoman, a real 21st century go-get-it girl who had made it in the city. She was probably on about 35, 45 K a year job as some marketing or sales executive. She looked the type…

After she had finally retrieved her ticket and put it in the machine, the bastard thing didn't let her though! She tried one more time, but it wasn't having any of it. She must have had her mobile sitting next to the ticket in her purse. Rookie mistake…

So after she went over to the ticket guard I was able to go through myself, ticket poised in my right hand; ready like a true professional commuter.

I started to walk down the left hand side of the escalators, passing the lazy people who stood on the right, not caring that they may miss jumping on a train that is just about to leave. I got halfway down when the person walking in front of me suddenly stopped. I looked past them to see that there was a large elderly lady standing on the left hand side talking to her exceedingly larger friend that stood next to her. Side by side, nobody could get past them.

What the hell is she doing? Everybody knows that you cannot stand on the left? That's side is for busy people like me to get down quicker, not fat ugly old people who want to have a natter!

If anything I was more annoyed with the person in front of me, who seemed incapable of telling this old bitch to move over to one side. Now there were people getting irritated behind, thinking that I was the idiot holding everybody up? I was going to get the blame for everyone behind me missing the first train available? All because this bozo in front of me didn't have the courage to tell the lady in front of him to move her fat arse?

Calm down Rick; don't lose it… Keep it together…

I gave a long, slow, hard sigh to calm myself before snapping at him. I knew it wouldn't help the situation. What would it really achieve? So I missed the first train, big deal. I would just grab the next one. It was not as if it was a long waiting time between them, usually two, three, four minutes top? Not enough to lose my cool over.

I got down the escalators and turned the corner, only to be greeted with that irritatingly chirpy sound of the train doors closing. I didn't even try to rush on; there was no room to budge in the carriage. The dam fat elderly twins had made it on as well…

I looked up at the timings to see how long until the next train was coming.

8 minutes! What the hell?

I looked quickly at my wristwatch, even though a clock was clearly displayed next to the train times. It was sort of a habit of mine to double-check the time, just to make certain it was correct. It was 08.44am. I had the weekly Monday morning meeting to attend for 10am. I usually got to work for 9.25am. My working hours started at 9.30am.

I still had plenty of time… Don't worry Rick…

I stood on the packed platform. It was still just as crowded the further down I went. I kept glancing at the updated time. According to my wristwatch over a minute had passed, but the overhead train time still said 8 minutes? Was there a hold-up, something wrong on the tracks? There was no mention of any delayed service on the transport for London website (I would always check the website first thing in the morning just in case there was any severe delays).

The time finally went down to 7, much to my relief. The other minutes that passed were all slightly more than the minutes past on my wristwatch, being more a 10 minute wait than an 8. This made me wonder whether I should ever trust the overhead train times ever again. I decided not to.

The train finally arrived, chugging along slowly up the platform. The doors slid open. I managed to worm my way in the crowded carriage; no chance of getting a seat, but at least I was on.

I was crammed in between a young teenager with headphones that were way too loud, and a fat suit that had a serious body odour problem. Unfortunately I was pretty much used to this position on my morning journeys by now. There was always a suit that had never applied any deodorant, always some snotty nosed kid in skinny jeans with extremely loud music blaring some latest trend music that was heavy in bass.

The only person that was missing was some annoying person trying to read a broadsheet newspaper right in front of my face, smacking me every time the page was turned.

No sooner than I thought this, a middle-aged lady (looked like a glorified receptionist or something similar) who was standing in front of me head on, whipped out a copy of The Times that folded out directly in front of me.

Ah Jesus Christ! Just my luck... Who the hell reads broadsheet newspapers anymore anyway? Twats... that's who. People who think they look more intellectual, just because they are reading a big boy newspaper instead of a normal tabloid. What a bunch of self-righteous twats.

I tried to steer my head away so I wasn't facing the back of the newspaper, but I was jammed in pretty tight had no room for manoeuvre. So I was stuck there, staring blankly at the print.

Don't lose it...

The train jolted to a halt, causing me to go head first into the newspaper. After apologising to the pompous receptionist (or whatever she was) I balanced back into my rightful position next to the body wreaking suit and snotty nosed teenager.

The lights flickered on and off as if they were trying to kick-start the carriage back up again. We were halfway between Seven Sister and Finsbury Park. The train usually was delayed between these two stops. I was never sure why, but always seemed to happen. It usually only lasted about two or three minutes tops, and then the train rarely stopped after that. All the way to my stop Brixton station, the end of the line.

Ten minutes! Ten minutes passed and the train did not budge an inch. *What the hell is going on here? There were no severe delays mentioned on the website? Nothing said on the radio. So why's this dam train not moving?*

The carriage was getting warmer by the minute, and everybody without a seat was getting agitated. There was only so long you could stand in one position on a motionless train for. When it moved it wasn't so bad standing up. The motion of the carriage moving sort of sent you into a hypnotic sway. Well, I thought so anyway. It was a reassuring feeling that I was on my way to work, on schedule and on time. But when it stopped...

The suits all had their phones out, getting their "I'm going to be late" text messages ready. I already had a template saved in my outbox for an occasion such as this one. Wasn't too sure when I would be able to send it though.

The fuzzy noise of the overhead speaker from the train driver began to crackle. The whole carriage was silent, waiting for a good explanation.

'Apologies ladies and gentleman for the delay to your journey. We are currently held at a red light here... Not sure how long we will be held here for now, but as soon as I have any further information I will keep us updated.'

That was it? That was all he had to say?

The whole of the carriage gave a sigh of frustration in unison. The teenagers got back to their headphones, the suits sunk their heads back into their broadsheets, and the young slutty businesswomen carried on applying their half-done make-up. I stood there, stuffed in like a tin of tuna. I couldn't even reach into my bag and get out my book. All I could do was stand as patiently as possible...

Don't lose it Rick; give it time. You'll be on the move again soon. Don't lose it...

A further seven and a half minutes later and the carriage was now literally a sauna. All the suits had miraculously found room to take their blazer jackets off, revealing the not so glamorous look of sweat patches and nipple erections. The overweight women were fanning themselves down with the free papers. The young kids mockingly didn't seem bothered by the heat at all (cocky little bastards and their youth). I stood there sweating, mostly on my forehead underneath my hairline. I felt hot all right, but I always used an antiperspirant that beat any sweat patch from ever showing. No, this sweat wasn't coming from my armpits one bit, only from my head.

I kept glancing at my watch, counting down the minutes I was going to be late; debating whether or not I could still make the meeting, or at least half of it. It wasn't as if I would be missed much. I hardly ever took control of the talking, or had anything terribly important to announce. All this time in the same company and I wasn't even a key player.

This is what made me sweat. I was never going to be a key player if I kept on showing up late. I was always going to just be another face to talk down to, hell even get laid off wish ease when the company gets its first financial crisis.

That's exactly what will happen if I'm stuck on this bloody train any longer!

My eyes darted towards the emergency brake lever that was in arms reach above my head. That £80 fine never looked more appealing.

What exactly would happen if I pulled it? We've already stopped? Would they have to break in and let us all off? What if somebody had fainted on here? What if we all fainted? They couldn't just let us all stay stuck in this carriage could they?

Unfortunately I hadn't the bottle to pull the lever, or the faith of the London underground to actually let us out of the carriage, emergency or no emergency. Either way it was a lose-lose situation.

A good 5 minutes strolled past slowly until I heard another noise that wasn't a cough or a sneeze or some loud rubbish music coming from somebody's headphones. It was that delightful crackle of the overhead tannoy. It sounded so crisp, so warm.

'Good morning ladies and gentlemen; on a further update of the delay, unfortunately the train in front had a one under and we are going to be held here until they clear up the mess on the line before continuing. I apologise for this delay, and hopefully we will be under way very soon.'

Another chorus of moans and groans echoed through the carriage. Most people looked confused, as (I assumed) they did not know what a 'one under' was. I knew what it meant.

A few years back I had got talking to this train driver who previously worked on the underground while in my local pub. He was celebrating his retirement or something. There were a few others with him, who would all cheer in celebratory that he only had 'two under' in his whole career. Intrigued, I bided my time and politely asked the gentleman as to what 'two under' actually meant. He told me that it stood for how many people had fallen on to the tracks in front of his train; be it suicide or just an accident. It was a phrase used by drivers to one another. Only having 'two under' was apparently something of an achievement. On average most drivers had about 5 or 6.

So that was the reason I was bloody late? Because of some selfish bastard decided to commit suicide on the Victoria line in the middle of the morning rush hour? Just because he's having a rough time doesn't mean he has to drag us all down with him. Jesus Christ... Some people...

Although I wasn't so sure that the driver of this train should of used the 'one under' term to a train-full of passengers.

Did he actually say 'one under?' And did he say they were going to clean up the mess? Surely that wasn't right?

Perhaps I had imagined it all. Perhaps I misheard it? It was sometimes hard to understand the crackly tannoy. Whatever it was, we sure as hell weren't going to be moving any time soon.

Although I was stuck on a crowded train, squashed in with all the other commuters, the sudden feeling of isolation swept over me. I was alone, by myself, with nobody around me I could talk to.

Claustrophobia started sinking in. I began to sweat profusely. I felt alone and trapped. Hell, I was trapped! We all were. All of us on the train were helpless victims being held prisoner by the evil powers of the London underground. I couldn't take it much longer...

Don't do it Rick; don't lose it... Keep calm.

I looked down at my watch. It was now 9.25 am, the time I would usually be getting off at Brixton station. My office was practically next to the station on the high road. By now I would be walking past the same faces in the street. Not a day went past without somebody preaching about the end of the world and another person offering to sell my drugs. I remember the first time somebody asked me for drugs. I naively thought he was looking for his friend Charles.

God knows why the offices had to be in Brixton. We look so out of place there. I remember when the offices used to be in central, right next to Leicester square. Now that was working in London. People always seem so jealous when you tell them that you work in town, but not any more. Not when I tell them where I work. I basically have no perks working in town now. I literally get on the train and journey from North London to South London, cutting out the glitz and glamour of central and the west end; having to sit on a pissing underground train for the majority of the day.

What the hell am I doing? When did it all go wrong? No. Don't think about that now. That's a slippery slope to start thinking like that. You have to get to work Rick…

I glanced at my watch again. 9.28am. It was closing in on 9.30am, the start of my working hours. I was going to be late for sure, but by how long? Half an hour? An hour? Maybe even 2 hours?

I started panicking. This was it. I was going to have another panic attack again; right there on the train in front of all those strangers who I knew all too well by face, but dare by name. I was going to explode. Burst out in a fit of rage. I could feel it bubbling up inside me…

The clock was ticking down. 9.29am. I knew I was going to be late, but it still made me nervous thinking about what they would be saying about me in the office?

"Rick's late again Trevor,"

"Where the bloody hell is he? He could have phoned"

"I always knew that Rick wasn't a team player"

"How many meetings has he missed now?"

"Well, at least we know who doesn't want a pay rise any time soon"

"Who shall we lay off next sir? How about the next person who turns up late to work?"

The voices kept circling in my head like cars on a racetrack speeding around my brain. I pictured the whole of the carriage as my manager's office, and all of the passengers were the staff giving me my final farewell. They were all laughing and smiling and waving goodbye at me. Not one of them was upset. They were all glad to see the back of me, all because I could never make it in on time. All because I was stuck on this bloody train!

I looked at my watch. The clock was still ticking. Time hadn't miraculously stopped. 20 seconds left. 19, 18, 17...

Keep it together Rick!

14, 13, 12...

Don't lose it; being late is not the end of the world...

9, 8, 7...

Don't...

5, 4...

Lose...

2...

IT...

1...

'That's it! I can't take it any more! They can't keep us down here! It's wrong! It's fucking wrong! I can't take being on this train any longer with you people! You're all a bunch of freaks! Every day I have to share the same dam journey with you people, and every day one of you coughs on me; one of you sneezes on me; one of you flicks your stupid broadsheet newspaper in my face; I am constantly sandwiched between the two of you who are always the sweatiest! And I always get stuck on this same bloody train underground! What the hell is going on here? Dam London Mayor, dam London tube strikes, dam bloody London! I can't do it any more. I can't take it anymore! I... Need... To... Get out of here!'

The train was horrifyingly silent. Every passenger did not know what to do. Half of them were looking away trying not to make eye contact, others were awkwardly fidgeting, some looked utterly disgusted with the outburst, and a few of the younger passengers were trying to hold in their giggling.

I stood there in shock, looking at the man who could have been me were it not for the distance between a few microseconds.

Desperate Dan... the fat looking gentleman with the infamous chin on him. Who would of thought it...

He was a ticking time bomb ready to explode at any minute. His little outburst had made me completely forget about my own situation. I could see Desperate Dan through two people in front of me. He was standing up in the aisle next to the seats, breathing heavily to regain his sanity; contemplating on his next move. And by the looks of things, so was everybody else directly around him.

I felt a sudden connection with him, as if the frustration I was feeling was being shared between us. I wanted to help, maybe say something to back him up, but I was speechless like everybody else. I was stupefied.

How could anybody have the bottle to do that? Was I just about to do that? Was I just about to burst out loud in front of all these people?

It was as if I had caught myself in the act before anything even happened.

But before good old Desperate Dan could even contemplate breaking a window to escape his transported prison, which I am positive was going to be his next action; the train's lights began to flicker again and the carriage started up and was on the move once more.

'Once again ladies and gentlemen, I apologise for the delay. We've been given the green signal so we should be fine for the rest of this southbound service to Brixton. Sorry for any inconvenience this may have caused for your journey.'

The carriage began to rock in that soothing motion, which I loved so dearly. Soon I would be off the train, off the underground, off this ceiled enclosure. Desperate Dan looked pretty sheepish at that present time, and it was awkward to watch. He could not even sit down, curl up and hide in a free newspaper. Everybody huddled around him seemed to tut in unison, as if he had caused distress for no apparent reason. After all, we were only going to be late for work. It wasn't as if it was the end of the world. At least we were all in work; something that was pretty hard to come by in this day and age…

Not sure how long you can stay in a job for if you keep turning up late though…

We arrived at Finsbury Park. People got out, people got in, barging each other to get a place on and off the carriage. Desperate Dan got off; although I knew for certain that it wasn't his stop (he always got off at Green Park). The doors shut tightly, and we were off towards our next stop, Highbury and Islington.

Highbury and Islington? I still have ages left go yet…

I quickly looked down at my watch. It was 9.4-

The train suddenly jolted to a stop. The lights flickered on and off. Everybody on the carriage gave out a heavy sigh. The overhead tannoy began to crackle again…

'I apologise once again ladies and gentleman…'

Don't lose it Rick; don't lose it…

The Babysitter and the Crocodile

'...Now for the last time, go brush your teeth and get straight to bed.' Said little Matthew's babysitter, starting to get irritated now. Who would have thought it would be this hard to get rid of the little brat?

'But it's only eight o'clock.' Argued little Matthew, refusing to budge from the settee. 'My Mum and Dad always let me stay up to at least half nine on a Saturday, sometimes until ten!'

'You're like an annoying broken record you are kid. Now do as you're told! Or else I'm gonna tell your parents how much trouble you've been tonight. Let's see how long they'll let you stay up after that.'

'But that's not fair!' Cried little Matthew.

'Life's not fair kiddo, you best start getting used to it. Now go on, up you get. And the longer it takes you, the more bad stuff I'll tell them about you.'

'You're lying.'

'Try me.' Grinned the babysitter. Little Matthew jumped off the settee in a huff, and stamped his feet all the way up the stairs towards the bathroom. *Stupid babysitter.* He could still see a patch of daylight outside the window. Even some of the other kids in the street were still outside playing. She was right about one thing though; life was definitely unfair.

Matthew slammed the bathroom door shut behind him, as hard as he could. He got his frog-shaped toothbrush, put the multi-coloured toothpaste on it, turned the tap on and began to brush his teeth. What was she going to do down there anyway, except call all her friends for a long chat on the house phone? Maybe he should be the one grassing *her* up. But why bother? His parents were never going to believe him...

He was just nearly finished when he heard the low growl. It was like a slow rumble that echoed throughout the bathroom. Little Matthew turned his head round towards the bathtub. He walked towards it, and with his free hand he pulled back the shower curtain that hung all the way around the front side of the tub. The crocodile was lying perfectly still in it, baring all its shiny white and pointy sharp teeth, as though he was almost smiling at him. Matthew slowly pulled the curtain back, turned the tap off and put his toothbrush and the toothpaste back on the side. He then, very gradually, opened the bathroom door and walked out, all the while keeping eye contact with the bath where the crocodile lay, wary of any sudden movements. He closed the door behind him and walked back down the stairs. The babysitter was sitting in Matthew's spot on the settee nattering away on the house phone as he suspected.

'Hang on Jenny... What the hell did I just tell you?' Said the babysitter, putting the phone down temporarily from her ear. 'Get back up those stairs right now! Have you cleaned your teeth yet?'

'Yes, but...'

'So go to bed then! You're already in enough trouble as it is. You actually want me to tell your parents that you didn't behave? I'll smash something and say it was you.'

'But there's a...'

'How about this framed picture of your nanny? I'm sure you'll get at least a couple weeks of being grounded for this.'

'There's a crocodile in the bathtub.'

'Matthew! Stop telling fibs and get to bed.'

'But I'm not lying!' Pleaded Matthew.

'Sorry Jenny,' sighed the babysitter after picking back up the phone, 'He's having nightmares or something. I'll call you back in a minute.' She put the phone down and turned the volume to mute on the television. 'What are you saying Matthew? You think there's a boogieman in the bathroom?'

Matthew shook his head. He knew it wasn't the boogieman; everyone knew that the boogieman lived in the wardrobe. 'No, not the boogieman, I said there's a crocodile in the bathroom.'

'A crocodile? Good god Matthew; how old are you?' Said the babysitter. 'Go to bed and stop fooling around. I mean it.'

'But shouldn't we tell someone about the crocodile?'

'Who then; the crocodile police? You're really starting to get on my nerves now. Come on; I'm going to show you that there's no crocodile and then put you to bed myself.'

She got up from the settee and nudged him up the stairs, with Matthew hesitantly being lead. They got to the bathroom, and the babysitter knocked twice on the closed wooden door.

'Oh Mr Alligator? Are you in there? Open up if you are!'

'*Stop it!*' Whispered Matthew. '*You'll annoy him.*'

The babysitter cackled with laughter, and began to open the door. 'Let's see how much we can annoy him then shall we? Oh snappy? Here snappy? Where are you boy?' She walked right in and peered around the bathroom. Once she was fully in, little Matthew slowly closed the bathroom door behind her.

'Hey numb nut, the lock's on this side of the door! You thought you could lock me in here all night? Oh, boy, you are in so much trouble. You are so...'

The low, rumbling bass of a growl shook through every wall upstairs, and even more so against the bathroom door, followed by utter silence. Matthew waited for a few minutes, but couldn't here another sound.

After a while, little Matthew thought that the old saying "let sleeping dogs lie" could also be said for crocodiles, so he slowly went downstairs, got some ice cream from the freezer in the kitchen, and sat up on the sofa to watch the late night horror movie on TV in peace; uninterrupted, until his parents came home.

Crooked Mile Road

The snow was falling thick and fast, settling jaggedly on top of the icy ground. The wind was howling manically, throwing the blizzard into frenzy. Nothing but pure white could be seen in the solid snowstorm. The weatherman had forecasted such a turn in conditions, but Malcolm decided to ignore the warnings; something he soon wished he hadn't. The sinking feeling of regret had become adamant while attempting to walk home through Crooked Mile Road. Never had such a long road been so discarded before. No salt had been laid, no footpaths had been cleared; all that was scattered on the road were heaps of snow tossed down from the sky. Everything but white powdered snow, and Malcolm...

The old B194 had proven itself to be a successful short-cut for Malcolm many times when travelling back in his car, and just as sufficient when needing to walk home from the office in Waltham Abbey, back to his house in Broxbourne. Why, even when a little snow started to fall that day it still seemed a quicker retreat back than accepting his co-workers offer in an accompanying bus journey; what with all the stop-offs and the long way round. There was no using the car though this time, as the company car park had been sealed off by the snow; barricaded like an ice queens fortress, letting no vehicles enter or dare escape. It looked at one point that it may have stopped, so why turn his back on his favourite old road? After all, as the road name stated, it was only a mile long.

But the force of the winter season was proving too much for Malcolm. He had many layers on, but the wind still slapped around his bare cheeks; mocking his feeble attempt to walk through unmarked. There was no going back either. Once he had initially set off down the first steep corner he knew there was no chance of an uphill retreat. The snow was too thick and powdery to climb, and he hadn't the energy to carry off such a task. There was no point in phoning one of his friends, who would have no sympathy anyway, for a lift, as most of the roads in the area were unmanageable. And even if they were, there would be no ventures taken through Crooked Mile Road. Many people steered clear from the road in the best of conditions. It had a reputation all right...

Malcolm could feel his shoes getting heavier with snow. His coat blazer pockets were being filled up and his scarf was practically frozen solid. He had a tear on his right glove, bearing his index finger. He tried to protect it but it was no use; the finger was already blue with frostbite. The only thing he could do was to keep on walking; keep on going. He would eventually make it. Sure it would take some time now (a lot longer and more painful than originally planned) but nonetheless he would get there.

Malcolm started to question why on earth he even braved it in to work that day in the first place. He was one of the only few that had bothered to make the effort. The weather wasn't even heavy in the morning, completely driveable with a bit of concentration and control behind the wheel. There had only been around seven of them who had actually bothered to turn up. There were no emails or phone calls stating that work would be cancelled, so why did everybody else presume that they could have a day off?

Whether he liked it or not, he knew that the ones who didn't turn up had made the right decision. Lucky for them, the weather prediction was right, and many people had been left stranded at work or taking agonising bus journeys around every joinable town in the county area just to make it home. Not them though. They were tucked up in their heated little houses enjoying their snow day off, as well as being paid exactly the same as if they had bothered to come in. This really annoyed Malcolm. He was never a bitter man, and rarely got jealous or angry with other members of staff, but given the condition he was in, he had every right to feel a little bit hard done by.

Malcolm carried on with his journey, slumping through the white powder and stomping heavily on its surface so not to fall or slip in. His suit was now completely ruined; the slush had drenched through his coat and now it was even leaking through on to his dry skin.

He noticed that he had not seen any wildlife, not that this surprised him. Usually he would spot a couple of rabbits, or maybe a fox, or even a baby deer jumping over the road in the distance. He presumed that they were all tucked up in their own little shelters and burrows, away from the cold winter. If not they would most probably freeze to death out in the open; a thought that continued to creep into Malcolm's head, worried of his own well being.

The crying wind started to pick up immensely, almost deafening Malcolm of all other noises (not that there were many others to listen to). It seemed to be roaring at him, warning him not to go on any further: or telling him to give up and admit defeat. Either way the roar was getting louder, as though closing in on him: stalking him all this time just waiting for the perfect moment to strike.

A new colour appeared in front of Malcolm. The blue and white sky had faint amber growing more present by the second. Malcolm turned his head behind him and was temporarily blinded by two bright beams of light that shone directly into his eyes. As his vision cleared, he noticed that a car was heading in his direction.

He was astonished. How could a car be driving on this road? The road itself wasn't even well marked on a clear day. How could he see in front of him? More importantly, had the car seen him?

Malcolm signalled high with his arms, so to make the driver aware where he was in conjunction to the road. It was hard to see where the pavement was and where the road actually joined. The car continued slowly towards him. It wasn't going fast at all, maximum speed at around five miles an hour. He would probably do more damage to the car if there were a collision.

Malcolm stood still as it approached, so not to get in its way. Astonishingly to Malcolm, the car seemed to be slowing down by the side of him. It was an old grey Nissan Figaro; and looked like it had been dragged straight out of the sixties. The wheels of the Figaro skidded gradually to a stop. The windows were completely frosted and steamed up. Malcolm leaned in further towards the passenger's side. He thought that perhaps the driver was lost and came down the wrong road; maybe they were after directions?

The passenger's side window jolted due to the frost but then eventually went down, revealing a blonde haired gentlemen sporting a long black coat, multi-coloured scarf and driving gloves. Malcolm was more surprised that it was a gentleman driver, as the car itself looked very ladylike; something that lady Penelope out of the Thunderbirds would drive. The man inside had a ridiculous grin on his face.

'Howdy!' Shouted out the gentleman over the whirling wind. 'Quite some snow storm we're having here hey partner!'

Malcolm was not quite sure what to say back at the man's obvious statement. Was he mocking him?

'You must be frozen out there sir.' Continued the gentleman. 'Where about's you heading?'

'Just to the end of Crooked Mile Road.' Said Malcolm. His teeth were chattering rapidly.

'Well hope in partner! I'm going to have to get to the end of this godforsaken road anyway. You might as well ride along with me.' Offered the gentleman. He leaned over and opened the passenger door.

Malcolm never usually accepted lifts from complete strangers, if anything he was against hitchhikers or anybody who gave hitchhikers a lift, but looking at the road ahead of him he did not even have to think twice before jumping in to the car. He could immediately feel the warmth hit him as he sat in the heated passenger seat.

'Thank you so much; I thought I was going to freeze to death out there.' Thanked Malcolm graciously. 'I think I misjudged the weather forecast a tad.'

The gentleman laughed out loud. He started to drive away slowly and jolted slightly in doing so.

'Woops! Sorry about that. Still getting used to this car. Haven't had it long you see.' Apologised the gentleman. 'Not used to these snow chains either. They get you through the snow, but sure as hell don't let you get anywhere fast.'

Malcolm rubbed his hands together over the hot air vent, paying close attention in defrosting his index finger. The radio was on, set on some station playing The Kinks 'You really got me'. It certainly fitted in well with the car's interior. The gentleman flicked one of the many switches up. The car aerial whirled its way upward, making the song a little less crackly.

'The name's Tony.' Said the gentleman, extending his hand in greet to Malcolm.

'Malcolm. Really appreciate this Tony.' The pair shook hands.

'Yep, this road can be quite a burden. You're lucky I found you there partner. Mind you, wasn't hard to miss a black man amongst all the white snow. Stuck out like a sore thumb there Malcolm my old chum! I suppose you lot aren't used to snow are you?'

This made Malcolm a bit uncomfortable, but he was used to it. It was one of those things he had accepted whilst growing up in a predominantly white middle-class area. He didn't accept it, but he had grown to tolerate it. It was a throwaway comment that had no racial hatred infused, more an observational remark if anything. But still, it made him feel awkward. The usage of the phrase 'you lot', as if every black man was manufactured to act and behave in exactly the same way, was what upset him. He was always known as 'the black kid' at school. There were a couple of times he got called a nigger, but that was by a minority that got along with no one. He was part of the popular crowd, and his friends would always stick up for him whenever it occurred, but it still hurt.

He knew that Tony hadn't meant any harm in what he said; this was clear by the way he said it so naturally. And after all, if he actually were racist he wouldn't have picked him up in the first place.

'No, I suppose not.' Swallowed Malcolm. 'Give me a sunny beach in the Bahamas any day.'

Two men laughed together, putting Malcolm back at ease. The radio station had started playing 'Green Onions' by Booker T and The MG's, another sixties track. The bass line seemed to shake the whole Figaro as it came out of the tiny speakers. It was no way means loud, but the treble on the speakers seemed to have been broken, causing the added deep frequency.

'Seriously though Malcolm, you should be careful on this road. You know of all the accidents and strange going's don't you?'

'I've heard stories.' Admitted Malcolm.

'Really?' Said an Intrigued Tony. 'What stories have you heard then partner?'

Malcolm stalled for a split second. He realised that he was getting into a sceptical conversation with a stranger he had only just met, and was quite frankly growing weary of him before they even started. He did not seem a threat, but it was something about him that Malcolm did not trust. However, he could not quite put his finger on it.

'Well, a few superstitious believers consider Crooked Mile Road to be haunted by a phantom ghost; supposing to be a victim of a motorbike collision, riding around on his broken vehicle or something, causing accidents for other drivers.' Malcolm chuckled, but hesitatingly stopped when realising that Tony was keeping a firm facial expression, staring out at the hard snow hitting the windscreen. He had heard that story from one of the lads in the office when he told him of his usual journey home through the Crooked Mile. Malcolm, although a deeply religious man, had always discarded such spiritual accusations, and a firm non-believer of the supernatural or paranormal.

'That's right partner. I've heard some similar variations of that story myself.' Tony finally replied. 'Legend has it that the phantom rides around at night, luring drivers to speed promptly to their death. But tell me Malcolm, have you ever heard of a motorbike accident being on this road at all? Did you ever read it in a local newspaper or heard about it on the news? Take a look at the side of the roads; do you see any flowers?'

Malcolm could hardly see out of the side window, and even if there were flowers laid down, the snow would have covered them completely.

'Do you know what a ghost bike is partner?' Asked Tony, but continued on before a response. 'It's an old bicycle painted completely in white, set up by the side of the road as a memorial in place where a biker has been killed. Have you ever seen a ghost bike on this road before? Take a look for yourself.'

Malcolm shook his head. He didn't even bother to amuse Tony by looking for a white bike in the heaps of snow.

'You haven't seen one partner because there ain't one there! It's all stories; old wives tales; fables passed around from person to person, and that's what really intrigues me about this road. How can one road cause so much spook? The name is pretty spooky in a rusty old way, and the road itself twists and turns so much for a small country lane in the middle of nowhere. Yes sir, this place is perfect for my new idea…'

'New idea?' Questioned Malcolm. He looked out his side window, judging just how bad it actually was outside compared to inside the car. The radio was playing The Ronettes, Be My Baby.

'I'm a writer partner. I tell stories; mainly of the horror and thriller genres.'

Malcolm tried his best not to look doubtful, but he found it tough. Tony did not strike him as a writer. He supposed there was no obvious look, but the all the writers and journalists he had met in the past all had a certain style about them. There was always an element of swagger but also a hidden nerdy persona. Tony had neither. He was definitely confident but in a more annoying tone, and he didn't look like he was or ever had been a geek. He was very tall and very muscular for his frame, as if he had kept himself in good shape over the years. This more than anything opted Malcolm to not question the drivers claim.

'Really? Have you had anything published then?'

'Not yet.' Snapped Tony. 'Still tweaking a few ideas, but very soon indeed, very soon. My latest book is about this very road, and it's a scorcher if I do say so myself. It's called "The Phantom Ghost Rider of Crooked Mile Road". Bit of a long title I know, but I like it. I'm just missing a couple extra key characters and it'll be there.'

Tony temporary halted in thought, and then turned to Malcolm.

'Do you want to be in it? I need a good rounded character with a bit of ethnicity thrown in. You could be perfect!'

There it was again; that friendly racial comment Malcolm thought he steered clear from the first time round. He looked at Tony with a thwarted expression; only to find the drivers eyes wide open with inspiration rolling out of them. The man had found his muse.

'It's perfect partner! You could be the phantom bike rider's first victim. The black guy always gets killed off in horror stories doesn't he?'

In any other situation, and he had many similar confrontations before, Malcolm would have stopped the conversation going on any further. The man was obviously a typical white middle class Wally and wasn't going to drop it. But here he was, caught out in the middle of the heaviest snow blizzard he had ever seen. Plus Tony was of a fair size, and was no doubt missing that certain sanity most people had. It was something in the tone of his voice that was evident of that, like he was being tested with every sentence. All the time's Malcolm had travelled up and down Crooked Mile Road; he had never known it to take this long.

He could just barely see out of the window and noticed a large field gate he recognised. They hadn't even made it halfway through the mile…

'Well? What do you think partner?'

'Why not.' Said Malcolm, trying his best not to initiate more talk.

'Fantastic! Why, what if the Ghost Rider wasn't driving his bike, but had a car instead, and picked you up by the side of the road? It could be a snow blizzard like tonight as well! He could offer to give you a ride to the end of Crooked Mile Road…but…well, I can make up something pretty horrific that could happen to you partner!' Tony started laughing and nudging Malcolm to laugh alongside him. Malcolm didn't see the humour, and was now considering conjuring up an excuse to get out the car.

He had clearly made a mistake. The man had a screw loose, even if it was only key people skills.

'Or! You could be my lead character! It would be like Night of the Living Dead; you could be my Duane Jones! The black ill-fated hero!'

'Damn…I've just remembered…I've left some paperwork at the office. I'll need to go back and get it. I'll just walk back, sorry for wasting your time…'

But as Malcolm's hand first grasped the door's handle, the shiny silver lock that situated above the door slammed down heavy in front of his eyes. He glanced over at Tony, who, while with one hand on the driver's car lock button, was looking directly back at him. The two men stared at each other, both with doubt flavouring their minds. Malcolm's was full to the top with fear over his driver's mental stability, while it was clear that Tony started to have a feeling of distrust in his passenger.

'Nonsense. You'll never make it back their now in this weather. Nothing is that important. You'll have to try and get it in the morning, that's if you're not snowed in tomorrow. I'm sure your work will understand that?' Said a very concerned Tony, although it was unclear what he was concerned about.

Malcolm stayed quiet, the reason being that he was trying to conjure up another excuse to get out the car. He couldn't help it; he was just too uncomfortable. There was just a strong feeling he had that this man was trouble.

'What's wrong partner?' Continued Tony. 'Don't you want to hear the rest of my story? Don't you want to be the main character?'

'No, no… It's not that, sorry.' Replied Malcolm promptly; so to assure Tony that he did not offend him in any way. 'It's just, I've had a really busy day, what with hardly anybody in the office today, and I just know it's going to pile up on me tomorrow.'

'Well so will the snow if you set out there!' Retorted Tony; snapping a quicker response than Malcolm's, as if competing. 'We're nearly halfway through good old Crooked Mile Road anyway. Just another half a mile and a bit, then I'll drop you off, okay?'

Malcolm looked outside and saw the branches on the trees swaying all separately like mad men trying to hang themselves. The snow wasn't stopping for a while, and he knew deep down there was no way he was getting back towards the office at Waltham Abbey. He returned his stance towards Tony, whose face now had a sparkle of desperation, as if Malcolm was refusing to ride with him, or listen to his story ideas…

'You're right…partner!' Malcolm said trying to win back some trust points from Tony. He hadn't much of a choice, so opting to ride it out with a nutty stranger for half a mile didn't seem the most obscure plan all day, bearing in mind it was his idea earlier to venture through Crooked Mile Road on foot.

'That's more like it Partner!' Tony's face lit up like an LED light. His eyes looked so bright that it even made his pale skin seem tanned. 'Right, well let's get back to our story then shall we?'

Tony began to discuss a list of other key characters he had come up with, including a love interest for the main character called Wendy, who he also thought should now also be black. He spoke about his ideas for secondary plots, how The Phantom Ghost Rider should have a past history that interlinks well with the main story line. He also described how Crooked Mile Road itself would have a strong reputation, much like it had in the present day, of being some sort of phenomenon like the Bermuda Triangle.

While Tony rambled on, Malcolm kept himself looking interested and part of the conversation, focusing on what Tony was saying, just in case he was suddenly quizzed on it. The Figaro couldn't have been driving no more than 3 miles an hour, with the build up of snow on the road slowing down the automatic car even more so.

The radio started to play The Who's 'Substitute', when it was interrupted by a breaking news broadcast that caught Malcolm's attention. Tony had not noticed, and carried on explaining the Mise-en-scène of the inevitable film version of his novel. Malcolm listened in carefully while all the time with his head tilted towards Tony to show him interest. The news broadcast stated the following:

'WE INTTERUPT THE MUSIC TO GIVE A BREAKING NEWS STORY. ALL DRIVERS AND PEDESTRIANS BE ON SAFE LOOK OUT FOR A TALL, BLONDE HAIRED CAUCASIAN PATIENT THAT HAS BROKEN OUT OF THE ABBEY ASYLUM THIS AFTERNOON. HE IS EXPECTED TO BE UNARMED, BUT CONSIDERED VERY DANGEROUS. DUE TO THE EXTREME WEATHER

CONDITIONS IT IS LIKELY THAT HE IS STILL SOMEWHERE IN THE AREA. THE MAN SHOULD BE WEARING A LONG, BLACK COAT JACKET AND MULTI-COLOURED SCARF, BELIEVED TO HAVE BEEN STOLEN FROM ONE OF THE DOCTORS EARLIER TODAY. IF YOU SEE THIS MAN, STAY WELL AWAY FROM HIM AND CALL THE EMERGENCY SERVICES TO UPDATE ON HIS LOCATION. WE REPEAT, KEEP WELL AWAY FROM HIM, AS HE IS CONSIDERED DANGEROUS. CALL THE EMERGENCY SERVICES AND ASK FOR THE POLICE STRAIGHT AWAY IF SPOTTED.'

The Who began to replay their track, sounding so innocent compared to what had just been stated. Malcolm stared at Tony, who had not acknowledged one sentence just broadcasted and was carrying on with his brilliant tale. Malcolm also stared hard at his blonde hair, long black coat and bright multi-coloured scarf that seemed to shine vividly, even more so than before.

What the hell was he going to do?

Tony's conversation with himself began to fade down to a quiet stop, as though he got bored of his own voice for a while. The windscreen wipers were harshly smacking the snow off, and Tony squinted more to focus on the drive.

'How long did you say you had this car for?' Questioned Malcolm. It slipped out his mouth spontaneously as he thought the very words. He immediately froze, but still could not take his eyes off the driver.

Tony glared back at Malcolm, with the same expression of distrust as before smothered all over his face, as if he was being accused.

'Only a day now partner.' He said very calmly and soft, as if disappointed in Malcolm. 'Only a day…'

The Figaro had become instantly fogged with tension. The pair sat both staring out to what they could make of the road; all the while weary of the next one's move. It was getting hot in the car as well. Malcolm wanted to remove his coat, but feared that any sudden movement would antagonise Tony. The driver was obviously feeling the heat too, as he leaned his hand over to the air conditioning, causing Malcolm to hesitantly jig back in defence. Tony started moving the sliding knobs, but was having trouble with some that were jammed.

'Come on... Stupid thing!' Said Tony to himself. He was trying to force the dial across, but it was clear that the car had become fragile over time and required a certain knack to adjust. It was also clear that Tony did not acquire this certain knack.

'You wouldn't think this shitty little car could heat up so dam quick would you partner?' He said, while still wrestling with the dials. 'Who the hell would buy one of these anyway?'

'You?' Said Malcolm, questioning his driver once more. He did not know what asking this would achieve, but he once again could not help it. He was going nowhere unless embroiled in a physical confrontation, whether it be forcing Tony to stop the car, breaking the passenger door down or going head first through the windscreen. Either way he was stuck with Tony, and needed to know what he was actually dealing with. Was this guy the escaped loon from the asylum? All fingers were pretty much pointing to him at that very moment. Or could it just so be that he was a general weirdo who had no communication skills and a love for horror stories? Whatever it was, curiosity had definitely got the better of Malcolm.

Tony turned at Malcolm with his large white eyes in charge. He looked startled, as if the game was up. But his facial expression soon changed to a wide-open grin, almost in a playful manner.

'You're right... You're God Damn right partner! What the Hell was I thinking?' Snorted out Tony.

Malcolm laughed nervously along with Tony. The driver finally managed to force the air-conditioning dial across to 'cool'.

'There, that's better. Just needed a slight nudge in the right direction.' Said Tony.

The Figaro started to drive round a large bend in the road, one that Malcolm knew all too well. If you were to be travelling at some pace, the corner usually proved quite daunting, especially if there was any oncoming traffic to swerve away from as well. Crooked Mile was renowned for being a dangerous road, and deep down it was probably the reason why Malcolm liked to use the short cut.

He was always known as a very cautious man, a non-risk taker. He had never had any financial problems and never went on any dangerous trips abroad, no bungee jumping, no rock climbing. He never really played many sports for fear of injuries, nor did his current job provide any health and safety worries. It was not that he was afraid of any of these things or ever regretted the lifestyle he had chosen, but more that the opportunity for anything dangerous never really arose. The road was his walk on the wild side. The trip to and from work was his daily rush of excitement and adventure.

But his faith in Crooked Mile was soon deteriorating. Although the speed that he found himself going round the deadly long corner was the slowest he had ever went, he was more afraid on this day than any of the others…

'You're awful quiet partner, something bothering you?'

'No… no, just had a rough day. Wanting to get home and get some rest really.' Said Malcolm, quite honestly apart from the nothing bothering him bit.

'Well I'm going as fast as I God Damn can, what more do you want?' Snapped Tony. 'Jesus, you people are so ungrateful.'

'Sorry, I didn't mean it like that.' Said Malcolm, not very surprised of Tony's outburst. 'I'm very grateful for-'

'-Very grateful my arse! And you've shown no interest whatsoever in my story at all. Do you even want to be in it? I'm making you my lead character for Gods Sake!'

The car stopped, skidding slightly in the snow, and the engine switched itself off. At first Malcolm thought Tony had braked hard, but soon realised the driver was just as surprised as he was.

'Damn it!'

Tony tried to start up the engine again, giving it plenty of gas, but the old car was not re-starting.

'Well, looks like we're going to have to jump-start this old banger partner. D'ya want to hop out and give her a push?' As soon as Tony finished huffing out his sentence, the car door locks popped upwards.

To Malcolm, it was like seeing his prison gates being opened for the first time. He could hardly believe it. He had been given the opportunity to step out of his cell. Did he trust him? Was this a test? He had turned quicker than a light switch from anger to seeking aid. Did he stop the car on purpose? It was highly unlikely that an automatic had stalled.

'Come on partner! I haven't got all day.'

Malcolm, who was momentarily paused staring at the opened door lock, snapped back and opened the car door. He put his fist leg out and felt his frozen shoe be reacquainted with the cold snow. It was like sheer bliss. But before he could turn his other leg round far enough, Tony grabbed hold of Malcolm's right arm tight. This shocked him; the first physical presence he had encountered, and the driver's grip was even stronger than once presumed. He looked up into the man's bright white eyes. His heartbeat skipped a few extra as he waited on what was going to be said next.

'Careful out there partner. It's mighty deep; I don't want my lead character getting injured now do I?'

The warning threw Malcolm. Was he being sarcastic, or was he actually being concerned? Tony loosened his grip, causing Malcolm's arm to throb back into position.

Malcolm reached his other leg round and pulled himself up, out of the car. He was out! He was free!

'Start pushing it gently and I'll try and give it some juice.' Said Tony, in an almost normal tone for once.

Malcolm trampled through the snow towards the back of the Figaro. They were not on any hill and the snow on the ground was so heavy that there was no way of pushing the car anywhere, however Malcolm did not want to argue.

He put both hands on the boot and began to push, with no movement whatsoever apart from his own feet sliding around. Tony kept trying to start the ignition but with no luck on his end as well.

Malcolm could hear Tony from inside the car ranting and raving, getting more and more worked up, even though none of the windows or doors were open. It was like hearing a foggy version of a fight breaking loose. Soon enough the window came rolling down and Tony stuck his head out looking back at Malcolm frustrated by his efforts.

'Come on partner! Can't you people do anything right?'

This comment sparked a switch inside Malcolm, which was reaching near on boiling point as it was. Another flashback of being called a nigger as a child crept into frame again. What the hell was he doing? Why was he still amusing this guy? This racist? This escaped lunatic!

Enough was enough. Malcolm was outside, he was free, and this guy was stuck in his stolen lady car in the snow. He stopped pushing and stood up straight, poised and ready. Tony looked back again and his white eyes were even brighter in contrast with the falling snow.

'What the hell are you doing? Start pushing you idiot!' Screamed Tony.

'I'll tell you one thing us people can do all right.' Said Malcolm, with a half grin of near success on his face. 'We can run faster than you arseholes!'

And then he shot off, kicking up the snow as he flew past it towards the near end of Crooked Mile Road. He could hear Tony cursing and shouting in the background, but there was no chance of him looking round, not while he had his momentum on his side. A couple of near slips here and there made balancing difficult in the snow, but he kept upright. He was now glad he never took off his jacket in the car. That would have proven difficult in obtaining before sprinting off. The conditions were awful, but all he kept thinking of was that Tony also had to deal with it as well if he was to start to chase after him.

But suddenly Malcolm heard a noise. It vibrated through his body as he heard it; the sound of a car engine starting up again. He had got the car working again...

He looked round and saw the same faint colour of amber growing from the distance as when he first saw the Figaro. Panic filled up and overflowed in Malcolm's stomach. He could feel fear inside of him. What was this man even capable of? He was considered 'very dangerous'!

Even if it was only going 5 miles an hour tops before, he was sure that Tony would be putting his foot down a hell of a lot more now. There was only one way of outrunning a car in this condition, Malcolm thought, and that was off the road.

He saw a gate that leaded into a field. It was slightly ajar, but he still jumped over it the long way, perhaps to disguise his footprints. He wasn't too sure. The grass was completely vanished within the snowfall. Up ahead he could make out a barn, and a converted house directly opposite it. He ran his way over to the building.

The sound of the Figaro's engine was dying out slowly, as if it was passing through. Malcolm, who was now completely out of breath, eased up on his pace, while still keeping a light jog going.

He could not help but wish he had never gone to work in the first place again. This thought made him angry, but more with himself than the weather. If he had just taken the long bus route home instead of Crooked Mile Road he would not be in this mess in the first place. One thing was for certain though; he was not going to be taking that short cut again, not even in the summer time.

As he neared the farmhouse he saw an old man tracing through the snow from the barn. Malcolm shouted over and waved to him in aid. The man looked startled at first, but soon realised that this stranger needed assistance.

Malcolm jogged up to him, stopped and held his knees in support.

'Sorry for barging into your field like this, but there's a mad man loose on Crooked Mile Road. He's in a car, still on the main road, but we'd better get inside. He may be out the car by now and I'm not sure what he's going to do.' Said Malcolm, while trying to catch his breath.

The old man looked confused, as anybody would. He obviously was not afraid of Malcolm, as he would have tried protecting himself by this point.

'You'd better come inside then.' Said the old man while nodding his head in acceptance. He turned and made his way to the main house, with Malcolm following from behind. The old man had a large heavy raincoat on; big black welly boots and a flat cap.

As they reached the front door of the house, the old man got out a large set of keys and traced through them for the right one. Malcolm was hoping that the old man would hurry up a bit, due to the fact that there was a lunatic loose, but the old man didn't seem too bothered about that.

The key was finally found, and the door crept open, having to be forced somewhat due to the piled up snow. They made their way in, and the old man slowly shut the door, putting the chain and two bolt locks across. He also locked the door from the inside keyhole and put the large set of keys in his front pocket. He then looked up at Malcolm.

'Right. We'd better phone the police then ey.' He said with no sense of urgency in his voice. 'What's your name lad?'

'Malcolm.'

'Name's John. Go and sit yourself down on the couch and I'll make the call. You look pretty shook up.'

Malcolm went and sat down on the flower printed sofa. The house had a very unique cottage feel to it, with an old working fireplace, along with horseshoes and mugs hung on the walls and staircase.

John went over by the phone next to the stairs. Malcolm overheard John talking to the police on the phone, stating the address of where they were and what he had been told. Malcolm felt as if he should really talk to them directly, as he was the one who witnessed Tony, but felt it would be rude to interrupt. As long as the police were coming, that's all that mattered.

John finished the call and went and sat down on the chair opposite to where Malcolm was sitting.

'What the hell were you doing out in this weather in the first place?' Chuckled John.

'Let's just say I'm not going to go the extra mile for work anymore.' The two men both gave a small laugh each. Malcolm felt relaxed again.

'Well he's not getting in here that's for sure! Can I get you a drink at all? Coffee? Anything stronger maybe?' Offered John.

'Coffee would be great please.'

John got up and made his way to the kitchen. Malcolm sighed in relief and slumped back into his seat. He browsed the old man's living room some more. It was full of quirky little pots and lamps scattered around, but not in a messy way. It was very homey.

Malcolm suddenly remembered a key point that he had not explained to John before he made the call to the police. The Figaro. Tony was driving quite a recognisable car, one that could easily be spotted.

So not to disturb his host, Malcolm got up and made his way over to the phone by the stairs. He picked up the receiver. It was an old style phone where you had to whirl the numbers round manually on a fingerplate. He pressed in the first nine, whirled it round, and the other two nines followed, but to no response. He hung up to try again but soon realised that there was no dial tone. He looked underneath to see if the phone cable had come loose. As he turned over the base he saw that the phone was not even plugged in.

Malcolm began to scan the room, seeing if he had accidently picked up the wrong phone; hoping that this is what he did. He could not see another phone anywhere, but two things in particular caught Malcolm's attention the most.

In one corner he noticed that there was an old child's bicycle painted entirely in white. He also noticed a clothes hanger in another corner by the front door. On it hung a large black coat jacket and a multi-coloured scarf draped across it.

John re-entered the living room with a tray of coffee, a sugar bowl and milk pot. He had taken off his flat cap, revealing a mop of blonde hair. Malcolm also noticed that the old man was distinctively tall.

A tall, blonde, Caucasian male, should be wearing a long black coat jacket and multi-coloured scarf...

'Do you take milk? Sugar?' Said John; unaware that Malcolm had moved places from the sofa to the out of use telephone.

Malcolm froze, fixated on John's hair. For an old man it was astonishing on just how blonde it still was. He could not move for fear of provoking his host.

'Milk... No sugar thanks.' He managed to spurt out. 'Tell me, how long have you been living on Crooked Mile Road for now?'

John put the tray down on the coffee table, and then looked up at Malcolm with his large bright white eyes in a disappointing expression, as though he was being accused.

'Only a day now partner.' Replied John in a very calm and soft tone. 'Only a day...'

Dinner Date

I am an artist. My paintbrush is my whisk. Chopping boards, graters, wooden spoons, pots and pans; these are the tools I use to create my masterpieces. My paints are that of food and flavourings, which I mix together to invent wonderful colours. Every last sculpture of mine is decorated and cut to fine detail and accuracy. The aromas that are produced are that of Mount Olympus, where the Gods themselves would be honoured to inhale such wonder. Every bite of one of my dishes leaves you longing for the next. The flavours that pour out onto the tongue set the taste buds screaming out, as if they have finally discovered what they were missing all this time.

My restaurants all over London boast the finest cuisine that money can buy. From my Scallops Ceviche with Avocado Crème Fraiche and Roasted Breast of Black Leg Chicken with Morel Tart Fine, along with Poached Rhubarb with Lemon Balm Ice Cream, my menus shout out straight away the quality and standard of what is expected.

I am well known throughout the west end amongst the inner circle as the best chef in all of the capital. People fly in from afar just to witness the rumours for their own eyes and, of course, taste.

I myself tend to keep a low profile when visiting my bistros, as I let my food do the talking, instead of gloating over people's dinners while I boast about how great I already know I am. I shy away in this light, and leave it to my famous hosts who entertain as well as pleasure the guests in an honourable fashion rather than breathe down their necks every five seconds demanding that they acquire service.

In the kitchen, however, I am a tyrant. I own everything and everyone. For, after all, my creations are in their hands, and I'll be damned if they do not present them picture perfect to my originals. Pots and pans have been flung in many a back room, egging on the cooks to construct the perfect dishes. Each and every one must live and breathe as if it was the first fresh one of its kind that has just been made. In the 18 years since I opened my first restaurant, never has any one of my orders ever been refused or taken back. The day that this would occur would be the day I would quit my life long passion and hang up my apron for good.

But fortune has indeed struck me well over the years, blessing me with success after success. My talent has run on everlasting it seems, and will do so for years to come, even after I am dead, being handed down to my apprentices who I teach in the only way I know how. They will be my only successors.

But all this talent and success comes with a great price. Like many artists, I needed inspiration. I needed something fresh and new. I yearn for that excitement and anticipation over a new recipe that I have just discovered for the first time, causing my taste buds to orgasm and scream out.

But alas, I was blocked. The ink in my pen had dried out. I was at a loss. I had tried and tasted every possible flavour there was. I wanted something new and extreme, something that nobody else could offer. Vegetables and side salads were not what I was looking for. Sure they're great, but can never stand alone as the highest price on the menu; the choice that everybody aspires to afford one day. I needed a new style of meat to bring to the table....

Amateurs at my restaurants would suggest maybe adding crocodile or kangaroo or ostrich. I did not give them the satisfaction of a response over such pathetic propositions. Others added in perhaps more exotic meats such as Bear or Lion, but still this was feeble compared to my standards.

It ate inside at me, picking away mockingly over my despair. There was nothing that I had not already sampled: Kobe Beef, Elk, Llama, Yak, Wa-Gyu, Alpaca, the list was endless. There was nothing left for me to try; except maybe one thing...

The thought entered my mind and back out again pretty quickly, temporarily brushing off the very thought. But the more I pondered, the more it returned. What if I was to sample the greatest taboo of them all? What if it turned out to be the most succulent of all the flavours? What if all this time I was missing out? Me, the greatest cook in all of the land, had not tasted the greatest meat? Then the idea seemed to fill up in my head and explode out like a leaking teapot.

What would a human taste like?

The very thought gave shudders through my body. Morally I knew that this was unacceptable thinking. But on the other hand, the greatest achievements and discoveries in history all had sacrifices along the way, they all seemed radical ideas at one point in their existence. How else were they to know unless they did not experiment? If I was to do this I had to completely agree and accept in what I was going to do. After throwing back and forth moralistic views I soon came to my own conclusion…

I had to know. For the sake of good food and everything I stood for, it had to be done.

After I had convinced myself, I now had to figure out how I was going to achieve this. What type of person would make the best meat? Before considering any of this, I had decided from the start it had to be woman, merely on the grounds that if all did not go to plan and a struggle or fight broke out, I fancied my chances against a woman rather than an equally strong male. She had to be plump as to get the added juicy joints, but not too fat that it becomes chewy. Skin should be immaculate, as this is a giveaway sign of her own healthy living and balanced diet. And likewise with animals, she must be fairly young; as meat tends to lose it's tenderness and becomes tough and stringy with age. So what I was preferably looking for was a firm and attractive female in her early twenties. Ripe and ready…

So where was I going to meet such a rare specimen? I thought that the best option I had was to lure her to my own home, where I could pre-prepare. I started looking on the Internet for 'singles dating' websites. After flicking through vast amounts of endless pornography garbage that seemed to go hand in hand with this, I finally found a website suitable for my needs. It even had a little search engine, where I could type in my 'perfect partner', and the area in which I was looking. I was astonished to find so many single women in London that were actually very attractive. I had prepared myself for a lot worse than expected, naturally assuming those who were on dating sites would have to be struggling in the beauty department from the word go. But I sat there corrected. It was beautiful. I felt like a customer in a French restaurant picking out his favourite lobster from the tank.

And then, I came across her: Jennifer. My Jen. She was utterly perfect; a twenty-two year old hockey player that lived in North London. She enjoyed long walks in parks and keeping active. She had a good appetite, which was visibly obvious, and was looking for a like-minded male who had a passion for cooking and the arts. She was not too fussy on looks, rather more longing for a decent man than a vain one. I had to snatch her up before someone else netted her.

I signed up to the ghastly site myself in order to get her phone number. For obvious reasons I used a fake name and details.

She sounded very polite and well spoken when speaking to her for the first time, very desperate though. She seemed impressed with the way I spoke about my hobbies of food as well as the added mention of sport; a persuasive lie that seemed to drop off the tongue quite elegantly. I can bore you with everything else we spoke about, but if truth were told I can scarcely remember. I just agreed with everything she had to say and laughed on queue whenever she did. It was if I was in a daydream, just riding along with the conversation whilst all the time thinking what side dishes could go well with her.

I offered to cook for her round mine when she was next free, which happened to be in the next four days. I was shocked in how trusting she was. I was all ready to battle out a more convincing presentation on why I should be able to entertain her, but it seemed people are more naïve nowadays. Who knows what monster she could have ended up with?

So my date was all set. I had chosen my willing lobster. All I needed to do now was to prepare. Such a task needed time and effort to give my Jen credit. She was going to be spoilt. She would dine like a goddess, as her last meal should be the finest she had ever had.

This part of the evening I was not afraid of. Years of entertaining and serving to the fussiest of critics had moulded me into a natural. What I was more concerned about was the manner in which my Jen would leave this earth. She must not be frightened one bit. It will be humane, dignified; not the least bit barbaric. A drip of sedative into the after-dinner wine to knock her out, and a simple incision across the throat and my Jen would be dead without feeling a thing.

I managed to drag down an old wooden table from the attic, which I placed in my garage. I cling filmed the entire top surface a few times over, to cover the bare wood when my Jen would be on top of it. All my utensils, knifes sharpened and waste bins were ready. All I needed now was my Jen…

The days past so slowly as I feared they would. I amused myself by visiting a couple of my restaurants during the day, and going about my business in fetching the drug at night. I shall not tell you where I got this, or who from. For much the same reason, as I shan't ever tell you my name.

There may be some detectives amongst you who can probably guess who I am, as I have given enough clues already, the clear sign being 'the best chef in all of London'. Others may also point out that I have already given away some of my restaurants menu details. But I am a clever man. These food comparisons are those of my own recipes and but only fiction to my real menus. I have backtracked all of my steps and not one piece of evidence can ever lead back to me. There are too many chefs in London to prosecute all of us...

So why am I telling you all this? Why would I even risk giving away any evidence at all? If you sculpted a statue, would you not want the world to see it, or at least to hear about it?

The day had finally arrived. I had goose bumps all over throughout the afternoon, as the evening drew nearer. My Jennifer was on her way. She would be treated like a Queen. I would be the perfect gentleman.

The doorbell chimed playfully, nearly making me burst with excitement there and then. As I opened the door, in stepped my Jennifer. She did not disappoint in the slightest. If anything the pictures I had seen of her prior to our meet did not do her justice. She arrived by cab as well – one less problem to worry about there...

After a shy introduction I helped Jen remove her coat. Underneath she was wearing a long black dress, cut short to reveal her strong calf muscles. I may have drooled slightly here at this point but luckily she did not notice.

I led her to the dining table, where I had laid out our starters alongside candlelight, an opened bottle of Bordeaux and sensuous background music of light jazz playing at a legato tempo.

For starters we both shared fried fillets of red mullet with fennel purée and a pink grapefruit vinaigrette; my portion slightly less than hers, for which she did not notice. We spoke about our jobs, what we did for a living, where we went out, what our favourite restaurants were, how long we both had lived in the city. I had to admit, Jen was perfect. She had a gorgeous smile that boasted a set of bright white teeth. Her hair was simple but effective, cut short with a slight hint of past highlights. She had excellent table manners, no elbows showing, no talking with a mouthful of food. Her napkin was used properly and not just merely put aside on her lap. She was an absolute treat. It astonished me how she had stayed single the whole time.

I cleared away the starter, refusing Jennifer's considerate offer to help, and finished preparing the mains of Sauteed Spätzle with Butternut Squash, Pumpkin Seeds, beurre Noisette Powder and Wilted Rocket. I decided before hand not to have any meat as to fill me up too much.

We chinned our glasses as she praised my presentational skills, and added more gratitude after one mouthful. We continued to discuss matters such as recent book titles, foreign cult movies, what music we were both fond of, current exhibits being shown. The more I spoke with her the more I began to fall in love. Not in a physical sense, but more of a mutual understanding kind of way. There are not many people that get the same things that I do, but Jen was one of them. She was a fan of the arts, culture, and I even admired her passion for sport, even though I found it tricky to keep up that lie.

For desert we had Lime mousse with rum and vanilla jelly, caramel ice cream with peppermint and chocolate crumbs delicately sprinkled on top. Again my serving was smaller than Jennifer's, but she could not glance away from her own.

It is fair to say that I pulled out all the stops for her that night, and Jennifer was more than impressed with myself. I acted as a true gentleman all evening, complimenting her in every aspect. I genuinely meant every word I said as well. She was a fine young woman and I had thoroughly appreciated her company.

I took our two empty wine glasses to the kitchen, where I had the sedative hidden in one of the bottom cupboards. I opened another bottle and poured out its contents into the glasses, along with the drug in Jennifer's.

I handed her the glass and saluted another toast. To the future did not seem appropriate. Instead I hailed to the good times. She smiled delightfully and sipped her drink, followed by a heavier gulp.

I looked away while enjoying the company of my own wine; waiting. A large thud hit the table and I turned round slowly to find my Jen lying head down in the remains of her lime mousse. I finished my glass of wine, enjoying the sweet sound of Miles Davis that trickled back into my ears, before carrying on.

I hoisted Jen out of her chair, through the kitchen and into the garage, where the old table was placed, and flung her on top.

I put on my apron that was hanging up in place as well as my food handling gloves, got my knifes out of the drawer and made the quick incision across the neck and larynx ear to ear, which was followed with a gush of bright red blood. Jen's body started to spontaneously shake on impact, but died down soon enough. The blood trickled into one of the large barrels that hovered underneath Jen's head where I had placed it. I started to pump and compress the stomach in order to assist the flow. Whilst this was going on I unclothed Jen, taking off all her jewelry and accessories as well. She looked just as beautiful naked. Her skin was pure white, like it had been frozen, preserved in a perfect state.

Jen bled out around six pints of blood (which I thought could make wonderful black pudding...). Once all was out I continued to cut around her entire head, from her jaw line to the back of her skull. Once loose, I gave the head a slight tug to ease it off from the spinal cord. I looked down at Jennifer's face, her eyes peacefully closed. I debated whether to keep her as a souvenir to remind myself of the fond memories, but for obvious reasons I could not.

After removing Jen's head into the waste barrel I washed the rest of her body down. Not that I thought Jen would be dirty or I was in any way inappropriately touching her body, this was standard practice when dealing with meat. I used a short bladed knife to skin her carefully, taking both layers of tissue off, and then discarded it into one of the larger waste barrels along with her hands and feet that I chopped off.

The next step was to gut her. I began with a cut made from her breastbone all the way down her stomach. Once this was done, I prized her open and began to remove the organs out: the large and small intestines, kidneys, liver, stomach –

The doorbell chimed, this time not so playfully. I was momentarily frozen, with my hand still inside Jen's corpse. What was I meant to do? It was clear that I was at home, the music playing, my car parked outside, and the lights all on. Could I pretend I was out?

The doorbell chimed again. I decided to answer it, as at this time of night it had to be of some urgency. I hung my apron back up, took my gloves off and made my way to the front door, locking the garage and hiding the key in my pocket. I opened the door to one of my neighbours who wanted to inform me that my car lights were still on. I thanked him for pointing it out to me, got my car keys, switched the headlights off, and made my way back to the garage.

My heart started to beat fast. The thought of getting caught had never even crossed my mind, and although the doorbell proved not to be threatening, it still got my adrenalin going. I moved a bit faster with the preparation. As soon as she was cut up it would be easier to store her out the way.

After removing the upper torso organs, the heart and lungs, I began to butcher the carcass. I cut up Jen into segments thusly: first the arms, followed by halving then quartering the carcass, cutting up the top quarters, cutting the lower quarters where most of the meat is stored. I rounded up all the leftovers and put them into the wastage barrel, ready to be taken down to one of my local farms on the outskirts of Surrey. They have plenty of hungry pigs that would be most pleased with my visit.

I finished cutting the sections into the ribs, thighs, arms, legs, fillets, and put each part into it's own separate container. I then made my way back to the kitchen. All the hard work sure built up my appetite.

My nerves were going through the roof with tense excitement. This was it. This was where the magic would happen. This was my studio, my workshop, my sanctuary, and my church. This is where I had created some of my finest work. And now I was about to reinvent another masterpiece. I felt so giddy. I had to calm down and focus. I did not come all that way to be careless and lose myself in the moment. Dear beautiful, sweet Jennifer did not die in vain. She would be remembered through me for all eternity...

I decided to start off with the ribs, a nice and easy preparation. Everything I was going to do initially would be very basic, so not to confuse the essential taste with more exotic or overpowering flavours that would usually be featured. No side dishes, no sauces, just the pure taste of meat.

The oven was already warmed up, so I placed my ribs onto a tray, and after a quick marinade, seasoned half a section with garlic, pepper, salt and meat tenderizer, and the other half with added paprika.

While this was cooking I prepared my leg of human. I made small incisions into the skin, deep into the flesh to allow the flavours to penetrate. I then made a tiny amount of rosemary and garlic bundles to use to stud the leg. I seasoned with salt and put it my other oven for roasting.

I left my two meals cooking away for a good fifteen minutes before starting the next taster. I heated up my large frying pan, smothering it with butter not oil. I rubbed the fillet all over with sea salt and freshly grounded black pepper before applying to the pan. It sizzled delightfully when immediately touching the heat, soaking up all the butter. I turned it over a few times, giving it longer than I usually would. I preferred my steaks rare, but thought best to make this one at least a medium for my own health. Once complete, I placed this delicacy onto one of my plates and drizzled on top a splash of extra virgin olive oil, cut in half and squeezed a tiny amount of lemon over one side.

My place at the dinner table was vacant, still in the exact way as I left it. I started to feel upset that Jennifer could not be with me to enjoy this proud moment. She would have no doubt had a mouthful herself out of plain curiosity.

I got out my ribs to cool off while I sampled the steak. I cut off a sliver and stuck it into my fork. My mouth went dry with anticipation. I was like a kid in a candy store who had just stolen the largest gob stopper in the shop. Was I prepared for this? The moment the meat touched my lips I was inevitably a cannibal. Dare I cross this forbidden boundary line?

I closed my eyes and opened my mouth while I drove the fork towards me. I could smell as it melted onto my tongue. I chewed slowly, memorising the texture.

Next up were Jen's ribs. She was a big girl, so there was plenty to go around, but I only sampled two of each.

I sipped the last of the Bordeaux while waiting for the leg to finish. When it finally came out the oven I carved very thin slices along with more chunky slices, so to get a good balance.

I wish I could go into more detail with what went on at these eating points, however I am afraid to say that I do not seem to be able to remember most of it. It all seemed like a hazy blur, like I was in some sort of trance that overpowered my body's actions. All I can tell you is the taste.

My verdict, as an open minded master chef of London; it was bland.

It had a certain amount of taste, but without the drippings of oil or butter, without the vast amounts of seasoning of salt and pepper, it was completely dry. It was not tender, but rather stringy and complicated. And as far as all the butchering went, there was not much meat to show for afterwards.

I was gutted. I felt betrayed by my Jen. I had such high hopes for her, but she had let me down. All that flirting she did with me over dinner, all that good conversation about culture and fine food, yet she could not even offer me any succulent meat of her own. What a let down.

I wanted to scream out loud. I wanted to throw the plates across my kitchen. I started to wish that I had killed Jennifer with less finesse. How dare she have an easy exit, after what she was putting me through? She was not worth all this effort, not by a long shot. After throwing my arms around for a while in frustration, I curled up into a ball on the kitchen floor and began to cry...

A month flew past. My restaurants were all going steady. There was no repercussion regarding Jennifer, at least not that I heard of. No police came knocking, no news in the local papers. Nobody seemed to miss her I thought.

I missed her. Half of me wished that I had kept her head, so I could still see her beautiful green eyes. It's a pity when young intelligent girls like that are not appreciated. But hey, that's the society we are living in I'm afraid.

Every now and then I would pick at Jennifer's leftovers, experimenting with some new ideas that would pop in my head. Although I still could not agree that it was anywhere near my favourite meat, I seemed to crave it religiously. It was like some sort of gravitational pull that controlled me, urging me on to have another few bites...

It occurred to me that every great discovery did not come on the first attempt. Why sometimes it takes years of practice before perfection is achieved. And that is exactly what I decided to do. I was not going to give up so easily. I was not going to hang my apron up just yet in defeat, for I am an artist, and yearn for excellence. My Jen did not die in vain. I made a promise to myself that she did not. But my Jen is running out fast, and another meal is in order.

I decided to give the Internet dating site another go. After all, my last date was a right dish...

Angel Dust

Rachel's mother Audrey had been dead for near on two years. She had lived with her daughter and son in law, Parker (Edward Parker but Parker to practically anyone who knew him), for her remaining time.

Audrey moved in to the house when she turned ninety, a remarkable age to get to but also an age to become a burden. After a couple of slips down the stairs, near scares of heart attacks and few unpaid bills, Rachel and Parker agreed the best place for her was their own home. It was not as if they didn't have the space for her. A seven bedroom detached house with a large back garden and an easy stroll into town; they felt obliged to take her in.

Their two children, Max aged eight and Nina five, adored having their Nan around, and Audrey's only grandchildren gave her lasting happiness. She could watch them for hours running around the garden, playing on the swings and chasing each other playing 'it'.

When Rachel and Parker went out in the evenings, Audrey would always babysit, letting her grandchildren stay up that little bit later and eat that little bit more ice cream. His father always told Max that he was in charge of the night, and to look after his sister and grandmother, under trusted instructions to go get help from their neighbours if Nanny was in need of any assistance.

She was at peace there, with her close family supporting her, and Audrey doing everything she could to return the favour by helping around the house; cleaning, washing, changing the bed sheets, laying the table. Nothing too strenuous, as she was on strict orders not to do so by Parker, but helpful chores that made Rachel's housekeeping that bit easier.

If truth were told Rachel adored having her mother around the house during the daytime. While the kids were off at primary school and Parker was working at the local clinic, it was nice to have somebody else rather than an empty house to gossip with. And even at the age of ninety, Audrey still had a sharp mind (although now and then respectively forgetful) and could hold a good conversation without having to start each phrase with 'back in my day' or 'I remember when', like most old folk at that age seemed to use religiously.

Parker himself always had a soft spot for his mother in law; never forgetting the first time he met Rachel's parents and how nice and welcoming Audrey was. His friends had told him that the trick to knowing what Rachel would look like when she was older was to look at the mother. Parker remembered this advice, and also remembered not being disappointed on their first meet.

The five of them were happy in their home together, and it came as a great loss when only nine months in, Audrey collapsed in the living room with a heart attack and died the same day in the local hospital.

It could be argued that Audrey was only there for a short while, and annoying habits, rows, forgetful memories and dried up conversations did not begin to occur in time for them to be noticeable. To the family she was not a burden, but rather the completion of their little family.

Two years had gone. The children, now aged ten and seven, had never forgotten their Grandmother, and often spoke about her. Nina, the youngest, would often pretend that she was still in the garden with her, pushing her on the swing or playing 'it' at a very slow pace. Max would also play football on his own, saying that Nanny was in goal, but not very good at saving the ball anymore.

Rachel and Parker both found it warming how the children had never forgotten her, and how she was still a part of their lives even after death. They too would quote little sayings that Audrey would mutter out, sometimes even lay the table exactly how Audrey would with the knife and fork the wrong way round.

But something else always happened within the two years as well; something that could not be rationally explained.

Every time the family ever went away anywhere together, be it a summer holiday in Portugal, skiing in Canada, or even a long weekend trip to Devon, the very same thing would occur each time.

On their arrival back they would find, without fail, a slight trail of dust covered on the right side of the sofa in the living room; the same position Audrey would always sit to watch her soaps. There were never any windows left open while they were away, the floor in the living room was wooden with no carpet, the couch was not in any corners, they even had an air purifier in circulation. There would be no other dust gathered in the whole house; only in this certain spot.

'Mummy, mummy look! Nanny's back! Look!' Little Nina would often say after they arrived back home, jumping up and down with excitement while pointing at the sofa. Rachel would smile at Parker, with her husband giving a sarcastic grin back. Rachel wanted to believe it was her mother's doing, while Parker did not want to believe it. He was not against it, but as a man of science and rational thinking, he thought that there had to be some simple explanation.

Parker would test this each time they went away, but it was unexplainable. He tried switching the couches before they left on occasions, even moving the couch to another room. He put sheets over the top of it, turned the cushions over, but each time they returned there it was; on the same spot and on the same sofa, with no other traces of dust left anywhere. He finally came to accept it; he did not accept that it was due to his deceased mother in law, but he accepted the fact that the dust would always appear after they had been away from the house.

'Get a spiritualist to come round and check.' Suggested one of the girls at Rachel's aerobics class. She even gave her a card: 'Madam Huson, Spiritual Guidance'. Rachel's friend highly recommended her, saying that she often went to Madam Huson to get her future read; and that she was always understanding and helpful.

Parker nearly spat out his laughter onto Madam Huson's card when Rachel showed it to him.

'Why would your friend need to go more than once to get her future read? Surely you go the once and that's it!' Argued Parker, brushing the Madam as a con artist who relished in the gullible. He believed that a spiritualist giving out business cards said it all.

But it was something Rachel wanted. She could not explain why, but she needed to know what it was; even if what she got told was possibly made up, she needed to know something.

After a few nights of sighs, debating and questioning, Parker finally came to a conclusion: if it was what Rachel really wanted, then Parker would back her completely.

You picked a good man; Rachel could hear her mother saying to her.

Madam Huson came round the very next day after receiving Rachel's call, even though it was a Saturday. Parker was out, not by choice but by work, and the children were out in the garden playing on the swings.

The moment the spiritualist entered the house she twirled and hopped around as if trying to wake someone up. All the while, Rachel carried on the conversation of what she told her over the telephone, about her mother and what she meant to the family. The Madam was listening but not looking, as she seemed to be involved in some sort of trance, feeling the walls and floors as she passed them by. Rachel soon fell silent and gazed in amazement while Madam Huson carried on with her work.

They entered the living room and the Madam collapsed, on purpose, onto the sofa, on the very spot where the dust would gather, although no dust was there at that present time.

'This is where she sits.' She said to Rachel, not asking but telling.

'Yes, that's where she always used to sit to watch her soaps.' Answered Rachel anyway.

'No! This is where she sits… Still! I feel her presence. Alive, she was a warm, loving person; that I can sense. She would do anything for her family.'

Rachel sat down next to where the Madam had fallen, and closely listened.

'Some spirits do not cross over, my child, only until they are ready. Until they are completely fulfilled and satisfied, they remain here with us. Your mother is still here in this house, in the garden, on this land.'

The Madam got up, and stretched her body, searching over all the other household objects, the lamp, the television, the coffee table, all of which she seemed to pass over quickly, and then returned to the sofa.

'You say the dust only appears here when you leave the house?'

Rachel nodded, unable to fully answer back just yet.

'Well this dust you see my petal, are spirit orbs; but what I like, and prefer to call: Angel dust! Tis' when a spirit sits at a certain spot for so long, that even themselves can conjure up the filth and dirt that's in the air, thus leaving a trace behind.'

'But… Why every time we're away?' Rachel managed to get out, with plenty of patience given by Madam Huson.

'My dear, you said to me that you took your mother in when she was in her time of need? For that she is forever grateful, but she unfortunately passed before she could fully return her gratitude. You mother, it seems, is protecting your house every time you go away, keeping it safe from harm. She still wants to help in any way she can.'

'But...' Rachel paused again, trying to take in what the spiritualist was saying. 'But... If she is still here, will I ever be able to see her; talk to her; listen to her?'

Madam Huson smiled wonderfully.

'My dear, you already do. You just don't know that you are doing so. Come, come with me.' She took Rachel's hand and led her towards the back window; as if it was the Madam's own house and she was showing her guest round it for the first time. They looked out into the garden, where the children were running around the grass together smiling.

'Look my dear,' she said, whilst pointing her long finger out towards the children. 'Your children; they can see her still, just fine.'

Rachel looked out and saw her two children jumping around, laughing and playing together, just like when she had seen her mother with them.

'See?' Asked Madam Huson.

'I see...' Said Rachel, and slowly began to cry tears of joy.

*

Smiths and Brooksie were two small time crooks. It was something that society made them fall into from the word off. Neither of them had the guts to pull off big jobs like a bank or an insurance scam, but neither of them had the education or guidance to become law abiding citizens and work an honest days pay. Therefore their life depended on being petty thefts, such as stealing pizza boy's mopeds, robbing small newsagents and hot-wiring old cars in parking lots. No job left them with much to show for their troubles. All they got was more heat in their backs and a bigger conscience on their shoulders. They both were starting to feel the weight, and both wanted out.

The trouble for them was that there was no way out. Neither would be able to bag a decent job, not with their life long history of criminal records, but neither had enough money to see them through for a while searching for any kind of job out there. There was only one thing left for them to do. Go out on a high.

This was it, they decided, one last big one. One last hit that would give them something to show for. One last moral broken that would help kick start a fresh new life for the pair of them. If they had enough money, they could start trading or something. They could buy and sell used goods down the market, legitimately, and maybe for once earn an honest pound under their names.

This was their dream. But where were they going to strike? What would be there last ever crime? There was only one place both men had in mind...

The Parker's place down on Green Avenue was the biggest house in the entire town. Everybody knew that old Eddie Parker was right for a quid or two. He was one of the doctors down at the local clinic; had moved in from the big city to a quieter place. News soon spread fast about who had bought the mansion on Green's; that sort of gossip even managed to spiral its way down to the crummy part of town, the neighbourhood where Smiths and Brooksie had been born and raised.

So this was it. They had made up their minds. If they were going to do this one last time, they were going to go out in style. One final shot at the big time. They were going to rob the richest family house in the entire town.

For months they began to prepare for it, keeping surveillance on the house, seeing if there were any patterns of absence for any long periods of time. This was soon found to be tricky, what with a housewife in there the whole time, only popping out here and there for groceries and the occasional clothes shopping. The only time she ever left properly on routine was each Wednesday morning for her weekly aerobics class (Brooksie couldn't help but admire the lady's figure while watching her go to and from the classes in her tight tracksuit. No chance of him getting a girl like that while he was still broke and a crook), but that was only for an hour tops and during the daytime; no time at all to grab any real large bulk, or search for any hidden family heirlooms.

They waited and waited, but there didn't seem to be any foreseeable opening. They couldn't give up halfway through, although it crossed both men's minds. They had wasted so much time and effort on the house, which could have been put in to better use by stealing purses, but they were determined to see it through. All they needed was just one lucky break.

But it seemed as though luck was again not on their side. All until that one fateful day, where Smiths by chance decided to follow Eddie Parker to work to figure out his daily routine for a change. The moment he witnessed Parker walk into that travel agents on the high street, he nearly hit his head on the roof of the car while jumping up in joy.

It was surprisingly easy to find out the family's holiday dates, what with both the kids being on all the social networking sites and the mum's gossipy aerobic class. Smiths and Brooksie were all set. All they had to do now was wait...

The day had finally arrived. The Jeep was packed with full suitcases and ski bags tied to the roof rack. Smiths and Brooksie were so prepared; hell, they even knew what time they were leaving. The family set off half an hour later than planned, but that was no shock due to the two manic kids they had running around everywhere.

Three days passed, very slowly and very tensely for the two crooks. Nerves and doubt had started to fog their little minds. Was this too big for them? Could they pull it off? They had to...

Night fell onto the avenue. All was pitch black, except for the streetlights and the front windows of each house on the avenue. Soon even these got brought into darkness as well. Brooksie had no trouble causing the town power cut. All he needed was a pair of pliers and the right electrical box to work from.

The two of them climbed over the back garden fence. They did not have to worry about how much noise they were making, as the whole street were too busy trying to sort out their own troubles.

Windows were usually no match for Smiths, but found the Parker's ones a struggle. After battling with it for quite some time, and getting quickly frustrated, he resulted in breaking the window with his elbow; clumsy, amateur work. But still, nobody heard; or bothered to hear.

They climbed through one at a time, finding that they were in the living room. Brooksie started nudging Smiths uncontrollably as they glared at the widescreen TV, surround sound system, CD players, speakers, and Blue Ray DVD player; not to mention the silver wear and fancy cutlery that shone proudly in its display case. Into the bag it all went, one by one.

They stormed upstairs and downstairs, raiding all the bedrooms, the office and games room. They had all of Rachel's jewellery away for a start (as well as some of Rachel's panties for Brooksie). The computer in the office went, so did all the games consoles. Anything lying around that looked like it had any worth or value whatsoever they took, even the kid's toy boxes, thinking that some may be collectables.

The whole house was spotless, minus the mess both men made clearing out chest drawers and closets, tipping each section onto the floor until they found something. They were desperate men; scavenging all they could find. Any thought of guilt or moral got flung out their minds the moment they saw their reflections in the big television screen. After that their primal urges took over and they did what they only knew how to do: steal.

They were just about finished. The loaded bags were all stacked up by the broken window, all ready to be carried to the van. Smiths had one last check before they were off. He looked around the living room, thinking how clean it all looked now that there was hardly any junk in there. So clean...

All except one little spot on the right side of the sofa, which seemed so out of place. Smiths wiped it off with his glove then made his way towards Brooksie who was waiting by the window.

'Come on Smiths, let's go!' Brooksie whispered, like a giddy school child that had just raided the tuck shop.

Smiths gave a smile to his partner in crime, and then playfully skipped in triumph towards him, much to Brooksie's amusement.

But his enjoyment soon vanished, as he saw his buddy being hauled up into the air feet first, as if he was caught in a rope trap. But, by utter amazement, nothing was holding on to him. There was no rope, there was no wire, but something or someone had got him.

Smiths dangled there in mid-air howling at Brooksie to help, but Brooksie was frozen stiff. To most educated people, they would rubbish the thought of any paranormal idea as soon as they could. But to the uneducated, all they needed was a tiny glimpse of possibility for them to believe. Brooksie here saw more than a tiny glimpse; he saw a freaking avalanche of a glimpse.

He ran into the Kitchen screaming, too afraid and too stupid to sensibly make it towards or through the window, looking for an exit. He did not even stop when he heard his partner being dropped to the ground with a hefty thump.

Suddenly a butcher knife that was in its rack, one of the few that they didn't bother to steal, flew out of its holdall and across the kitchen directly into Brooksie's left leg. He howled with pain as it pierced through his skin and teared into his muscle.

In the other room, Smiths had managed to get up and made a beeline for the bags in a blind panic, but got knocked over for his troubles. At first he thought he must of hit one of the pullout tables, so he tried again but got knocked to the ground once more. He couldn't believe it. He had to battle for his bags against the air! It was like there was a force field around them, protecting the goods inside.

He then saw his partner hobbling towards the window, dragging his bleeding leg behind him. The image startled Smiths, concerned for his own well being rather than Brooksie's.

'Help us Smiths! Get this thing out my leg!' Shouted Brooksie, with both his arms stretched out searching for aid.

'Get the bags!' Shouted Smiths, 'We're outta here!'

Brooksie ignored Smiths requested and leaked out of the window head first, crawling through the garden towards safety, which to him meant anywhere over the garden fence.

Smiths tried again to grab the bags. He had come this far. He was this close. He wasn't just going to run away now. He was desperate.

He lunged at the stolen goods, but the bags flew into the air. He stared in disbelief, realising that the bags that were now hovering was what had happened to him just a few moments earlier. It didn't sink in before due to the mad rush, but as he gazed up in wonder, fear trickled down through his entire body.

Suddenly, all the chest of drawers and cupboard doors started flapping repeatedly together. The sound of wood smacking was so overpowering, Smiths had to cover his ears in protection.

Get out! He thought he heard someone say. It was hard to hear over the harsh noise, but it sounded like an old woman's croaky, deep voice.

Get out now! Leave this place! He did not know whether he was imagining it or not, but he definitely heard it crystal clear that time.

Like his partner Brooksie, Smiths was also uneducated. And, like most uneducated people, he was as superstitious as they came. But educated or otherwise, if a paranormal poltergeist lifted up your stolen goods and demanded that you left, you sure as hell listened and obeyed.

Smiths jumped through the window, shattering a few pieces that had not yet been fully broken off. He ran through the garden, leap-frogging Brooksie who had only crawled halfway across, and hurled himself over the fence.

Both men never mentioned the incident to each other, or to anyone else for that matter. Brooksie would tell people that his scar on his leg, which now caused him to have a slight limp, was when he and Smiths went fishing together and he fell on top of the guttering knife. Smiths would vouch for this every time.

Were they going to keep on committing petty crimes? Would they try to live decent, honest lives from then on? Or would they have another go; one more shot at the big time? One thing was for certain: they would never step foot on Green Avenue, or even anywhere in that part of town, ever again.

When the family returned home from their ski trip in Austria, they were greeted straight away by Roger, their next-door neighbour.

He informed them that he heard what sounded like a break-in when the power cut occurred, saying at first he could hear what seemed to be loud banging from inside the house, and then a heavy crash like glass breaking shortly after. As he rushed out with his flashlight to see what was going on, he saw two men jumping out of their garden, one helping the other who appeared to be injured. They drove off in a small van parked directly outside, but it was too dark for him to catch the number plate. He called the police immediately.

'The funniest thing though,' he said, 'Was that when I went in to check out what they had stolen, I found five full bags of your stuff just lying by the broken window. They had it all there, but just didn't want to take it with them? You should have seen the look on their faces though. They looked petrified! Something must have spooked them good in there!'

Worried and relieved at the same time, Rachel burst into the house to find that the living room window had been covered up with wooden planks, and all the items in the bags were now in separate boxes of which the police had supposedly placed them in.

The children came running in and went straight for the boxes of toys, sieving through to make sure they were all there. Nina, the youngest, stopped checking and began walking around the house, searching for something else.

After a while Nina re-entered the living room.

'She's gone.' Said Nina.

'Who's gone sweetie?' Rachel said, concerned that the robbers actually did get something.

'Nanny. She's gone. She's not here anymore.' She said, almost close to crying.

After all the fuss and excitement going on, Rachel completely forgot to check the spot on the sofa. But as she did, she noticed that there was no patch of dust that usually was there, greeting the family's return.

After Parker had thanked Roger a thousand times, he left the ski bags on top of the roof rack and entered the house to have a look at what had happened.

'Daddy, daddy! Nanny's gone.' Said Nina to her father, running up into his arms for a cuddle. Parker lifted his daughter up onto his chest, and walked round the room with her in his arms hushing down her crying.

'Darling look, the dust is gone?' Said Rachel, pointing to the sofa. 'Do you think she's gone for good now? Why did she leave? Why didn't the robbers take anything? What happened here darling?'

Parker took in all the questions at once. He thought for a while. He thought about his old mother in law Audrey; he thought about what could have spooked the robbers; and he thought about the words Madam Huson gave to Rachel. He then gave out a wonderful, reassuring smile to his wife and children.

For Parker, as a man of science, logic and rational thinking, had a pretty good idea what had happened…

The black cat at the window

Mary had always lived a solemn, quiet life. She had no brothers or sisters to rely on while growing up, and both her mother and father had died when she was old enough to be independent, but young enough to still need them. In her early twenties she rarely socialised like so many young girls did, keeping herself to herself; with which she was content. She did have boyfriends on brief occasions, but they were of a similar status and never really swooped Mary off her feet. Each time she parted from one it was a simple natural occurrence. There were never any mad tantrums or heavy arguments, but rather a simple goodbye, see you around soon. Most people who ever met Mary would say to others how nice she was, although only because a bad word would never leave her lips.

Mary lived alone in a two-bedroom house in Somerset. She worked behind the counter at the grocery shop in her local town; again with which she was content. It was a job that gave her the money she needed to afford the upkeep of the house, plus the additional benefit of the owner, Mr Huckle, giving her the occasional free groceries. She knew all the locals in town mainly by face but rarely by name. Some would often talk to her and ask how she was, to which they would get a simple response but nothing to instigate the conversation any further.

It would be fair to say that Mary was a loner. She would be the first to admit this, but never regretted her lifestyle choice. For Mary had a hobby; a hidden passion that kept her entertained and enthused during all those years of solitude.

Mary loved to paint.

Ever since she first held a brush she was obsessed with painting. She yearned for it every hour of the day. It made her feel at peace; it relaxed her; it felt right. Every spare moment she had she would be painting away at her latest piece, finely tuning the finishing touches to add to her own creative collection. She loved to look back over her work and see what she was capable of accomplishing. But she never showed her art to a living soul. She was too afraid that it would be harshly judged; that people would not like her drawings; that they would say she was wasting her time. Instead she would paint away in privacy, admiring the beauty of the colours and get lost in her own little dream world.

She rarely had any visitors around, so her painting never got disturbed. But one night this was soon about to change...

Mary had just finished painting her latest work in the spare room that she had converted into a mini studio. It was where she stored all her drawings and ideas, all her brushes, stencils, pallets, canvases; all neatly ordered on the shelves and tucked away in the drawers.

She could feel her heart racing louder with every stroke taken, as she could sense the possibility of one of her greatest achievements nearing completion. She panted deep breaths on the finishing tweaks and took a step back to admire what she had accomplished.

Mary almost sweated out tears. It was beautiful. It was very subtle, but to Mary, very beautiful. It was a portrait of an old French gentleman walking through the cold streets of Paris; so proud of his city despite his poverty. Mary much preferred pictures that told a story, rather than all the new minimalist and modernism movements she had occasionally heard about. A painting wasn't a painting unless it was of something, not just squiggles or rough patches thrown on in no particular order. Mary despised that kind of style, believing it to be far beyond cheating, but more mocking and disrespectful towards the great art.

Mary yawned out an air of tiredness, and glanced at her old grandfather clock that was positioned in the hallway. It was nearly ten o'clock, and time for rest. She covered her canvas and made her way to her bed - painting always made Mary tired - and fell right asleep the moment her head hit the pillow.

The grandfather clock harshly struck at the early hour of three, causing Mary to wake up in shock. She was sure that the clock had lost its chime a few years back. But before she could question why this had happened, another sound entered her ears; it seemed as if it had come from her bedroom window.

It was a soft meow; so delicate and innocent. At first Mary was unsure she had heard anything at all, but this was soon followed by another tiny cry. Mary scrambled out of bed, curiously made her way over to the window and pulled the curtains apart. Sitting there, on the ledge of the window, was a large black cat. Its bushy black fur coat shimmered proudly in what was left of the moonlight. Its whiskers looked straight and groomed, and its legs boasted huge paws, which hid away powerful claws to match. Its tail swayed hypnotically behind, twitching playfully in the cool wind. It sat there, staring directly at Mary with its wide glowing eyes.

Mary had never been a fan of cats. There was something about them that she did not trust, especially black cats. She had thought of them as very symbolic creatures, perceived as evil omens, being the familiars of witches or demons acting as their spies or their couriers. Mary was not a superstitious fool, but at the same time had a certain amount of respect for old wives tales. Some people believe that old fables are usually based on truth, and have merely been distorted through the passage of time. Mary wouldn't admit that she was one of those people, but more rather did not want to takes any chances.

The cat carried on meowing, scratching away at the glass for attention. Mary presumed that it was one of the neighbours cats, although not entirely sure which neighbour, as she could not recall seeing it strolling around before. She presumed it had got stuck, but had no idea how it got there in the first place. Either way, Mary thought she would let it in through the window and try to guide it down the stairs and out the front door, leaving her in peace.

Mary slid the glass window open to let it in, but it refused to enter. She was slightly offended that it did not accept her invitation at first. *Did she look threatening? Was her room not good enough for it?*

Instead it just stared at Mary, gazing into her eyes. They were so shiny and bright. Most cats were usually like this, but these eyes were even more so, most probably due to the darkness of its fur.

Mary soon grew grouchy due to her tiredness. She had a busy day in the morning and the last thing she needed was to be kept up by a howling cat. Impatient of its decision-making, Mary tried to grab it to pull it in, but the blasted creature hissed at her reaching hands, warning her not to touch.

In a huff Mary slammed down her window and closed the curtains. *If it wanted to be out there in the cold then fine*, Mary thought. She had never been a cat person in the first place. She detested them. It was not as if she was even a dog person by contrast, but rather not a fan of pets in general. The last thing she needed was an uninvited guest at her window. Mary hoped that if she ignored it then it would eventually get bored and wander off to wherever it had originally come from.

Mary thought wrong.

The cursed feline did not leave, and would not stop meowing all through the night, letting her know that it was still out there. At one point Mary even tried undoing the window again so if it wanted to come in it could. But instead the dam thing just sat there and the howling was simply louder than before, causing Mary's night of sleep to suffer.

The next morning Mary woke up still tired from her night's lack of sleep. Although exhausted, she knew she had to get up as usual for work. As she drew the curtains, the beam of the sun hit her directly in the face. When her vision was restored, she was surprised to see that the black cat had gone, vanished from the window ledge. She did not recall hearing it creep in at any point, so she decided to search the house for the cat, but could not find it anywhere. Every other window and door was locked, so if it had come in at any time during the night, it still had to be somewhere in the house.

Mary was baffled.

She double-checked the height of her bedroom window, poking her head out into the morning breeze. It was quite a fall to the ground. She could not see any flattened cats at the bottom of the house, so she thought best not to worry about it and get on with her day. After checking the grandfather clock's chime to see if it had miraculously fixed itself but being confusingly disappointed, Mary got ready and made her way to work.

All day at the grocery store Mary was tired. She shamefully drifted off whilst behind the counter, for which Mary apologised deeply to Mr Huckle. He immediately forgave her, because it was the first time she had ever fallen asleep in all the years she had been working for him. The customer count was not particularly high that day, so Mr Huckle told Mary to go home and get some rest. She refused, but he insisted. He wanted his best worker back to her top game for the morning.

When she got home, Mary had a quick peek at her latest painting. As she removed the cover off the canvas, she held her breath as her masterpiece was revealed. She adored it. The old French gentleman had seemed to come in age overnight, as if more alive after the paint had dried. The backdrop of Paris seemed to have settled well, moulded together to create the perfect scenery.

But there was something else that caught Mary's eye. Something she had not noticed before; something that she could not remember ever drawing.

By the side of the gentleman's feet was a black cat, walking along the concrete pavement. It was coloured in and painted perfectly to fit in to its surroundings.

Mary shook her head in disbelief. She was sure that the cat was not in her original sketch; but there it was, boldly drawn like everything else in the picture. Confused and tired, Mary retired to her bed early for a good nights sleep.

The clock struck three, echoing throughout the hallway and into Mary's bedroom, causing her to wake up, interrupted once more from her dreams. But before she could even think about drifting off again, the sound of meowing came from the window. She could not believe it. The dam cat was back, exactly the same time as the night before. It was as if it had waited for Mary to return. She decided not to even entertain it by opening the curtains or the window on this occasion. *If she ignored it then it would get bored and just go away.*

Mary thought wrong.

All night long she could hear its claws scratching away at the glass, begging to be looked at, ordering to be paid attention to. Mary tried not to make any sound, hoping that the cat would think that it had lost, and she was sound asleep, not worrying or thinking about it. But no, it seemed the more quite she was, the more louder it got.

Mary gave up attempting to lie still, and tried to scare it away by opening the curtains and window fast, and then flapping her hands trying to shoo it away. But it did not budge an inch. She could not push it off the ledge, for she could not reach it, plus she was not a monster; but the thought definitely crossed her mind on more than one occasion.

It seemed as though the cat did not want her to sleep. Mary occasionally drifted off at times due to being exhausted, but these moments were only temporary, as the same haunting strings of meows that had originally tired her would soon wake her up again.

Morning came. Mary lied in bed staring up at the ceiling with bag-filled eyes. The sound of meowing had finally stopped. The cat had eventually gone. She knew she had to get into work. She did not want to let Mr Huckle down by calling in sick; he was kind enough to let her go early the day before. And anyway, it wasn't as if she was even ill, but she knew she would be soon if her sleeping pattern did not improve any time soon.

Mary got ready for work as usual. But before she left the house, she decided to have another quick peek at her painting to cheer her up, to get her through the day. She always turned to her paintings for support. In a strange way they made her feel better, as if there was a purpose, a reason for her to carry on.

She unveiled her piece, and smiled in content to herself. But the smile soon faded. For on closer inspection, it appeared that the black cat had grown in size, nearly doubled in fact. Before it had seemed to be purring by the gentleman's ankles, and now it had reached his knees. Mary, convinced that she was imagining it all, quickly covered the painting and made her way to work.

The day was long for Mary. She drank numerous amounts of coffee to keep her from falling asleep. There were surprisingly more customers that day, giving no chance for Mr Huckle to let her go early again, although he was genuinely concerned for Mary; letting her have breaks in between the small rushes. She managed to drag herself through the hours and just about make it to the end of her shift.

When she got home there was no peeking at any of her paintings, no comforting glances at any of her sketches. Mary needed sleep. She went up to her bedroom, folded into her bed and her heavy eyes automatically fell into a deep sleep.

The grandfather clock struck three; along with the sound of the black cat meowing right on cue. Mary could hear the soft whimpers echoing through her bedroom, quietly torturing her. The dam cat was back once more. She had had enough. *If the cat wanted to sit on that window, then fine.*

She grabbed her sheets and pillows and marched into her painting room, moved her canvases, stands and pots of brushes out of the way and made a space on the carpet floor, which had a few splashes of paint on but no fresh colour stains to worry about; she had not painted recently. It was a hard surface to lie on, but at least there was silence.

But then she started to hear a howl of pity coming from the windowsill of the paint room. Mary's eyes opened only to find a cat shaped silhouette by the window. She could not believe it. The cat had followed her round. It was stalking her...

Mary dragged her sheets to the kitchen downstairs, but moments later the cat appeared by the kitchen window. She searched the house for a room without a window, but all had one; some even had two or three. Each room Mary went into, the cat soon followed.

She eventually managed to curl up in the hallway next to the grandfather clock, slumped out by the top of the stairs. She lay there uncomfortably trying to rest as much as she could, but Mary could still hear it. Through the walls, through the shut doors, Mary could hear it outside, moaning and whining.

The grandfather clock, which was directly next to where Mary was resting, bellowed an almighty chime, signalling the hour of four. It's shattering clang rippled through Mary's body. Confused and upset as to why the blasted clock decided to only work in the early hours of the morning from now on, Mary pushed the grandfather clock in frustration; causing it to topple over and smash its numbered face on the stairway. Silence filled the house once more...

The nights and weeks that followed, without fail, the cat would turn up at one of the windows of the house; and every night it would turn up at the early hour of three. Each night Mary could hear it outside meowing; purring; scratching; howling. She could hear its tiny paws marching up and down on the window ledges, creaking the surfaces on every step it took. Mary would open the window and shout at it, screaming the question *what did it want!* Every move she would make towards it would trigger a hissing or a claw swinging. It would defend itself by perching away from reaching distance. Mary tried throwing pots and pans at it, but every shot missed. It was as though there was a force field around the cat, denying any impact. It never even twitched. It just boldly sat there, staring at Mary, stalking her into numerous restless nights.

Mary's days became shorter. Her work at the grocery shop became lesser. Mr Huckle had to cut down on her hours, for he insisted that Mary had some problems or issues that she needed to sort out.

Mr Huckle was right.

All Mary could do when she got home was fixate on her cat situation. *Where did it come from each night? She never saw it during the day. What did it want from her?*

Mary even bought some cat food home, leaving it outside her back door to see if it would show itself in the daylight. She thought that if she could catch it then she could show it around the neighbours to discover its real home. But it would never show. Only in the early hours of the morning would it visit her.

Slowly over the long months Mary began to grow obsessed. Perhaps this was from the lack of sleep that her mind was not fully functioning properly. Perhaps Mary's personal choice of isolation from the outside world did not help matters. Maybe she needed some company. Could it be that the black cat was symbolising this? *Of course it couldn't. She wasn't a superstitious old biddy. She wasn't going to become a crazy old lady with a cat...*

Mary didn't have it in her to call an exterminator. Besides, she didn't even know whether a cat could be classified as a house pest. And even so, what was she going to tell them? That the cat only came out at three? That it is nowhere to be seen during the day? That they would have to sleep over to get rid of it? Most people thought she was mad enough as it was, without crazy stories of haunting cats thrown in the mix as well. A story like that would be enough ammunition to check her in the nearest nut house they could find.

Mary needed support. She needed guidance on what to do. And then she remembered her paintings. *She had grown so obsessed with the cat that she hadn't even painted for weeks!* Painting was the one thing that Mary could rely on. It was her medicine, her cure. Whenever she felt alone, felt down, or felt worried; Mary turned to her paintings.

One night, instead of trying to sleep, Mary went into her paint room and set up a blank canvas. She felt giddy when she picked up her brush, just like the first time she ever started to paint. But before she could start anything, she needed inspiration. In the corner of the room, standing proudly awaiting to be displayed, was her masterpiece of the old gentleman in Paris. She smiled, remembering such beauty she had once drawn.

Mary went over to the corner and lifted the cover off the canvas. She shrieked hysterically and recoiled in horror. There was no old French gentleman; there were no crooked roads or pavements; there was no cold portrayal of Paris. Instead, there was only a portrait of a large black cat, its eyes staring directly into Mary's…

Mary had always lived a solemn, quiet life. Mary liked to keep herself to herself. She recently quit her job in the grocery shop, as it was getting in the way of her true passion in life; what she had always wanted to do all day, every day.

Mary loved to paint. It's what relaxed her and made her happy. Mary much preferred to paint pictures that told a story. A painting wasn't a painting unless it was of something. And what she loved to paint the most was the black cat that sat patiently by the window, letting Mary draw portraits of it all day long.

In fact, this was now the only painting Mary ever did; with which she was more than content…

The Big Bad Wolf

Peter Matthews woke up with a fright. His head was face down on the pillow, stuck to it by the sweat dripping from his brow. Peter could feel his throat had dried up and was in desperate need for some water, but he could not move to reach his glass by the side of his bed.

He was frozen solid from his nightmare: the same nightmare that had haunted him all his life. He could still hear the humming in his head. He could also feel the cold air breathing on the back of his neck, waiting for him to turn over. His feet were just hanging out the edge of the duvet, to which Peter quickly tucked them back in. The humming was getting louder.

Was he still dreaming?

Peter felt the rest of his body to find himself all covered in sweat. He did not know what the time was, but he hoped it would be morning soon. The nightmares went away in the daytime…

He attempted to quiet down his breathing, but the more he tried the louder it got. He knew that it was in the room with him still.

If he was quiet, it will go away.

He could not help but be annoyed with himself. Peter was now sure that he was awake, and that the nightmare was indeed over, but he still could not move. Neither could he sleep, as he did not want to go back to the terror. All he could do was lie there hoping for the day to break.

The humming was slowly fading, along with the cold breath. It was soon replaced with stone cold silence, all but the wind blowing faintly through the window curtains. Peter slowly rolled onto his back, peeling his body off the sweaty bed sheet. He was now facing directly up at his ceiling, still not ready to turn to the rest of his room.

It could still be in the room somewhere, hiding; waiting for him to move.

He could begin to hear the faint sound of growling, coming from the corner of his room. The night was still thick with darkness. Peter needed to get to the lampshade. The light made it go away. The growling started growing louder, along with the return of the humming.

It was all in his head. It was all in his head.

Peter tried reassuring himself, but it was no good. Whether it was in his head or not, it felt as real as ever. It was in the room with him, getting closer. The humming was pounding in his head, chanting over and over:

'Who's afraid of the big bad wolf; big bad wolf; big bad wolf? Who's afraid of the big bad wolf; big bad wolf; big bad wolf...'

Peter finally got up and made a burst towards the lampshade as the humming and growling got to its loudest peak. As soon as the light was on, the room fell silent again. Peter scanned the whole of his room, only to find it bare.

He fell back into his bed, but did not sleep for the rest of the night; neither did he turn his light back off.

'He's seventeen years old for Christ's sake! He should have grown out of theses night terrors by now!' Moaned Peter's Dad Jeremy while sitting round the dinner table the following night. 'Sleeping in school is unacceptable Peter, not when you've got you're A levels to study for. You need to grow out of this.'

'Don't be too harsh on him Jeremy.' Said Peter's Mother Sally, sympathetic towards her son.

She could remember the night terrors ever since Peter was three. She also knew, unbeknown to her husband, what stalked Peter in his nightmares. Sally had always felt guilty for letting Peter watch Walt Disney's Silly Symphony of the Three Little Pigs. Although quite reasonable to let a toddler watch, not a night went by that she did not feel responsible.

Peter sat in the chair between his parents with his head down playing with his mother's shepherd's pie. He did not like it when they discussed his night terrors at the dinner table, and kept very quiet when they did.

'It's got to stop.' Repeated his father, while pouring a large glass of red wine down his throat.

'We've tried everything; noise machines, KID Chamomile, aroma therapy, going to sleep earlier, tofranil, benzodiazepine, nothing seems to work. It's just something Peter's going to have to grow out of in his own time.' Said Sally defensively.

'No wonder he hardly has any friends; he can't stay round anyone's house while he's screaming all night. And now he's letting it interfere with his school work.'

Peter bowed his head further into his dinner. He wanted to crawl away, but would know that wouldn't make things any better. He was in enough trouble as it was, what with his moody old maths teacher, Miss. Crannington, phoning up his parents about sleeping through trigonometry.

His dad shoved a forkful of pie into his mouth, but then paused halfway through chewing. He held the empty fork up in thought.

'What about psychotherapy? That's the one thing we haven't tried. Maybe the boy's got some emotional problems he needs getting off his chest.' Said Jeremy, rather proud of his suggestion.

'That's nonsense,' snapped back Sally. 'If he wanted to get anything off his chest he would have done so by talking to us.'

'Don't be silly darling. The boy can't even tell us what the nightmares are about, let alone sharing what they might mean.' Sally looked away in secrecy at her husband's comment.

'My son is not going to see a shrink, and that's final.' Authorised Peter's Mother. The rest of the meal was eaten in silence.

Peter was in the school library. He felt tired from lack of sleep, but he had a lot of catching up to do on his work that he had missed out on in class. He was sitting alone on one of the desks in the middle of the bookshelves.

Crowded around a separate desk was a group of kids in a few years below, who were staring at him and whispering to each other. Peter tried to ignore them but could not help overhearing some of their comments.

'I heard that he's nocturnal, like a bat.'

'Don't you mean like a vampire?'

'Look how pale he is, I bet he is a vampire.'

'Is that why he has no friends you think?'

'No, it's because he smells!'

'Smelly Vampire!'

'Shush, he'll hear you!'

'What's he going to do? Suck my blood?'

'Yeah!'

'Then make you smell his armpits.'

The old librarian, Mrs. Smithson, who was behind the front desk, shushed the group of kids. They simmered down, but carried on whispering to themselves and chuckling occasionally. Peter looked up at Mrs. Smithson, who in return gave a friendly wink back. She was a frail old woman, with silver trimmed hair and thick spectacles fresh from the eighties. Peter smiled and tried to focus back to his math books.

Just as he was getting into it he started hearing some rustling noise from the group of kids, along with childish laughter. He braced himself, then about a few seconds later a scrunched up piece of paper came flying at his desk, just missing him. Peter frustratingly closed his book and turned round towards them, to which they started laughing.

'Shush, he's looking at us!'

'Don't make eye contact! That's how he lures you in!'

'What a freak!'

'Smelly Freak!'

Mrs. Smithson shushed them again, this time louder and with more authority. They fell silent. Peter turned back round to his desk and opened back up his book. He breathed a sigh of relief, and then raised his head towards the front desk to thank Mrs. Smithson, who at the time had her head down in her own book.

As she rose up, Peter sat there stupefied. Mrs. Smithson's face had changed. Her face was hairy, her nose was now a snout, and her teeth were sharp and pointy, dribbling with drool. She gave Peter a razor sharp smile and winked at him the same as before, only this time it did not feel Peter with reassurance.

'Are you afraid?'

Peter turned round and was faced with one of the children, a small blonde haired girl, who was mocking him moments before.

'Are you afraid of the Big Bad Wolf?' She questioned Peter.

Suddenly all the children started laughing and singing together:

'Who's afraid of the big bad wolf; big bad wolf; big bad wolf! Who's afraid of the big bad wolf; big bad wolf; big bad wolf! …'

Peter got up from his desk and ran towards the library exit. He ran past the bookshelves as fast as he could, but no matter how hard he sprinted he wasn't going anywhere. It was as if he was running in slow motion.

The children's laughter and singing got louder. He looked behind the front desk to see Mrs. Smithson, now transformed fully into the Big Bad Wolf, rising from the chair and creeping slowly towards Peter. Peter carried on trying to run as fast as he could, but struggled to make any ground.

The wolf was right behind him, its claws fully stretched out. It started laughing, displaying its wide-open jaws. Peter stopped running and closed his eyes tightly. He felt the wolf grab the back of his head, and then he woke up screaming.

His Mother ran into his room and turned on the light, followed slowly by his Dad. They calmed him down, passed him his drink of water and gave him a towel to clear the sweat off his body. That night, Peter slept in his parent's room, just like he was five again, but still could not sleep.

Dr Bernstein sat back relaxed in his chair, clicking his pen in his left hand. He examined Peter's body behaviour while the boy was sitting in the armchair looking out the window. He immediately noted the lack of confidence in the young man. Peter was skinny in the arms and legs, but which were slightly toned. His face looked drained from life, the eyes being a tell-tale sign of this, and his dark hair looked tremendously uncombed like jagged wire. It was apparent that Peter had given up on his appearance a long time ago. Dr Bernstein put down his pen and sat up straight.

'So Peter, tell me about your dreams.'

Peter bypassed the question, still sitting staring outside towards nothing. Dr Bernstein waited a good minute before continuing.

'You can take as much time as you like. I want you do feel comfortable in here. Whatever is said between us will not leave these walls. This is all on your time.' He said reassuringly.

Peter finally turned and looked at the psychiatrist for the first time since being alone with him. Dr Bernstein was an elderly gentleman with a distinguished nose, bushy sideburns, baldhead and wide framed glasses. Peter thought he sort of looked like a friendly vulture. There was immediate warmth to him, to which he did not know why. Perhaps it was all part of the job: a friendly welcoming image. Either way Peter did not feel threatened. He wanted to open up to someone.

'I've had nightmares... ever since I can remember. I'm afraid to go to sleep at night because I know I will have them. During the daytime I'm fine, besides from the fatigue.' Said Peter. 'It's not the dark I'm afraid of, but that's when the nightmares occur.'

'I see,' Said Dr Bernstein, cupping both hands in unison. 'And what, if you wish to share, are the dreams about? Is there a running theme or a certain episode you keep visiting?'

'Well, yes. All my dreams involve around one thing, but the places and scenarios always change.' Peter dropped his head in embarrassment. 'It's silly I know, but all my nightmares have the same figure in them: The Wolf.'

'A Wolf?' repeated Dr Bernstein. 'I see. What type of wolf exactly?'

'It changes shape quite a lot, but it's more or less the same each time.' Peter's head dropped further, and looked away. 'It's the Big Bad Wolf.'

Peter was amazed as he turned back to see Dr Bernstein's face exactly the same as before: no laughing or raised eyebrows. It was as if he believed him.

'Every time I hear the humming noise of 'Who's afraid of the Big Bad Wolf' I know it's coming.' Peter continued. 'It's like routine now. I know it's crazy, I mean, I've seen the cartoon during the day many times and I find it funny now. I even like the Wolf in it; I think he's funny! But for some reason it always haunts me in my dreams.'

'So you say the wolf in your dreams is a cartoon character?'

'Sometimes… sometimes he's very real looking. But all the time he's standing upwards, bigger than me. He can hide anywhere; he can be anyone or anything; he can turn up at any time. I may even be having a pleasant dream and then he will suddenly appear. It's frustrating. I'm seventeen. I shouldn't be scared of a fictional character in a cartoon. Nobody else is, so why me?'

'That's not entirely true.' Said Dr Bernstein, raising his index finger high. 'Strangely there is not an actual name for this phobia, but it is very common. I have had many patients with the fear of certain fictional cartoon characters. One of the most common of all is Pinocchio. The donkey scene in particular disturbed a lot of people. Why I even had someone many years ago who was afraid of Betty Boo. But it's not necessarily the physical image of these characters, but rather what they represent to the viewer. In your case it sounds like a childhood fear that returns to remind you of such terror you once had. What you must do Peter is to confront your fear. Have you ever seen a real life wolf before? They are much more real than any cartoon character.'

'No.' Peter shook his head and folded his arms in protection over the thought of doing so.

'Well I think you should. In fact I have an old friend of mine who works as a keeper in the local zoo just a few miles from here.

I'm sure I could arrange a trip there for you. I know they have wolves on show there.'

Peter shuddered even more. He knew it might help him, but he was not ready for that just yet, so shook his head again.

Dr Bernstein leaned back in his chair.

'Peter and the wolf.' He said, with a friendly grin. 'Don't worry, we will get there.'

Peter's mother watched from the kitchen window, while washing the dinner plates in the sink, as Peter left the house to begin one of his frequent jogs around the local park. Each time she would warn him to watch out for the farmer's rabbit traps hidden in the leaves, and each time Peter would agree that he would. Sally could not help but still be concerned every time though.

She would be the first to admit that she over mothered her son too much, but again could not help this. He was her only child and not a day went by without Sally thinking of his wellbeing. In the back of her mind she felt as if she had failed him as a parent.

'You worry too much about that boy.' Said her husband Jeremy in a patronising tone, who was standing over Sally.

Jeremy's views were in complete opposite of his wife's. Not that he ever said it, but he was embarrassed of his only son. He hated the fact that he was a loner; that he was a coward.

'I can't help it Jeremy. He's our little Peter.' Said Sally.

'Well let's hope this psychiatrist helps out; otherwise I don't know what we're going to do. We could send him to that home where they can help him?'

Sally slammed the dinner plates into the sink in frustration then swung round facing Jeremy in the eyes.

'You promised me that you would never bring that up ever again!' She said without blinking once.

Jeremy apologised softly. It took a lot to upset his wife, but he knew he had hit a sore spot again. Although he occasionally thought it, he would never mention the home again.

Peter was far enough away from the house and deep into the woods by now. He glanced round to make sure he was completely out of sight, and then got out a packet of malboroh lights from his jogging bottoms along with his small lighter in the other pocket.

He lit the cigarette after a couple of attempts from his lighter, took a deep inhale and laid his back up against a tall oak tree.

Peter had been smoking since his mid-teens. He only started smoking because he thought it looked cool; practically every cool movie character he saw smoked. When he first started he was not sure whether he really enjoyed it or not. He did not dislike it, but at the same time did not really get what all the fuss was about. Peter only really started to fully appreciate it when he discovered the full extent of stress, mostly in the form of bullies at school.

He did not like lying to his mum every time he went 'jogging', but secretly enjoyed it when he told his dad. He knew that he would not approve of him smoking one bit. He also knew that his dad thought of him as an embarrassment. Between them they sort of had a mutual agreement in not mentioning it ever for the sake of Peter's mum, who was key in holding their small family together.

Once he was finished with his cigarette he tossed the end into a nearby bush, shoved the packet and lighter back into his pockets and casually jogged on for a while until eventually heading home.

Peter examined his surroundings. He appeared to be in an old wooden barn, free of any livestock. It was completely empty apart from three separate stacks of hay laid up against a separate wall, and an old barn owl perched on top of one of the wooden beams by the ceiling. It seemed strangely symmetrical for a farmhouse. The barn doors were closed and the only ray of light came from one of the roofs windows; the one that wasn't covered completely in dirt. The place looked familiar to Peter. It reminded him of a place that he used to visit in the West Country when he was little with his parents; an old farmhouse called Mrs. Kingsman's.

Mrs. Kingsman was the owner of the farm who, with the help of her husband Mr. Kingsman, ran a working farm as well as a small bed and breakfast for traveling hikers. His parents were always into hiking when Peter was young. Peter didn't find the walking much fun, as he was more of a runner, but loved being able to stroll around and explore all the cattle, green fields and hay barns. Anything on Mrs. Kingsman's premises was his to freely roam. He used to have hours of fun finding new hidden places to where he could discover and name his own. He had once found a small river running through one of the lower fields, to which Peter built a great dam all by himself. It took him all one afternoon to create such a structure, and to his amazement was still working strong the following morning. Memories flooded back to Peter in a rush of the great times he spent in solitude, just himself and nature at peace. No bullies, no homework, no bossy teachers; just the great outdoors.

But those memories soon evaporated quickly from Peter, for he soon realized that he had not been to the farm for years, and this was not a holiday.

This was a dream.

Peter started to panic. He could feel his heart racing. This was the worst scenario when he knew he was actually dreaming. Many people would believe the opposite, but knowing he was sleeping made it a lot worse. Whenever he was unaware that he was asleep, there was still a glimmer of hope that he would not see the wolf, as he had never seen the wolf whilst being awake. He knew that the wolf did not exist; that it was all in his head. And when he dreamt, it was all in his head; which meant that the wolf was not far away.

If he didn't think about it, it wouldn't appear...

There was a large thud on the barn doors that vibrated through the air. Another followed shortly after. Peter looked up and saw that the owl had not been startled by this, and was still nesting on top of the beam. It started to hoot very softly in Peter's direction, as if questioning him.

He was at the farm... It wasn't here... The wolf wasn't here...

There was a further thud, then silence: all but the owl, which was still hooting. Peter was frozen stiff like in so many nightmares. He wanted to run away but could not lift either of his legs. Instead he stood still square in the middle of the barn.

It was here...

The hooting slowly changed into whistling. A long, high-pitched whistle, like a boiling kettle, that deafened Peter's ears, was followed by the tune that he was all too familiar with. This made him frustrated more than anything at this point now. He knew it was inevitable. He knew the wolf would turn up, complete with the humming that drove him mad.

He wanted to wake up; he kept telling himself to wake up.

It pierced through his eardrums and filled up like a balloon ready to be popped. Louder and louder it got, until it finally stopped suddenly.

This was it…

This was the queue for it. Peter knew who was coming any minute now. But something out of the ordinary happened. He found that this time he could move slightly.

As remarkable as this was, it still only left him one option, and that was to hide into one of the three stacks of hay. Before he could decide there was a heavy thump on the bar doors, which triggered Peter to jump into the nearest stack, furthest away from the entrance.

The doors swung open and the owl made a swoop down out of the barn, leaving Peter all alone. The sun hit the inside of the barn and lit it up like a motel vacancies sign. In approached a dark, shady figure that was out of focus to Peter's eyes. He knew exactly who it was though.

The walls of the barn began to melt, trickling down slowly to display the outside fields, leaving Peter more vulnerable with nowhere else to run and hide to.

The figure crept up charismatically towards where the first stack of hay was, which had now transformed into a pile of twigs and sticks in replacement.

It gave a big huff and puff, and blew away all the sticks and twigs in one foul swoop. It then examined the empty area underneath. Once satisfied it turned and walked towards where the second stack of hay was dumped, only this time it was a stack of bricks.

Once Peter realised this, he then checked to see if his stack had altered, but only find that it had stayed exactly the same: as a pile of hay.

Shit. He had jumped in the wrong one!

The almighty shadow huffed and puffed but could not blow down the bricks. In frustration it quickly swung his neck round and stared straight at the pile of hay where Peter was hiding. Peter ducked but he knew that he had been seen. He also knew that it could blow down hay as easy as sticks, if not easier.

It ran towards the haystack with its tongue-flapping wild out of the corner of its mouth. A howling noise of triumph roamed the air as Peter closed his eyes as tight as he could, while the sound of a hurricane filled all around him. He waited for the inevitable. It felt so cold as the wind blew upon him. It felt so close that Peter could feel the drool dripping on his head. It felt so real…

'You know Peter; I did a little research of my own about the three little pigs. The most well known telling of the story was by a man called Joseph Jacobs, which appeared in the English Fairy Tales collection back in the eighteen-nineties. The fable starts off with the title characters being sent out into the big wide world by their mother to seek their fortune. The first builds a house of straw, but the wolf comes along and blows down the house and then eats the first little pig. The second pig builds a house of sticks but with the same consequences. Then the third pig decides to build a house of bricks. The wolf cannot huff and puff hard enough to blow his house down, making the wolf attempt to trick the pig out, but to no avail. Finally the wolf resolves in coming down the chimney of the house, whereupon the pig places a big pot of boiling water to where the wolf plunges into and then cooked for supper. Now obviously in more recent retellings, such as Walt Disney's adaptation, they had written out the death and violence in the story, but the underlying fundamentals are still the same; the pigs are vulnerable in their own houses and the wolf still wants to eat them. Being sent out into the world by their mother is a common theme within fairy tales, with the absence of guidance or protection in an existence fraught with danger lurking at every corner. Perhaps this could be contrasted with your own family life, being nurtured as an only child and not having experienced true independence? Perhaps the episodes you encounter are a reflection of your concern of being alone and vulnerable? Or perhaps they are your own self-made fables of a warning of what could be prowling out there ready to pounce on you the minute you eventually leave home? Whatever the reason may be, the one thing you must always remember is that the wolf never wins. Eventually in each revision of the story, the wolf never succeeds. Although in your dreams he appears to be winning each time, the one thing you must remember is that the wolf will eventually lose. So you can either do two things; you can either keep going as you are and eventually someday down the line, maybe in a day, week, month or year, the wolf will inevitably lose. Or you can outsmart the wolf by confronting it head on. Whatever you decide, one thing is for sure; the nightmares will stop, but it is up to you Peter, to decide when you want them to.'

Dr Bernstein's words sat in the back of Peter's mind all through the drive home from the clinic, and the more he thought about it the more it sank in deeper. He admitted to Dr Bernstein that the truth of his lack of self-reliance hurt him a bit, not in a patronising way but more of admittance if anything.

His mother, who had picked him up, could sense her son was in deep thought and wanted to discuss how the session went, although she had been given strict instructions by Dr Bernstein not to question Peter. Instead she drove agitatedly in silence while her son stared away from her out the window, pondering over his dilemma. She knew that the therapy must had been working on some level, but could not help but feel as if it was pushing Peter further away from her. Whether this was the case or not she did not know for certain, but she knew how it felt.

They returned home and pulled up onto the drive. They both got out the car, still without saying a word to each other, when Jeremy pulled up next to them. He got out the car and walked round to the passenger side to pick up his suitcase.

'So how did the psycho do today Pete?' Said Jeremy, knowing full well he was breaking Dr Bernstein's instructions.

'Jeremy!' said Sally, trying to hush her husband.

'What? Oh Jesus Christ Sally, I'm paying for the damn things, I should have a right to know. Hell, It was my idea!'

Peter ignored his Father and shuffled fast inside the house and up the stairs towards his bedroom. Sally gave Jeremy a disappointed glance and chased after her son.

She opened the bedroom door to Peter sitting on his bed changing into his running shoes, already with his jogging bottoms and top readily on.

'Don't listen to your Father Peter. If you want to tell us then you can do, but if you don't want to then that's fine. As long as it's helping then it's worth it. Right?'

Peter stopped tying his trainer's laces and gave his mum a thankful smile. He got up and gave her a kiss on the cheek then jogged past her.

'And watch out for the farmer's traps!' She shouted down the stairs to him.

Peter began his run as per normal, lightly jogging along the footpath that bended far round, completely out of sight from his house. He stopped halfway through next to a familiar large oak tree, but decided that he would venture off of the footpath and further into the forest amongst the trees for a change of scenery.

He started off with a light jog that molded into a heavy pace run, which in turn became a full on sprint. Peter did not know why he was sprinting but he was not stopping.

He kept running and running, deeper into the forest, into the unknown. He was swerving side-to-side avoiding the plants and shrubbery, as he swept past. His trainers were filling up with the undergrowth scattered neatly on the floor by Mother Nature, weighing him down a bit but not denting his pace. He could feel his pulse start to beat faster and faster, until it was in unison with his strides. He had not felt so alive for a long time. He felt as if he could have kept on running forever.

He eventually started to slow down after nearly losing his balance a few times. He stopped completely next to a fallen log, held his hands on both knees and took heavy breaths, sucking in much needed air.

Once recouped, he stretched upright and got out a well-deserved cigarette. As he inhaled he thought profoundly again about the words Dr Bernstein gave him.

He had grown to trust the doctor and respect what he had to say. From their first meeting a good relation was born, and over the weeks so too a good friendship. He could confide with him all his personal thoughts and opinions, and proud to say that he was his patient.

Dr Bernstein wanted to help him; Peter could see that. This gave him more of a motive to resolve his problem. He did not want to let him down.

Before, he did not mind letting his father down and although he felt sorry for his mum, he had been more comforted by her rather than aided. With Dr Bernstein, there was hope. There was a cure somewhere. There was a way out.

After disregarding the remains of his cigarette into a nearby bush, he headed back the way he came. Although Peter had never really ran far into the park before, he had a rough idea about where he was and knew if he cut in a bit he should discover the path again.

After walking along a while he started to jog casually in order to get to the path quicker. He thought that he would be able to see the foot trail by now, but it was nowhere in sight.

He soon passed a very familiar looking fallen log, and immediately realized it was the one he had stopped at for his cigarette. Confused and frustrated, Peter decided just to follow back the way he first ran in. He backtracked his footprints that he had stamped in the mud just moments earlier. They lead him a good several feet until they had seemed to vanish. He looked a little further on, just in case the ground was too hard to imprint on and tracks were clearer further up, but to no such luck.

Peter walked the way the footprints looked to be heading until it lead him to a long heavy bush, to which he never remembered passing and surely would have fallen in to if it was the direction he was mean to have run from.

Peter was lost.

How could he be lost? The park wasn't even that big?

He scanned each direction, trying to find any familiarity. He looked up at the sky. It was getting dark a lot quicker than usual. There was still light, therefore enough vision to get home in time, before it was pitch black. But darkness was creeping closer, and Peter could feel it.

He started to run again, as fast as he did the first time, in the direction he thought he might have come from.

If he kept running in one direction, he will soon be at the edge of at least one side of the park.

His heart started to beat again, but not in time with his strides like before. He was completely disorientated. He felt out of balance, but kept on running. Light shadows were beginning to form on the trees that canopied over his head. He felt as if they were chasing him, and he would be caught up if he stopped.

Unsettled, unbalanced and unstable, Peter clumsily caught his right foot on a sticking out twig that was half buried in the ground, causing his body to hurl forward, only to be stopped by a low grown branch that knocked him unconscious.

As he came to, he was in complete and utter darkness. It had caught him up and swallowed the area whole. Not one ounce of the light of day was to be seen anywhere. It took a while for his eyes to adjust.

Peter huddled into a tight ball for protection. He was scared. He had never been in the park at night before, and it looked so different. The friendly, huggable oak trees now looked like gigantic creatures with long and windy tentacles. The fluffy green grass now looked like a carpet of jagged metal. And the gentle sound of humming birds whistling to each other was replaced with the noise of loud crickets, scattering rodents and hooting owls.

He needed to get home. He wanted to be home.

But before Peter could even think of getting up, another sound crept into the air: a faint sound of growling.

It filled Peter's eardrums, vibrating through either side. He did not even consider the possibility that he had imagined it. He knew what he had heard and he knew what it was, although he did not know in what direction it came from.

He slowly crept up on his feet, careful not to make any noise. He still did not know where to move once fully up.

It could have come from anywhere.

Directly in front of him, he saw movement within the long grass and plants. It appeared to be heading towards Peter, who was frozen stupefied.

Soon enough, a dark shadow stealthily formed out of the remainder of the shrubbery and revealed itself in front Peter.

It was a wolf: a real wolf.

Not a cartoon version or an upright standing wolf, but a real life wolf. Its teeth were as sharp as he ever had imagined. Its silky black coat was dark and bushy. The slight vision of his claws seemed to glisten in the moonlight.

It was stalking Peter; closing in on him; hunting him. It was summing up when to strike.

It was all a dream; it was all just a bad dream.

Peter's dreams always felt so real, but this was beyond all the rest. There were no transforming librarians or melting walls. It was just himself and the wolf surrounded by the trees. It was as real as it had ever felt.

Peter could also do something that he could rarely do. In all the circumstances he had found himself in with the wolf he was helpless. He had no chance of getting away or no chance of protecting himself. But this time Peter could do something that he had never been able to do before. He could run.

He felt it in his feet, in his legs and in his arms. His pulse was beating hastily around his body. His adrenalin had finally kicked in. Just like the wolf, he was ready.

The wolf set itself into pouncing position. Peter was poised too, prepared to move if he had to. A good minute passed with both in the same stance, eyeing each other up, until the wolf finally lunged itself towards Peter.

Peter leaped out of the wolf's path and set off running as fast as he could. He was running faster than he ever had done so before now, with no fear of slowing down out of breath. His body agreed that this was be all or end all, and accepted the pace without showing any signs of fatigue.

The wolf howled as if to initiate his hunt, then started the chase. Peter dared not to look back. He did not want to, and he also knew it would slow him down.

Although he could not see the wolf, he knew that it was gaining in on him. He could hear fast pattering of tracks in the mud getting faster. The rumbling sound of growling was growing louder, with the occasional roaring snarl thrown in.

Peter had to get to higher ground in order to have any chance of escaping. He swiftly scanned the trees as they flew past him, seeing if there was any gap or branch leverage, but there was nothing that looked it could aid him.

The wolf was now by his feet. Peter could just make out the glimmer of his sharp silver teeth in the corner of his eye. It could have sprung on him and took him down whenever he wanted. It was binding its time, focusing on the perfect moment. It was a skilled hunter, and knew that timing was everything. It hunted to survive. It did not make mistakes. If it made mistakes, it did not eat. If it did not eat, it did not survive.

Peter's body was trembling, going into spasm from overloading. He could not keep going for much longer. He knew the wolf was right next to him and knew it had the advantage. Peter closed his eyes so tight they started watering with sweat that stung.

It was all over…

SNAP!

Peter fell to the ground immediately when he heard the sound and skimmed across the dirt, staggering to stay up but failing to do so. He was down.

But to his surprise, the wolf had not got him. He looked behind and saw the beast lying on the ground, barely moving. Relieved but confused, Peter could not help but sneak over and see what had prevented the wolf attacking him.

He noticed the wolf was whimpering silently, as if embarrassed in doing so. He also saw that its back right leg was caught in one of the farmer's rabbit traps. It was an old rusty, inhumane trap with large sharp spikes either side, which were tucked deep into the wolf's thigh. In all the years Peter had been running in the park he had never seen one before, but was thankful to see one now.

The wolf was trapped. It could not move. It was helpless. It had lost.

By now Peter had regained his breath back and was ready to run again, although he could not help but stare down at the beast. All his life he had been petrified of the big bad wolf, and now here it lied in front of him, as powerless as he could have never imagined.

Even though the wolf did try to attack him, Peter felt sorry for the animal, and started to consider what would happen to it now.

It would probably be shot at first sight from one of the farmers. Is that what he wanted?

The wolf's head was slumped in the mud, acceptance of defeat. It did not growl or bark at Peter, but it did stare at him. His big black eyes were looking right into Peter's. It was as though it was looking for forgiveness, and for help.

Peter weighed up the situation.

If he was to free it, there's no way it could chase him now. Not with the heavy wound it would be carrying. But would it still try to?

He thought long and hard, and finally decided on what to do.

He knelt over the wounded area, the wolf still whimpering softly but not complaining in how close Peter was. Peter's heart was beating fast again. There was more adrenalin inside him, now more than ever before.

He held both sides of the trap with either hand, and stretched out as hard as he could. The wolf made a howling noise when the spikes slid out of its thigh. The howl gave Peter a frosty chill down his spine, but carried on.

He extended the trap as far as it could go, until he heard a clicking sound. It was fully open and free from the wolf, which limped out of it dragging its hind thigh.

Peter got back a good distance for safety. The wolf turned and looked at him in the eyes, as if to express its gratitude, and then limped off very slowly.

It turned and looked at Peter once again. For some reason, Peter felt as if the wolf wanted to follow him. He did not know why this was. He was weary as to whether or not there were more wolves in the park, as many did hunt in packs, so at first held back.

The wolf did not move. It wanted Peter to follow him.

Why did he want him to follow it?

Peter started walking slowly in the same direction as the wolf, as if in a trance that he could not control. The wolf began walking, still dragging his back leg that's thigh was loosing a lot of blood. He was leading Peter somewhere.

All the way, Peter kept a safe distance away from it, but never stopped following. It took him through the forest and past the long grass, until it came to a path. It was the same path Peter knew very well. It was where he usually stopped and had his cigarette, next to the big oak tree.

Peter stopped walking, but the wolf carried on. It made it's way across the path and into the forest on the other side to rest alone, without looking back once. It had done its job.

It had led him home.

Dr Bernstein greeted his good friend with open arms at the entrance of the wolves' enclosure at the zoo.

'Thomas, you are one in a million.' He gave him an appreciative hug, and then shook his hand. 'Thanks to you sir, the boy is cured. He no longer has the nightmares and can now sleep in peace. His life is slowly being restored, all thanks to you and Koara. I knew she would be good for him. She is such a playful and peaceful creature. I hope she's not too badly hurt though. The boy said she was caught in a rabbit trap?'

Thomas exchanged greetings, but looked at Dr Bernstein quite confused.

'I'm sorry Doc, I know I said I was okay to go out with Koara in the park when you called and told me the kid was going out jogging, but she wasn't feeling well. I had to keep her in. I didn't trust the boy alone with any of the other wolves so I just left it. I was going to call you but got caught up in getting Koara better for the morning show.'

Dr Bernstein looked even more confused than Thomas.

'Are you telling me that the wolf Peter saw in the forest was not Koara?'

Thomas gave out a small snort of laughter.

'No. And I would be very surprised if he saw any wolf at all out there. This is England, not Canada. We don't have wild wolves roaming around the woods here. Why? Did the kid say he saw a wolf?'

Dr Bernstein stroked his chin in thought. He knew there was no possibility of a wolf wandering the local park. But Peter was so adamant that it happened.

'Do you think he dreamt it?' Suggested Thomas.

Dr Bernstein smiled.

'I hope so.'

Jeremy was watching the television downstairs late one night, along with a few bottles of beer. Peter was in his bedroom fast asleep and his wife Sally had just gone upstairs to go to bed. Now that his son was sleeping properly he could have his peace and quiet to himself again in the evenings.

Although Peter was cured, he still occasionally got picked on in school and he still did not have any friends. In the eyes of his father, he was still a loser. But now he had no excuse for being one.

After nearly nodding off a few times, Jeremy finally gave in and headed up to bed. His wife was already tucked up on her side, hogging the majority of the duvet and resting on three of the four pillows. Jeremy got undressed and jumped into his half of the bed.

'How about sharing some of the duvet for a change Sally?'

His wife remained silent.

'Oh, so you're giving me the old silent treatment tonight then? Good. Don't have to put up with your moaning all night.' Jeremy pulled half the covers over his side and rolled facing away from Sally.

'Are you Afraid?' Said Sally very gently.

'What?' Questioned Jeremy, turning over to confront his wife. 'What in Christ's sake are you on ab-'

He froze. His eyes widened, nearly coming out of their sockets. His mouth stretched with shock. His face went white as his own sheets.

Facing him, in the place where he thought his wife was lying, was a creature with a rough hairy face, big pointy ears, wide dark eyes, great big teeth and a drippy tongue.

There was an immediate humming in his head that was getting louder and louder. It would be the same tune he would here in his mind for a very long time. It would be the same song that would haunt his nightmares every time he fell asleep. And he would be too embarrassed to tell a single soul about it.

'Who's afraid of the big bad wolf; big bad wolf; big bad wolf? Who's afraid of the big bad wolf; big bad wolf; big bad wolf…'

A Brief Conversation at the Inn

'I head that they have fangs the size of tigers, and a hideously formed body of a man.' Told the first gentleman to Manning, while waiting for his ale to be poured.

'Aye, the body of a man, but the face of a jackal,' daringly said the women standing next to him, 'with razor sharp claws instead of fingers.'

The second gentleman, who had already retrieved his ale, added: 'they stalk on you and pounce when you are alone and out of sight, away from any group. That way they cannot ever be seen, or whispers of men who had gotten away and lived to describe the beast ever be told. That is why we travel together, as a group.'

Manning raised his head, along with his own beverage of the house special, and said 'Then, my dear travellers; how does it come to all three of you, such imaginative descriptions of these horrifying beasts?'

The three new arrivals glared at each other in silence.

'Whispers can be awfully loud sometimes, I suppose.' Shrugged Manning, and returned back to his drink.

The three travellers paid for their drinks and retired to the armchairs surrounding the roaring fire, keeping themselves to themselves.

There was no need to be greedy on this night, thought Manning, not when the house special was fully in stock.

Manning raised his ale in salute to where his reflection should have been in the glass mirror hanging behind the bar...

<u>Wrapped</u>

Robbie Simmons left the doors of the office and stepped onto the cold wet pavement of Camden's busy High Street. He gave a good stretch of his entire body, which had stiffened up from being in the same slumped position sitting next to his desk all day. His eyes had to adjust to the outside light before starting his journey home due to staring at his computer screen for so long.

Robbie had seen from the small window next to his desk that it had been raining heavily, and seemed to look as though it was beginning to clear up. It was still raining, but nothing compared to earlier on in the day. The rain was not a problem at all for Robbie, as he had his smart foldaway umbrella in his Dunlop bag that he got out and popped open within a matter of seconds, careful not to whack it in front of anybody walking by. It shielded his neatly combed hair from the damp raindrops perfectly.

He began to walk up the high street, under the railway bridge towards Camden Town underground tube station. He only got a few feet before realising how cold and windy it was outside as well. Robbie was only wearing a slim jumper and skinny jeans, with little padding of layers underneath, and soon felt frozen. He immediately felt anger towards the weatherman's poor morning report of a good sunny spring day, which Robbie had stupidly taken for certainty.

What he needed now was some more items of clothing to keep him warm on his journey home. Travelling on the underground was not a problem, but he knew that when he got off at High Barnet station he still had a fair walk back to his home; and he did not fancy braving it in the day's harsh weather conditions. He thought it best to quickly stop off at the Camden Lock indoor market and have a look for a cheap coat or woolly jumper at one of the many clothes stalls.

As he walked in, passing many wannabe trendy groups of teenagers all wearing the latest craze that was deemed socially unacceptable for the time, he saw that he was awash with choices.

After restraining himself from searching the vinyl stalls for old sixties records, he noticed that over half of the stalls were primarily selling clothes and accessories. There were plenty of small booths dedicated in selling gloves, mittens, umbrellas, chains, bracelets, rings, wacky t-shirts with obscene pictures and writing scribbled on them. But nothing that appealed to Robbie, or looked as though it would keep him the least bit warm. There were a few hooded jumpers for sale, but all had either a band's name or slogan printed in bold on the chest; and Robbie had no interest in any of the named bands that they were promoting. Also he did not want to get into trouble by wearing a hoody around Camden or Barnet. He thought about certain little gangs of hoodies that hung around starting fights with each other, robbing and threatening anyone that as much as dared to walk past them wearing the wrong colours.

He didn't want to go through anything like that again...

Robbie was just about to give up and face the cold walk home, when at the corner of his eye he noticed a small little booth tucked away in one of the corners. He was not sure what it was, but something was drawing him in to go and have a closer look.

As he walked up to the stall, he soon saw a stack of large racks with every type of scarf hanging on them that he could possibly imagine. There were silk scarves, cashmere scarves, velvet, beaded, cotton, embroidered, sequined, knitted, satin; all in every single colour imaginable; royal blue, coral red, dark chestnut, golden brown, hunter green, cardinal, mauve, medium carmine; the list was endless. They were all sectioned perfectly into their own unique style as well.

Robbie had always been a fan of a good scarf, and his eyes lit up with delight the moment he saw all the available options. He started considering which one to pick immediately, and questioning whether he needed two or three extras just in case to match with his other outfits. He started clicking his fingers to keep control of his excitement while he examined each potential purchase.

And then he saw it.

It was an old vintage looking stripy multicoloured knitted scarf, just about big enough to wrap around your neck with. It was the only one of its kind, with no other replica visible on display.

Robbie reached out with both hands and picked it up gently, as though it was made of diamond glass, careful not to damage or break it. He held it up high so it folded open in front of him.

It was perfect...

'Ah, I see you like?' Said a voice from behind Robbie, causing him to jump as though he had been caught doing something he shouldn't have been. 'No, no, don't worry, you can touch; go on touch. Very soft, no?'

Robbie turned around to see the stall owner, who was a little old Chinese man wearing slim-framed glasses and a wrist of golden chains, sporting a ready-rolled cigarette in one hand. He smiled reassuringly at Robbie.

'Very nice taste sir; very nice taste indeed.' He then pointed towards the long length mirror propped up by the side of the stall. 'Go on sir, try it on for size.'

The old Chinese man steered Robbie, who was still clutching the scarf firmly in his hands, towards the mirror. Once in front of his own reflection, Robbie then loosened his grip and swung the scarf around his neck. He momentarily felt embarrassed as he considered which style to wear it, as if the Chinese man would think that he was a fraud. Would he go for the casual neck wrap, maybe a smarter ascot knot, or a stylish square knot?

He noticed the Chinese man was giving him a smile of encouragement, so he quickly settled for a standard European loop to save time.

Robbie automatically felt warmer. It was so soft and smooth around his neck, an automatic feeling of protection and comfort rushed over Robbie.

It definitely felt as good as it looked.

'Ah, it fits you perfectly!' Said the little Chinese man excitedly, a kind of reaction you would expect from a suit tailor rather than a market stall owner in Camden. 'I can see that this scarf likes you very much.'

Confused at this peculiar comment, Robbie took the scarf off over his head and quickly decided to instigate a price negotiation to move on before any awkwardness kicked in.

'So, how much do you want for it then? I can't see a label or tag anywhere…'

'For you good sir, I do you a good price.' He said, while removing his rolled up cigarette from the grasp of his hands and placing it neatly behind his left ear. Robbie had heard this line before many times, and he was no stranger to haggling down for a bargain, but was shocked with the price he offered. 'I sell to you for four pounds.'

Robbie was thrown back by how cheap it was, and immediately started scanning the rest of the stall to see if there was anything else he liked, and soon spotted a standard navy blue cotton scarf; not as nice as the vintage multicoloured one but a practical item that would fit most of his wardrobe nicely.

'How much is that one then?' Said Robbie, pointing to the hanging navy blue scarf.

The old Chinese man turned around to face his stock and squinted his eyes following where Robbie was pointing.

'Twenty pounds.' He said after observing the scarf. 'This section here is all twenty pounds. The scarves on that rack are twenty five, and the ones in the middle there are a bit cheaper at sixteen.'

'So why is this scarf cheaper than the others?' Robbie questioned, rather confused. It didn't make much sense. It was obvious that the vintage scarf was the best looking one, and the way it had been knitted was pure perfection.

The old Chinese man smiled a big grin at Robbie.

'Because my good sir, that scarf deserves a good owner; and I can see by the look in your eyes when you were trying it on that you will look after it well.'

Robbie wasn't going to argue with the man. He wanted the scarf, and the old Chinese man wanted to sell him the scarf.

Perfect!

'It's a deal. I'll take just this one then please.' Robbie said without haggling. He didn't want to jeopardise the good deal in any way by offending the man, so got out his wallet and fished out three pound coins and two fifty pence's, and then handed them over to the little Chinese man who slid them neatly into his front money pouch worn around his waist.

'Very good choice sir; that scarf will provide protection for you wherever you journey; you look after it, and it will look after you. Make sure that you and only you wear it; okay?' The Chinese man's face seemed to drop as he said this, as though wanted what he was saying to be taken seriously and understood.

Robbie, again not wanting to offend him, nodded sternly in response, as if acknowledging what was said.

'Good boy sir, very good boy!' He said, and his face lit up again as before.

Robbie whipped his newly bought scarf around his neck, gave a grateful farewell to the old Chinese man, made his way out the of the market and back on track towards the underground station.

Robbie propped up his umbrella as he got outside in the rain again, and walked proudly through the crowds of people hovering around the station entrance, with his chest boldly propped up displaying his new accessory. Even though it was a small piece of clothing, it gave off plenty of warmth around his neck and upper body that seemed to circulate around the rest of him. It was as if he was wearing a full-bodied parker. It did not make him sweat either. It seemed to know the exact temperature to be comfortable.

It was indeed perfect.

After shaking off his umbrella and a quick rummage around in his bag, he got out his travel card and went through the ticket machine. He made his way down the escalators, checking the posters on his way down for any good shows or events taking place, most of which he had already seen.

He got down to the platform, which was absolutely packed with people. Everybody was huddling close to the yellow line; all gathered where they guessed the doors would land. Robbie observed the platform, debating where to stand so he could squeeze on the next train.

Most underground trains arrived very frequently, usually spaced between a few minutes, but that never mattered. If there was a train at the platform, everybody on the platform always wanted on, including Robbie. He decided to walk all the way down towards the other end, excusing everybody he accidently bumped in to as he did so, where the least amount of people were gathering.

The rumble of the station, frantic blowing gust of air and sound of screeching coming from the dark-lit tunnel signalled the coming of the train. It grinded to a halt and the automatic doors hissed open, followed by hoards of commuters piling in and out any way they could.

Robbie squeezed on the last carriage and propped himself up at the end of the last aisle. The doors slid shut after beeping frantically and the train gradually began to move.

It was not until after East Finchley station that Robbie could sit down, with many passengers filtering out by then, but was soon up again as he annoyingly noticed that the train he had gotten on was destined for Mill Hill East, the wrong train. He got off at Finchley Central and waited on the platform for the next train to High Barnet.

Robbie soon noticed that the platform itself was less than busy, with only a handful of people left waiting; who had all probably made the same mistake he just did.

He got on the next train that arrived shortly after, with High Barnet clearly marked in bright bold letters on the front of it. The carriage he got on was practically empty, all but a couple of people scattered about the seats.

Robbie sat down furthest away from everybody, got out his mp3 player and started listening to the relaxing sounds of Fleet Foxes. As he did this, his eyes glanced curiously across the near empty carriage, focusing on the remaining passengers.

There was a young couple giggling to themselves with a few shopping bags hung on their arms; an office lady that looked eager for her phone that was gripped tightly in her hand to regain signal as soon as she got out the underground; a middle-aged guy who was wearing a leather jacket that did not suit him one bit; and a scruffy-looking man with a bushy beard wearing a torn green coat and a tilted can of cider resting on his lap.

The last guy looked like trouble…

The scruffy-looking man's eyes caught Robbie's stare for a split second, causing Robbie to instantly look away and keep his head down.

The train stopped at West Finchley, with everybody in the carriage getting off; all except the man in the green coat.

Robbie could feel the man's eyes staring at him; looking him up and down. The sound of his cider can cracking open caused Robbie to jump slightly, for which he could hear made the man chuckle slightly.

He didn't mean to seem fragile, but Robbie could not help it. Ever since he was robbed two years back, held at knifepoint by a gang of desperate hooded jumper wearing youths, he was always weary of even the slightest dodgy-looking stranger; and this man was looking very risky.

The train began to slow down, a bit too earlier than expected, and then grinded to a halt halfway through the dark tunnel, with the overhead lights flickering on and off.

'Apologies ladies and gentleman for the delay; we're just held at a red light here, waiting for the train in front to leave the platform. We should be moving along very shortly.' Stated the driver over the crackling tannoy.

Robbie started to hear over his music a sound of fidgeting coming from the other end of the carriage, where he knew the man in the green coat was sitting. Robbie, all the while still looking away, could also hear him getting up and staggering towards his side of the carriage.

The man slumped down in the seat directly opposite, still staring at Robbie with his weary eyes.

'Nice scarf...' Said the creepy man to Robbie, while taking a swig from his can.

Robbie looked up and gave a smile of acknowledgement, and then returned his eyes to the ground.

'Bloody trains ey,' Continued the man. 'They always do this don't they? All these poxy tube drivers going on strike every chance they get demanding more money; and for what? This! You can't go on the underground once without having a delay these days. And these bloody underground arseholes are demanding more money! I say fire every one of them who goes on strike and replace the lot of them.'

Robbie smiled politely at the man, trying his best not to instigate him to talk any further.

'I mean, at least give us one year's good service, something worthy of a pay rise; you know what I mea-?' The man burped. It smelt of stale cider. 'I mean, what's the point of demanding things when you're not even good at your job?'

The man took another large gulp of his cider, and then held it up in front of him; shaking it in the direction of Robbie.

'Fancy a mouthful?' Offered the man.

'No, thank you though.' Replied Robbie as best he could.

'Ah come on boy, who knows how long we're gonna be sitting here for? You might as well make the most of it.'

'No really, I'm okay thank you.'

The man sat resignedly back upright in his seat, with an expression of disappointment on his face.

'Oh, I get it. I know your type boy. You think you're better than people like me.' Accused the man. 'You think that just because I'm wearing a ripped up old coat and drinking a can of cider on the train that I'm scum! Right?'

Robbie's heart began to race. He had tried his best not to get involved with him, but by being too cautious only made matters worse. The man's eyes were fixated on him. Robbie could feel the glare again as he tried desperately too look away; standing down, admitting defeat. The lights began to flicker again as the carriage began to move once more. The man began to laugh.

'Hey, I'm only yanking your chain mate! If you don't want a drink that's fine, just trying to be sociable here. Don't mind me.' He put his hands up in apology.

Robbie smiled as best he could without looking uncomfortable. The underground sign for Woodside Park fluttered past the window until coming to a halt and the doors opened. The man did not leave, and nobody else got on. For a split second, Robbie considered getting off early and waiting for the next train to come along, just to get away from the strange man.

Only a few more stops left. He could ride this out...

The doors shut and the train began to move again.

'What you listening to boy?' Asked the man, pointing at his own ears as if using sign language.

'Fleet... Fleet Foxes...' Robbie managed to sputter out, while removing his headphones in courtesy.

'Oh yeah? I've never heard of them! What are they like?'

'Well, they're a folk group; kind of like a mixture between Simon and Garfunkel and The Beach Boys. It's... it's good; very relaxing.' Said Robbie, gaining a bit more confidence in his voice as he spoke, probably due to the subject at hand.

'The Beach Boys you say? I fuckin' hate The Beach Boys!' Said the man very aggressively, followed by a howl of laughter that made Robbie feel instantly at unease again.

The next stop was Totteridge & Whetstone. As the train approached the platform, the man got up out of his seat (much to the relief of Robbie), tucking in his green coat so not to get it caught between the seats. The doors spread open, but the man simply stood there and gave out an almighty stretch, followed with a few cracking sounds from his body.

'Ah, needed that! Feels like I've been sitting on this train forever.'

Robbie knew the feeling...

The man stayed standing as the carriage commenced moving, still drinking his cider while swaying along with the train. Even though Robbie was listening to his music, he could still sense the awkward silence, as though the man was waiting for him to talk.

The train whistled as it flew through the black tunnel, chugging along and screeching as the wheels clashed against the metal tracks. The strange man in the green coat had a goofy smile on his face while looking at Robbie; making Robbie wonder how many ciders the man had already drunk before hand.

Soon enough, Robbie could see his stop, High Barnet.

'Here we are boy; end of the line!' The man commented.

Robbie got up from his seat, holding his bag tightly as he walked past the bearded man towards the carriage doors as they opened, hopped off the train and began walking with pace towards the exit. The strange man got off just as quick, with his steps closely behind Robbie. There were a few others that got off as well from the other carriages, but not enough people to hide behind and get lost in a crowd.

He walked up the escalators and through the ticket machine towards the outside. It had turned dark since Robbie last left the over ground, and was still cold and wet as before.

He reached Barnet Hill and crossed the main road towards the path that led to Vale Drive. But despite having his headphones in, he could still hear the sound of familiar footsteps behind him.

'Hey boy, looks like we're both heading in the same direction.'

The man's voice spilled on top of Robbie's chest like a heated rash, making him feel instantly uncomfortable and afraid. He didn't even turn round. His legs picked up pace and hurried as fast as they could. He got out his mp3 player and turned the volume up as loud as it could go.

He could just pretend he didn't hear him and keep walking. Nobody can be mad at that could they?

'Hey kid! What's the rush?' Laughed the man mockingly. 'Wait up!'

And then a heavy thump shook the footpath like a mini earthquake. Robbie turned round in shock to find the man in the green coat flat on his face, not moving an inch. Cider ran down the path, coming from the inside of one of the coat's pockets and dripping down his bushy beard.

The man was obviously a complete and utter drunk.

Robbie turned round to continue walking on, but something made him stop. It was something that he felt inside, a conscience perhaps. He knew that he could not leave the man lying there; not like that. There was nobody around for miles, and the path was blocked away from any main road. Despite how much of a threat he first appeared to be, he was now harmless and needed help.

'Hey… are you okay?' Robbie asked, while taking out his headphones and creeping cautiously towards the dumped pile of man in the middle of the footpath.

A long and painful groan came from below, and the man began struggling to get some sort of balance to push himself up.

'Oooo… Hey boy, come help a waster like me up. I need some help from your kind self.' Pleaded the man pathetically. Robbie was still hesitant, and if it were not for his polite and selfless upbringing he would have walked on as if it wasn't his problem. But Robbie had been brought up proper by his parents, who were both dedicated Christians and full helpers of the local community, and he knew that this waster needed some support.

'Come on kid, I was only messin' earlier; just me and my drunken way, that's all. I'm sorry mate…'

Robbie made his way over, with his hands reached out ready to prop him up. The man stumbled into his arms and pulled himself up using Robbie's body.

'Thank you kindly young sir, what a true gentleman you are; such a kind heart.' The man thanked Robbie greatly, and smiled at him showing off his missing teeth and numerous silver and gold fillings behind his greasy beard. Robbie smiled politely back, but this time he actually meant it.

He was glad he was helping him out, and felt sorry that he misjudged the man from his first appearance. It was all too easy to do that, but as a devoted Christian he should have known better. He should be seeking people like this man out, and helping them in any way he could.

But Robbie suddenly felt something touching his chest that soon dramatically changed his mind back.

He could feel the cold and sharp touch of a knife pressed against his shirt. He looked down to see the object twinkling brightly back and him. Robbie looked up at the man. He was grinning more than ever, but this time there was no grateful smile, but more a mockingly triumphant one.

'Too bad kid! You got a good heart; shame you had to run into someone like me.' The man grabbed the back of Robbie's neck tightly, holding him in a steady position so he could not run anywhere.

Robbie started shaking as he began having flashbacks of the last time he was at knifepoint. The gang of hoodies were all laughing at him as though it was all some sort of game or joke they were playing; that they relished the fact that he was so scared. It was like playing piggie in the middle, but Robbie was not trying to catch anything. Instead he remembered just closing his eyes tightly and letting them rummage through his trouser pockets and take off his bag with all his belongings in. He did nothing to stop it. He just wanted it all over as quickly as possible.

And now it was happening all over again… the nightmare was happening again…

'Now look here boy, you look like a pretty sensible lad, despite your gullibility. Now let's not make this into some big deal. When I tell you to, I want you to pass over your wallet, your Walkman and your phone. You got that?'

Robbie nodded, avoiding correcting the name of his mp3 player.

'Good. I'm glad we're on the same wavelength boy. You're also going to write in your phone your four-digit pin number for your cards; got that? And no false numbers, as I will find you; marks my words boy, I'll find you.'

Robbie nodded.

'Well, okay then. If you're lucky and do what I say then I might not stab you; I haven't decided yet. But your odds improve each time you…' The man burped again. '…Cooperate. Right… put everything you got in your bag.'

Robbie nodded, and put all his items in his bag.

He got out his phone last, typing a saved message with his four-digit pin number in it, showing the man as he did so, and then put it in the bag. He actually put in the right digits as well; he was too scared to even think of any other numbers, and knew that the man would know he was lying if he did so.

'Okay, now hand the bag over.'

Robbie slowly pulled the bag strap over his head and passed it to the man. He could smell his alcoholic breath blowing rapidly in his face as he did so. The man's eyes widened as he got given his goody bag. Giddy to see what he had collected, he opened it up and had a quick glance.

'Well, well… Looks like I've bagged myself a good one here tonight ey boy! You a rich momma's boy are ya? Always get what you want yeah? Well, I would feel sorry for you, but I'm pretty sure mummy can buy you all these things the next time she goes shopping ey boy.' He looked envious at Robbie, as if disgusted by the sight of him.

'Yeah I know exactly who you are, college boy. Straight out of Uni with a debt to clear in your own slow time and not a care in the world, while proper workers like me have to suffer. You students piss me off so much. You're always whining and protesting about some stupid Africans and sponging off the government. You're why this countries turned the way it has. You're the reason we're in trouble. You smug little shit...'

Robbie stayed silent, forcing to keep in his tears.

'I ought to get rid of the lot of you, one by one. Starting with you...' He held the knife up to Robbie's face, twirling it around in front of him. Robbie let out a sputter of a cry he could not hold in any longer, to which received laughter from the man.

'Go on, get out of here, and don't let me catch you around; I won't be so nice next time.'

He let go of his neck, but before Robbie could walk a step away the man quickly grabbed his arm in what appeared to be another quick thought.

This was it; he was not going to let him go at all...

'Hey,' the man smiled, showing off a dentist's worst nightmare set of teeth. 'I do remember being quite fond of your scarf. Probably the reason you got my attention in the first place. Pass it over boy.'

The dam scarf... If only he had just braved the cold on his own. Why couldn't he have just gone straight home?

Robbie untangled the scarf from his neck and gave it to the man, who held it approvingly. He wrapped it round his large neck, over the top of the green coat and gave another conquering smile.

It didn't suit him one bit...

'A perfect fit!' Laughed the man, coughing slightly.

But then the man's face started to change. He suddenly looked growingly uncomfortable, as though he was getting claustrophobic all of a sudden. He tried to take the scarf off, but for some reason he could not pull it away.

Robbie looked on in amazement as he saw the scarf seem to come alive and coil tighter around the man's neck, like an anaconda gripping its prey. The man worryingly dropped his newly won Dunlop bag and tried to cut the scarf with his knife, but soon got it knocked out of his hand by the scarf's movement, rapidly twirling around faster.

The man reached out towards Robbie in aid, towards the boy he had just named and shamed as a pathetic student, pleading for forgiveness, for mercy. His eyes said it all. He looked at Robbie in a different light now, as though he was the magic wizard behind conjuring up such sorcery.

His face began turning blue and his eyes were beginning to come out of their sockets. It looked as though he was trying to shout for help, but his throat was completely blocked by the knitted fabric.

The man sputtered and coughed ferociously, gave one last gasp of air before getting thrown into a body spasm and crumbled to the floor once more... This time however, he was not getting back up.

Robbie stood momentarily in shock at the motionless threat that lay still before him. He could not believe what he had just witnessed, and half of him expected to wake up at any minute.

His eyes were fixated on the scarf, which seemed to be coiling loose from the man's twisted neck. It looked alive, like a living, breathing, pulsing creature.

Robbie crept closely towards the broken mess on the floor, careful to retrieve his rightful bag. It was his bag after all, and he would be dammed if anybody else were going to take it from him if he left it there.

As he bent down to pick it up, the scarf startled him. It seemed to flood down the body of the man in the green coat towards Robbie, as though it was an innocent lost puppy seeking its master.

It flopped by his feet, next to his bag he was ready to pick up. He grabbed the bag, slinging it on his shoulder in the same position as before. He looked down at the scarf, its multicoloured material flapping playfully in the light breeze.

It still looked so cool...

There was something that made Robbie confident all of a sudden. It was as if he had his spark back; something that made him complete. And each time his eyes met the multicoloured, knitted vintage scarf he seemed to acknowledge this feeling more so than before.

He was not afraid anymore.

It was as if the scarf was calling to him; wanting Robbie to pick it up and sling it round his neck like a proud placement. And deep down inside of him, he knew he would be safe.

It was like the old Chinese man had said; the scarf liked him. It would provide protection for him wherever he went. If he looked after it, it will look after him.

To Robbie, a man of good faith, trust and belief, this made perfect sense. He picked up the scarf, slung it round his neck, and boldly made his journey home, feeling comfortably warm and well protected...

I Dreamt of the Beast

I, Anthony James Hoskins, write this statement being of sound mind, body and soul. The alcohol in my bones, although evidently still lurking upon my skin, has dried up fully, and now that I am whole again do I fear more than when I was still intoxicated. For the dream, which could dictate the word nightmare over a thousand times and then repeat a further thousand, that I shared with my conscience last night was that of sheer terror.

Before my interrupted slumber I must admit to my actions. I had on the night attended my Great Uncle Sidney's eightieth birthday celebrations, wherefore it would be fair to say that I was fully into the merry spirit that accompanies such a function. The expectation of enjoying the fine drinks such a grand bar should hold got the better of me, and so within the first hours I had totally overindulged. I took advantage of the complementary free house until came the time of dipping into our own pockets for a pour, for which I generously offered everybody in the party a round on myself. However, this generosity was but a placebo into the real reason of letting myself carry on with the liquor without looking like a complete drunk. Much to the contrary, I looked like the perfect gentleman to all; who showed their appreciation by returning to myself a drink of choice as a token of gratitude, which was greatly accepted.

The list of mixtures was endless. I do believe, were it not for a few wallet-tight guests who did not return this gesture, I could have possibly tried every alcoholic beverage in the venue.

Unfortunately for myself, alcohol does to me what it does to so many good men; its poison turned my world from an optimistic perspective into a frost of dark thoughts and paranoia. The group of men, who had gathered round laughing along with my jokes, were now laughing at me. The onlookers who peered from time to time catching a glimpse of the entertainment were now judging and condemning my actions. Everybody in the room, who were all close family and friends, were now against me.

I sipped cautiously as I eyed all movements, waiting for someone to open up and say what they really thought of me; that I was just a big fraud who drank too much. They all secretly knew my addiction. They all knew I liked the sauce a bit too much. But who was brave enough to say so?

My cousin Harold, one of the finest young gentlemen in all of London, must have seen me sway and stagger slightly whilst leaning myself on the edge of the bar, and by doing so asked me, as any young concerned gentleman would, whether I was well. Looking back it is clear that it was said with the best of intentions, but at the time I was a raging bull ready to pounce on the first sight of red waved in my face.

At first I started to push, which soon developed into swinging punches, for which I ashamedly admit impact. My close friends and relatives were holding me back, trying to calm me down, and restraining me from committing further wrong doing. Even as I write this down do I cringe with embarrassment, but I must be honest about my actions before continuing on.

I soon broke free of the crowds grasp, and staggered aimlessly towards the exit, thus bidding my night adieu. I crumbled through the cold dark streets of London town, scraping my coat jacket upon the cabs stacked up on either side of the streets as I carelessly strolled by. I cursed every name under the sun, and cursed the sun as well while I was doing the rounds. I blamed everybody at the party for ruining my night, and swore that the day I would meet cousin Harold again it would be his very last.

The wind was sweeping through my head as I continued my journey, and at first it occurred to me that this was aiding my drunken state, sobering me up with its calm breeze.

Only until I entered my residence did I understand how wrong I was. As soon as the front door slammed behind me, the light wind had left and I was once again alone with the stuffy feeling of still indoor air.

I had banished the night as unsuccessful and agreed with myself to stand it no longer, and rid its very existence immediately by going to sleep. With the state I was in I presumed that I would be out as fast as my head began to dent the pillow.

I could not have been any further from the truth.

I tossed and turned, battling my sheets into submission, but I was losing tremendously. No matter how hard I shut my eyes, I could not sleep. My mind was a whirl wind with dark thoughts, mainly consisting of my ex-wife, Madeline. She was the reason, the spark that ignited my drink problem.

The thought of Madeline being with her new husband Clark menaced me in a torturing cycle, viewing the same picture on repeat. I planned in my head what I would do if I ever came face to face with Clark. I knew what he looked like, but had never been fully introduced. What an introduction that would be, I thought.

I prayed that I would not think these thoughts much longer, for I grew tired of hearing my own threats. They echoed through my mind, hammering away trying to cling on permanently. Soon enough though I had grown weary of fighting and the inevitable slumber began. But if I was to know in advance the dream that would follow, I truthfully consider I would have forced myself to stay awake.

I sat up straight in my bed, leaning on the bedstead. I knew I had started to dream; hoping that I was. Every part of my room was as it should have been and how I had left it before I slept. The curtains were drawn; there was a pile of clothes stacked by the side of the bed, the cupboard door was left slightly ajar. But I knew for certain I had to be in a dream.

The room was lit, not by my candles, but shone in a dreary grey that seemed to hang in the air like fog. And there, sitting perched at the end of my very bed was a man half human half goat.

His lower body was that of cattle, with two powerful hoofs as feet and strong bushy legs. The torso was as muscular physique of man that I had ever seen, covered in a thick mane. Proudly hung around his huge neck was a shiny medallion symbol shaped in a pentagram. His face was a long hairy snout with two gigantic horns spread proudly either side, exactly like a male goats. But his eyes... his eyes were neither that of man nor goat. They were those of a beast; wide open and the darkest colour black my eyes had ever witnessed.

It was the devil himself.

I sat there not moving an inch. He was facing out towards my window, as if waiting for me to wake up. I had not known whether he saw me rise or not, but I wanted to creep back down into my bed and go to sleep. I had to remind myself that I was already asleep, and that it was all just a dream I was having; a very real, utterly frightening dream. It had to be a dream...

Finally, the devil's head turned slowly round until he was fully facing me. His eyes seemed to look right through me, as if he could read every thought I had ever owned. I feared to blink as not to insult him.

What do you want? I thought in my mind, although I had not the voice to amplify it.

'Carry on.' He replied to me, in a deep and dominant tone, that of which I had never heard before, but can hear as clear as day whenever I try to remember. It was said not as a passing comment but more in a persuasive, intriguing manner.

Carry on with what? I again thought without projecting.

'Carry on,' He repeated, this time more demanding, as if wanting me to listen carefully. 'You are a bitter and angry man. You have given up on your own life and wish to damper others. You are on your way…'

I am on my way? On my way where?

'Carry on…' He repeated once more, as persuasive as before.

I still had not blinked as my eyes were caught in shock. They were trapped by the sheer horror of such a foul, grizzling beast that sat there before my very sight. His nostrils would flair every time he breathed a heavy breath. I could feel the breeze smack me in the cheeks as he breathed outwards towards my direction. The room was ice cold, and I was struggling to keep the slightest bit warm, even though my bed sheets are the finest and thickest that money could ever buy. I forced myself into dismissing this encounter; that it was just a silly dream.

You can't be who I think you are. I know. I know for a fact that you are not he. The disguise you wear before me is that of the peaceful Horned God, celebrated and worshipped by the Wicca religion. You sir, are merely an image of what the Christian church conjured up as the devil to scare away and banish Wicca believers to gain control. I admit now that you frighten me, there is no denying that; but this is only because of the horror and pain the church has told me the beast is capable of, all the while showing me pictures of such an outfit. You sir, are nothing more than a Christian make-believe.

I said these words in my foolish head, not considering how disrespectful this could be to whoever sat before me, be it the devil or simply a monster. At this point I was more aware of how close he was to my very feet, near touching them with his hindquarters. I could feel him move as he adjusted his seating, and then finally stood up by the side of my bed looking down on me. My eyesight was temporarily blinded by the reflection of his proud medallion, for which I could not understand the cause being in complete darkness. He was just as tall as he was wide, nearly having to duck so not to hit his head upon my ceiling. I prayed that I did not offend him.

'Oh Anthony!' The beast bellowed out a laugh, which shattered my very soul. Each note was like a booming roar in my ears. 'I am whatever you believe I should look like. In your case I am what your pathetic church has made you set to believe. No mere mortal could ever bear eyes upon my true appearance, for his very soul would be crushed in an instance.'

He had not said it, but had persuaded me enough to believe that he was truly the devil. I felt anger towards the church for creating such a horrific description, and at the same time cursed the Wicca religion for being the original founders.

What do you want with me devil?

'I am here to tell you that I have reserved a special place, one awaiting your arrival. We are all waiting for you here Anthony; soon you will join us.'

Where? I asked so naïve, and forced myself to believe in my own innocence. Without answering me, the beast walked forward towards my window. Every step he took with those massive hoofs shook the floorboards like an earthquake. I can still feel the vibration rippling through me now it was that powerful. The back of the beast was completely covered in hair, thick dark hair, a cross between a wolf and a stallion.

He grabbed the drapes that hung either side, which I presumed was keeping out the night sky. With one almighty thrust downwards, he tore down both drapes, showing me his answer.

What was beyond the window I cannot say. It is not that I am in sworn secrecy, or that I cannot visualise it no longer, but more the fact that it was indeed indescribable. For what all the church had preached to me, for the imagery I was perceived to believe, nothing could have prepared me for such horror. No mere mortal words could describe what the beast had shown me. All I know for certain, was that it was hell in all its glory.

He turned and faced me head on once more, and began that haunting bellow of laughter, which had still not left my ears from the first time. He looked as though he was proud of his work, like an artist displaying his masterpiece to the uneducated. I held on to my covers tightly for fear of falling out. It was as though the only sanctum of safety was my bed. I tried to close my eyes, steer my sight away from it, but I was powerless. It was his dream, not mine. He controlled it. He was the one who decided my fate.

'Carry on, Anthony!' He snorted out, while grabbing my bed sheets off and pulling me closer and closer towards the window. 'Carry on...'

I woke up, heart racing as if it was set to leap out of my chest. I was dripping with sweat from head to toe. It took me a while to calm down and get used to breathing normally again.

I surveyed my bedchamber. The drapes were as I left them. The pile of clothes was still stacked up by my side. The wardrobe door was slightly ajar. And I knew for certain this time, that I was not dreaming.

It was daybreak. The sun came beaming in through the window, but I still dare not pull the drapes apart, for fear of what I might see again. I took the time to ask myself what the dream all meant.

I had a place reserved by the beast himself?

It occurred to me that all this time I had thought nothing of my actions. I had considered that my dark thoughts and occasional physical mishaps were simply one-offs, and were not to be repeated or remembered. I had been attending church as per normal and therefore assumed that if I kept this side up then I would be safe from damnation.

The dream spoke to me on two levels. Firstly, it was the devil egging me to carry on my ways of self-abuse, regret, violence and hatred. He could see my potential, even if I was blind to it. It was true that I had been carrying some deep, dark and disturbing thoughts around with me everywhere I went, only to hide behind fake generosity, for which money had never been a problem. I was on my way for certain...

My second thought, and the one I much prefer due to sheer terror of the latter, was that it was not the beast at all. I proposed to myself that it was a warning, sent out to teach me of my ways, for if the devil truly wanted me to indeed carry on my actions, it would have not shown me such terror and scared me off route.

I know what you may be thinking; it was only a dream and that I am getting worked up over my own sub-conscious. Very well. I would indeed choose the same conclusion if being told this tale.

However, now that I am truly awake have I found something that has ruled out my second thought completely, and banished any thought of my encounter being merely a nightmare. At this precise moment it is not the day I fear, but the night. For when night falls I may end up dreaming again, and this is what I fear the most.

You may think of me what you wish, but I, Anthony James Hoskins, will change. For years I had blamed the bottle for my sinful ways, but I now see the truth. From this day forth I shall no longer bear a grudge upon the past. I shall treat my fellow brother with respect, and help aid him as much as I can.

These are not just scribbling downs of a mad man, but a changed man. A man who will now devote his life to put right whatever he has done wrong.

I did not need proof for such a vivid and terrifying dream, but it seems as though I have been granted one against my will. For only moments ago, I found something. Something that inspired me to begin this statement; to cleanse my soul and own up to my actions for once, and explain my ordeal to anyone who wishes to read this, should I not be here to explain in person.

For when changing my sweat-soaked sheets this evening, I have found an object under my pillowcase, an object that I hold firmly in my hand right now for fear of losing, for the owner of such an object would not best be pleased with me if I did so.

In my hand, I hold the devil's pentagram medallion, and I dread more than ever that he wishes for its return, along with myself the next time I fall asleep.

Lightning Source UK Ltd.
Milton Keynes UK
UKOW030147101012

200329UK00001B/80/P

9 781906 755492